# LANDFALL

## LISA SILVERTHORNE

# LANDFALL

# LISA SILVERTHORNE

*AWARD-WINNING AUTHOR*

In the wake of Hurricane Katrina, first responder, Professor Kadence Harlowe puts her losses aside to rescue survivors and help New Orleans recover. When Kadence wins the services of a hot young East Coast executive in an online charity auction, she finds herself struggling between an old heartache and a new attraction.

When weary young financial executive, Nate Logan offered his services to a charity auction, he never dreamed he'd land in New Orleans cleaning up Hurricane Katrina. Or fall for the beautiful and fearless Kadence Harlowe. As Nate risks his life alongside her in flood-ravaged Louisiana, he begins to question his old life and its forced priorities.

Kadence and Nate's relationship is soon tested by secrets and the unthinkable: another deadly hurricane bearing down on the Gulf Coast. And they are right in the path of a twenty-foot storm surge.

**Novels by Lisa Silverthorne**

*A Game of Lost Souls series:*
*Contemporary Romantasy*
THE CINDERELLA HOUR
THE PRINCE CHARMING HOUR
THE EVER AFTER HOUR
THE FALLEN HEARTS SEASON
THE RISING SPIRITS SEASON
THE ETERNAL SOULS SEASON
THE ROYAL WEDDING HOUR
THE HEAVENLY HONEYMOON HOUR
THE DIVINE NEWLYWEDS SHOW
THE CELESTIAL COUPLES SHOW
THE ENOCHIAN APOCALYPSE SHOW
THE ANGELIC ANNIVERSARY SHOW
THE PERDITION PICTURE SHOW
**Complete Series!**

*Curse and Crown series:*
*Epic Romantasy*
THORN & BLADE
STORM & STEEL
FLAME & DAGGER (2026)

*The Spiral series:*
*Dark Contemporary Fantasy*
BETWEEN
REPRISE
AVENGE

*The Resurrectionist Papers*
*Paranormal Romystery*
GRAVE RECKONING

**Science Fiction Writing as L.S. Silverthorne**

*Experiencing True Purple series:*
RECOMBINANT, Book 1
HELIX, Book 2
SPLICE, Book 3

***Standalones:***
REDISCOVERY

# ACKNOWLEDGMENTS

For one of my best friends, **PATRICIA DUFFY NOVAK**. For talking me off the ledge more times than I can remember, for being there during the best and worst times in my life, for helping me fix so many broken things, for making the long trek north when no one else would, and for making me laugh when I'd forgotten how.

For my writing twin and adopted brother, **RON COLLINS**. For walking along the strange, sometimes lonely, writers' path beside me all these decades. For tirelessly participating in my crazy writing dares and making me believe in the power of persistence. And pushing me to never forget that I am a writer.

# ONE

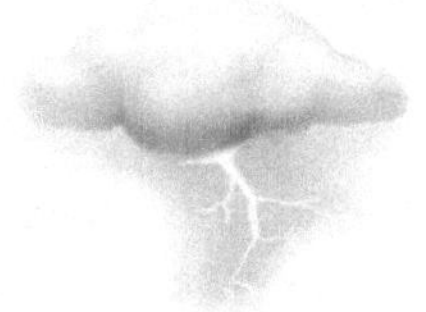

*Wednesday, August 31, 2005 —*

First responder, Professor Kadence Harlowe trudged through waist-high water in Ninth Ward, one of the hardest hit New Orleans neighborhoods, searching for hurricane survivors. Her hip waders sloshed in the early morning heat, barely keeping out the murky water as she moved toward the flat, aluminum Go-Devil boat. Three other volunteers climbed in ahead of her. LaWanda Arceneaux had called them back for another rescue call: a woman trapped in her attic.

The third day after Katrina made landfall was dawning. The air stunk with death, raw sewage, and crude oil. Kadence kept a mask over her nose and mouth to minimize the smell as she swung one leg over the side and pulled herself into the boat. Things she didn't want to look at floated past in the dark, oily-sheened water, the whole scene surreal.

Thankfully, Katrina made landfall well to the east of her Louisiana home, but the magnitude of devastation humbled her in a way that she'd never felt before. She had to come help these people anyway she could.

"How you doin' today, Professor?" LaWanda Arceneaux, a curly-haired Louisiana paramedic asked. "A little different than the classroom, this?"

Seated beside the outboard motor, LaWanda was a short, wiry athletic woman with golden brown skin and thick, shoulder-length hair that turned coppery in the sunlight. LaWanda gripped the edge of the small fishing boat that glided through the flooded parish, only rooftops and eaves visible above the dark water. The boat carried Kadence and her two firefighter buddies from Lake Charles.

"It's definitely a change from teaching college kids," Kadence said with a chuckle, pressing a strand of rusty red hair back into its clip, one that had escaped her ponytail. "A good way to give back. To pay it forward."

The heat roiled and Kadence dabbed at the sheen of sweat across her forehead. The outboard motor purred in the overwhelming silence of flood waters. Not even the chirp of a bird to break the eerie calm.

LaWanda laid a hand against her arm. "You have, Kadence, believe me. We need more first responders like you and the boys here. You've been out here searchin' and helpin' for days. And we appreciate the help."

Tall, lanky firefighter, Jim Hawkins, one of her best friends, slouched on the other side of the motor, axe handle hanging from his jeans. His sun-washed hair was cropped short, nearly a burr cut, a day's beard shadowing his long, tanned face.

"You're welcome to volunteer at my department anytime, ma'am," he said with a wry smile, tipping his blue fireman's baseball cap at her.

Kadence turned around and poked him in the gut. "Gee, thanks, Jim—I'll keep that in mind." For over two years, she'd been a first responder at Lake Charles station house eight where Jim worked.

"How much farther, LaWanda?" asked Marty Keller.

He was shorter and stockier than Jim, darker, scruffy in a bushy-haired, stray-dog kind of way. They were both good guys and they looked out for her. She'd worked alongside them many times, at accident scenes and fires. They'd earned her trust.

"Not far," LaWanda said, pointing toward a one-story white house with a rusty water line lapping high on its crumbling siding. The water eddied around the rain gutters, the grey roof barely above the flood waters. "Got a call about a woman trapped in her attic. Got two cats, too. We'll have to get around that fence there and come around to the roof's edge."

"You get us close enough and we'll climb onto the roof," said Marty.

"I'll take cat duty," said Kadence, laying a hand on the two beige cat carriers sitting at the front of the boat.

She'd rescued dozens of two legged and four legged survivors over the past few days. Most seemed dazed. She could only imagine the horrors they'd been through when that storm surge hit.

As the boat floated closer, the hoarse, exhausted cry of an old woman cut through the sweltering, morning heat, the air already thick and soupy. Like she could spoon it out of her way.

LaWanda steered the boat closer to the house.

"Help me! Somebody…please!"

The weak voice was muffled and Kadence couldn't tell the direction it came from, much less how close they were to the woman.

She craned her neck, trying to see past the roof point for a sign of the survivor. But the rooftop was empty.

LaWanda cut the motor. The buzzing sound emptied into eerie silence.

"Help me, please—the water's so high!"

A cold chill blew across Kadence's heart at the desperate, tear-strained voice when she at last realized where the voice had come from —inside the roof.

Kadence grabbed hold of the roof's water-logged edge, dragging the boat to a stop. It bobbed at the edge of the house as Kadence climbed out and onto the roof.

"Jim—your axe! She's trapped inside that attic!"

Jim stumbled to his feet against the swaying boat and climbed out onto the roof, his long legs making his attempt much smoother than Kadence as she gained her footing. Marty tumbled out behind him and all three of them ran across the roof.

"Keep talking!" Kadence shouted, hoping the frightened woman could hear her voice. "So, we know where to punch the hole!"

"I'm here!" the tired voice shouted again. "Please—hurry or we'll drown!"

Still somewhere ahead, Kadence realized as she crouched low, head down, ears focused on the woman's voice.

When she reached the top of the roof, she stepped over the point and onto the other side, toward the back, left side of the house. She'd gone no more than two paces when the woman's voice shrieked out another call for help.

Kadence grinned. She was right over the trapped woman.

"Jim, she's here!" Kadence shouted, motioning Jim over. She leaned closer to the remaining twisted shingles. "We're going to cut through the roof now! Stay back and hold on, okay?"

Jim slammed the head of his axe into the soggy grey shingles, tearing through the remnants of paper and wood. Katrina had already ripped away most of the shingles. The sharp rap of metal against wood gouged the silence, wood splintering. Shingles fell away until a fist-sized hole broke through to the attic. Kadence saw the shimmer of water less than a foot from the ceiling.

And it was still rising.

"Hurry, Jim!" she shouted as she and Marty yanked at the surrounding shingles.

The hole widened, splintering into the size of a grapefruit. Then a basketball until a dark, wrinkled hand stuck up through the hole.

"Stay back just a few more moments," Kadence called. "We've got to widen the hole enough to lift you through."

"First, take Percy!" the woman shouted, lifting a sopping wet brown tabby cat through the hole.

Kadence took the flailing cat from the trembling hand and cradled him to her chest as she rushed down the roof toward the boat. LaWanda opened a carrier and held it out for her, allowing her to slide the shivering, terrified cat inside. She closed the door and grabbed the other carrier, rushing back toward Jim and Marty.

The hole was as wide as Jim's shoulders now. Enough to lift out the woman.

"Here's my Diva," said the old woman, lifting out a drenched, annoyed tortoiseshell cat.

Kadence opened the carrier door and scooped the struggling cat into her arms, claws raking her skin. After a couple of false starts, a hiss, and more scratches, she managed to push the terrified cat into the carrier. Moments later, Jim and Marty lifted the old woman out of the swirling waters engulfing her attic.

She was frail, feather-light, humped shoulders and mostly curly grey hair cut close to her scalp, but smiling as Marty lifted her into his arms. Jim walked alongside him, helping to ease her into the boat. Kadence followed behind, carrying the mewling tortie cat. She set the carrier beside the first one in the boat and climbed in beside the old woman.

Kadence put her arms around the woman as she began to sob. "It's okay. You're safe now."

LaWanda sat beside the woman and wrapped a blanket around her shoulders. She opened a bottle of water and pressed it into the woman's shaking hands. The woman sucked down most of the water in a few gulps.

"I don't know what I'd have done if you hadn't come when you did," said the old woman.

"We're glad we could help. What's your name?" Kadence asked.

"Elsie Paige," said the woman, her shoulders hunching as the tears tracked down her dark, wrinkled face.

LaWanda introduced herself then Kadence and finally the two fire-fighters.

Elsie's hands trembled as she gripped the bottle of water, looking from LaWanda to Kadence. "All of it's gone, it'n it?"

Kadence stiffened as LaWanda nodded and hugged the old woman tighter. She glanced back at the house as Jim started the outboard and the roof receded on the horizon. The motor buzzed like a hornet and they glided away from the old neighborhood.

Too close to Lake Pontchartrain, the elevation not high enough to survive the levee breaks that had flooded the neighborhood. The land became a bowl for the escaping water. She feared the final body count once the water receded.

But seeing this poor woman in her torn blue house dress and scuffed up shoes made her eyes sting. She'd been pulled from a dark attic with water up to her chin, praying someone would get to her before she drowned. *How many others had clung to their attic ceilings, the water rising like a phantom to entomb them?* Shuddering, she wiped back tears. Elsie Paige had nothing now. No home, no clothes—nowhere to go. And no way to buy another home.

*What would it be like to be on the streets with no one to turn to, no one to help you rebuild your life?*

At last, the boat reached the edge of the water. Kadence saw Jim's red Ford F-250 parked up the hill with dozens of other cars. His boat trailer was still backed to the edge of the water where they'd put in before dawn.

Kadence and LaWanda climbed out of the boat and LaWanda guided frail, shaken Elsie onto dry land.

"Thank the Lord," Elsie cried, raising her hands to the sky. "Never thought I'd touch dry land again."

After Marty and Jim loaded the boat onto the trailer, Kadence picked up the cat carriers and set them in the back seat of the extended cab. LaWanda helped Elsie into the front seat while the rest of the group piled into the back.

For thirty minutes, they drove in exhausted silence until Jim pulled up to a staging area northwest of New Orleans. Small town. Old salt box houses. One gas and sip, a drug store, and an old school, the square, three-story building all red brick and windows. The air smelled sweet and clean here, scrubbed of the decay and death that surrounded New Orleans.

An ambulance was parked in front of the school, doors thrown open and people clustered around it, fanning themselves in the awful, heavy heat. Others sat in folding chairs looking shell-shocked and dazed. So many of them had lost everything like Elsie and more. Many still had loved ones missing. Others stayed with their dead until they could be transported to makeshift morgues.

A paramedic, a tall, thin woman with short brown hair and big brown eyes moved toward Elsie as LaWanda guided her toward the ambulance. She wore a blue uniform shirt and pants. They sat Elsie down inside the ambulance and the paramedic examined her.

Kadence glanced back at Jim's truck, hearing the muffled mewls of

Elsie's cats. They needed food and water. Kadence noticed a paper cup setting inside the ambulance door. She snatched it and tore most of the cup away. She then filled it with bottled water from Jim's truck. Opening one of the carriers, she set the makeshift cat dish beside the tortoiseshell cat that lapped at the fresh water. She rubbed the black and cream ears while the fluffy cat drank.

When Diva finished drinking, Kadence refilled the cup and slid it inside the tabby cat's carrier. He purred, his paws kneading the plastic as he pressed his face against the cool water, rough pink tongue flicking into the cup.

After twenty minutes, the paramedic lifted Elsie out of the ambulance.

"She's fine. Nothing broken. A little dehydrated and in need of a few good meals."

"Thank you, Candy," LaWanda said to the tired paramedic. "We'll get her inside and get some food into her."

Elsie stood on the cracked sidewalk leading to the green double doors propped open. Inside on the concrete floor, a white fan whirred inside. She folded her arms against her thin frame, glancing around at the strange town and places she didn't know. She looked lost and frightened.

Kadence moved toward her, standing at her elbow, a hand on her shoulder.

"Elsie, do you have anyone we can call? Somewhere to stay tonight? Someone who can keep your cats?"

The old woman shook her head, her eyes welling with tears and she brushed them from her warm brown gaze. "No, honey. They's all gone now."

LaWanda stood beside Elsie, ready to help her inside the shelter in the old school building, but she looked as sad as poor Elsie. Kadence had known LaWanda only a few months, but she knew that look of helplessness in the woman's eyes. She hated to send this old woman into the sea of cots and despair, left to fend for herself at her age while FEMA failed to provide assistance. She could be stuck here weeks.

"We'll take care of the kitties for you, ey," said LaWanda. "Don't you worry none, Elsie."

Elsie nodded as LaWanda steered her toward the open doorway and Kadence's heart twisted into a knot.

"Elsie, wait," said Kadence, walking up behind her. She reached out a hand to Elsie's arm and gave it a gentle squeeze. "You and your cats are coming home with me. I've got a big place, plenty of room."

Elsie's whole face brightened. "I cain't trouble you like that, girl."

Kadence smiled and brushed a hand across Elsie's wrinkled cheek. "I'm glad to do it. Please, come stay with me. We'll need to pick up some cat things, but we'll be fine. Okay?"

Elsie nodded, tears rushing down her cheeks. "I'd like that, Kadence."

LaWanda embraced Kadence in a hug, whispering "thank you" in her ear. "I couldn't bear seeing her go in there."

"Me neither," Kadence said in a low voice.

LaWanda let her go, holding her out at arm's length. "You been here for days, Kadence, barely sleeping. I think it's time you go home for a few days and rest. They'll be plenty to do when you come back, don't you know."

Kadence nodded. "Okay. I really should get Elsie settled. I'll see you in a few days."

Jim and Marty waved at her. "See you soon, Kadence," Marty called.

She turned to Elsie. "Come on, Miss Elsie," she said. She slid the two cat carriers out of Jim's SUV. "My car's just down the street."

"Where's your home?" Elsie asked, shuffling alongside her with wobbly steps.

"I've got an old house south of Lake Charles—near Moss Lake. About three hours from here."

Kadence led Elsie to the burgundy Honda Accord parked across the street from the old elementary school. She set the cat carriers on the sidewalk and fumbled out of her hip waders. Her legs were hot, sweaty as she peeled off the dark green waders. She dropped them in the grass and fished out her car keys from her cut off Levi's.

The door locks snapped open as Kadence popped the trunk. She tossed in the hip waders and closed it. She opened the back door and set each carrier inside. Both cats howled as she set them on the seats and hurried around to help Elsie into the passenger side.

"You must be starving. Let's get some food and supplies for your cats. Then we'll head for Lake Charles."

"Cain't thank you enough, girl."

"You can stay as long as you like, Elsie. It'll be nice having some company in that big house," said Kadence after climbing into the front seat. "Including the cats." She clicked her seatbelt into place and started the car.

She'd pick up 49 North to US 10 West toward Lake Charles. There'd be plenty of stores and restaurants on 49 where she could get Elsie and the cats a good meal. There was no telling how long ago they'd eaten. From there, a good soft bed and some quiet time were just what Elsie Paige needed. That would give Kadence more time to figure out how to get more help down to the Gulf for others like Elsie. She'd start that tomorrow. For now, Elsie and her cats needed food and rest.

She pulled away from the little town and Elsie pressed her face to the window, watching everything slip past. Her thin shoulders finally sagged and she sank back into the seat, her eyelids drooping. Kadence worried what the poor woman might dream about. She had no idea what Elsie endured before being rescued. Three days had passed since Katrina made landfall. *Had Elsie been trapped in that air pocket in her attic all this time?*

She'd do whatever she could for Elsie, but the magnitude of the disaster felt surreal and overwhelming. *How would this mess ever get cleaned up? Would people ever recover?* They wouldn't without help, she knew. News crews buzzed like flies on carcasses all along the impassable highways leading into New Orleans. Hundreds of people lived on those highways and streets now, with nowhere to go while the world watched from their living rooms.

Someone needed to bring the right attention to these people and get them the quick help they needed to get back on their feet and get on with their lives. She understood that need to get on with life, even though she hadn't quite managed it yet. Eleven months was still too soon for her. She still saw his face in those quiet moments when the heat haze hung low in the fading sunlight, the air smelling like asphalt and gardenias, the nights growing longer even with September a whisper away.

But not as long as the night when the call came into dispatch.

She bit her lip, fighting the sting of tears as that September night rushed back to her, memory of screaming sirens, howl of the fire truck, hiss of tires against wet pavement. The pounding of her heart in her throat at the familiar yellow mustang, crumpled like a paper wad against the embankment.

"It's green, honey," said Elsie, a hand on Kadence's shoulder.

Kadence felt the steering wheel between her fingers again as she glanced up at the stoplight and pressed the gas pedal. A sign pointing the way to highway 49 made her veer right.

"Thanks," said Kadence. "I guess I was lost in thought."

"About something you lost?" The angles of Elsie's long face and creased high forehead sharpened. She knew how to read people and she was good at it.

Kadence stared at her a moment, making another left as the highway stretched out ahead. State Road 49.

"Yes," she replied. "Like you, I guess. Did you live alone?"

Elsie nodded, laying her thick, arthritic hands in her lap. "Since February. My sister Myra Jean passed with the colon cancer. Charlie, my husband, died four years ago this March. Heart attack."

"I'm so sorry," said Kadence. "You've had so much loss and now this."

Her face brightened. "Got one daughter though. In Denver. And three grand babies. She wanted me to leave before Katrina, but I wanted to stay in my home." She laid her hands to her face. "It was a foolish thing to do, this."

"Well, you can call your daughter when we stop to eat. She must be worried sick."

Elsie nodded and Kadence fell silent again, letting her mind hover on the memory of steamed clams on Holly Beach, golden sunsets glistening on surf-soaked Louisiana shores, his arms around her in the warm August breeze coming off the Gulf. If she squinted at the horizon, she could almost see his face, the silhouette of his lean frame barefoot on Holly Beach, and remember the three years they'd shared.

But those years were gone now. Buried under layers of grief and memories and the pretense of moving on. She'd done the best she could, pretending, avoiding, dodging. But on a day like this, in the face of *Katrina's* devastation, the pain tumbled back to her, mixing its somber charcoals and umbers with the darkest shadows until she could no longer separate her pain from those around her. Only in the face of their sorrows could she escape her own.

She glanced at Elsie who hummed softly to herself above the huff of the air conditioner and wondered if they could help each other.

# TWO

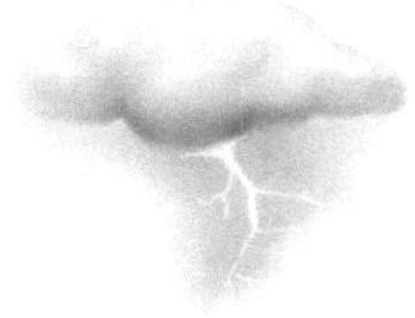

*Tuesday, August 23, 2005 —*

AT FIVE A.M., NATE LOGAN STUMBLED INTO HIS ARLINGTON, VIRGINIA penthouse, reeking of the cinnamon-cedar smell of Opus X cigars. He didn't smoke and wasn't much of a drinker, but that never mattered. It was just business, as his father always reminded him. Before reminding him of his duty to the firm—and the family.

His roommate, Ren Stewart was in the kitchen in a navy bathrobe, making coffee. Black kitchen cabinets and grey granite countertops were sedate against the dark blue walls, glass tables, and white sofas of the living area. And the panoramic view of downtown Arlington and its dark, glittering skyline, edged a burnished orange. Sun wouldn't be up until about 6:30 a.m. The room smelled of rich Kona coffee and bacon.

"You're up early," Nate called, tripping over his black Ferragamo's as he kicked them off. The tie was long gone, his white dress shirt missing two buttons. He tossed his navy-blue suit coat onto a chair and collapsed on the couch, leaning his spinning head back against the cushions.

"You do remember that seven o'clock appointment with Gloeckner Investments, right?"

Ren's voice had a chill to it that annoyed Nate. They were roommates—best friends since fourth grade. They went to high school together. Got their bachelors at Georgetown together. They'd accepted positions at Nate's father's investment firm after finishing their finance MBAs at Harvard. Together, they took over management of the firm's overseas partnerships when Nate's father was elected to the U.S. Senate and together, they made it thrive. Ren was the most honest, hardworking guy he knew. Busted his butt to get a Harvard scholarship. He'd always admired Ren, wondering if their family statuses had been reversed, if he'd have measured up like Ren.

Sometimes, Nate wished he could trade places with Ren. He'd bootstrapped his way up and people respected that. Sure, Nate worked hard, too, wanting only to stand on his own reputation and not Senator Lee Logan's, but it wasn't the same. He'd never have that chance to prove himself. Everyone would constantly accuse him of having life handed to him. He sighed. *And maybe they were right?*

Nate slid the Blackberry out of his shirt pocket and flicked it on, the early appointment glaring back at him. Okay, he'd forgotten, but he'd done his job last night, getting the Huffman account firmly signed aboard. It had taken a lot more time and persuasion than he'd expected, but he landed the account.

"Yeah, I'm on it," said Nate with a groan. "I'm just going to rest my eyes a moment." Shake off the cigars and lack of sleep. His chest still hurt and his head throbbed from all that smoke. Just his luck that Huffman was a chain-smoking insomniac.

Only fifteen minutes and he'd take a shower. Maybe the day would end by seven tonight and he could fall into bed and sleep? He groaned. Unless Corrina called, dragging him out to yet another engagement party or wedding planning annoyance where his opinion (if he had one) even mattered. Or his father, asking him to entertain yet another unscheduled, potential investor.

"No big deal, right?" Ren snapped, pouring coffee into a thick, red ceramic mug. "Just another day without sleep."

Nate jerked his head up from the white couch, brushing a tangle of pale blond bangs out of his eyes.

"What's that supposed to mean?"

Ren walked into the room, his dark hair still wet and uncombed. He carried two steaming cups of black Kona coffee in his hands, thrusting one out to Nate who gratefully accepted it. He took a quick sip, the hot liquid soothing his raw throat as Ren perched himself on the arm of a white leather chair.

"It means," said Ren, "that you're dead on your feet. Again. What was it last night, Nate? A charity function? Some favor to Corrina's father—or yours?"

"Hey, I do my job," Nate snapped, slamming the red ceramic mug onto the glass coffee table in front of the couch.

"And everybody else's, too. When was the last time you slept eight straight hours, Nate?"

When he was seventeen. When life was simpler and he didn't have the responsibility of the family business on his shoulders, when he didn't have to prove he wasn't an over-privileged brat at every turn. Even to Dad's old friend, Judge Coleridge, Corrina's father. Not even a Harvard MBA and a Fortune 500 company had been enough for that old man. Nothing was too good for his darling, Corrina, the Judge had told Nate's father at a Capitol Hill party after he'd introduced Nate and Corrina.

Ever since that party, Nate had been trying to prove himself worthy. Worthy to his dad that he could handle the company, worthy to clients who looked at him as some spoiled rich kid, and worthy to his fiancée that he was competent and reliable. Sometimes he wondered if it was him or the Logan name that Corrina loved.

"Not everybody needs eight hours sleep," said Nate, glaring at his best friend, always so serious and determined to fix the world one person at a time.

"Too bad that doesn't include you, buddy," said Ren, rising from the chair. "You're killing yourself with these late hours and you know it. You work too hard, Nate."

Nate ignored him, picking up his mug, and taking another sip of coffee. "I'm fine, Ren. I'll be at the meeting, wide awake and as convincing as hell. Just like I always am."

Ren shook his head, sighing. "It's not your persuasiveness that I'm worried about."

"What are you, my mother? I'll sleep later," said Nate, rising from the couch.

"When? On your way home? Fifteen minutes between meetings? Nate, people are worried about you."

*Worried? Worried that he wouldn't measure up.*

"I'm fine," Nate snapped and moved toward the bathroom. "See you at the office."

---

NATE, DRESSED IN A CHARCOAL BRIONI SUIT, DROVE HIS STEEL-GREY BMW SUV down Wilson Boulevard toward the glass and steel Logan Financial building. He parked in the garage, the air smelling like asphalt and grit and headed into the wood paneled, dimly lit elevator for the tenth floor, feeling a little more tired than he'd hoped. It was ten till seven and already he was exhausted. He gripped his stainless-steel travel mug, still hot with coffee, and pressed it to his mouth for a quick drink. When the elevator opened, he walked toward Logan Financial's tall glass doors and slipped into the empty foyer.

Cherry wood floors glistened against burgundy leather chairs and moss walls. The air smelled faintly of citrus, soft classical music almost a whisper as he walked past the reception desk. Marina wouldn't be in for another hour. As he walked down the long hallway, Ferragamo's clicking against the hardwood, he saw Ren's door ajar, but kept walking toward his office.

He opened the door and flicked on the lights. The windowed south wall shone with early morning sunlight that glistened across the circular cherry desk that stood beside the window. He hunched down into his chair, tossing the black leather briefcase onto his blotter. A silver-framed picture of his father stared back at him, thick salt and pepper hair and plenty of laugh lines. Dad remarried when he was a sophomore at Georgetown, Kitty something or other, fifteen years younger than him. Nate had little use for the woman who was all about appearances. And money. Dad's, that is.

Beside Dad, sat another silver-framed picture of his mother, Millie. She lived in the south of France for the moment with her millionaire husband. Her soft blonde hair was short and curly (like his), a little windblown as she stood on the deck of her boat. On the other side of the desk, beside an antique gold clock was Corrina's picture. Her bobbed hair was bleached white-blonde, her grey eyes intense as she posed in her ivory, debutante ball gown, looking over one shoulder. She made a point of telling him about four times that evening that her dress was Chanel. Like he cared. He hated having to buy expensive suits and shoes. He rolled his eyes. For the firm.

The red voicemail light pulsed on his black desk phone, but he ignored it, instead finishing off his coffee as he retrieved the Gloeckner file from his file minder.

A soft knock echoed through the quiet office.

"Yes?" he called.

"It's Ren," the muffled voice responded.

"It's open."

Ren stepped inside, dressed in a blue pin-stripe suit and freshly polished brown leather shoes. His dark hair was short and gelled. He carried a brown leather portfolio in the crook of his arm.

"Gloeckner reps are in the conference room," he said. "You ready?"

Nate nodded. "Always," he said, setting down the silver travel mug. "Let's do this."

Ren motioned him forward and he walked out the door, down the hall toward the glass-enclosed conference room, Ren behind him.

---

THREE HOURS LATER, NATE WALKED OUT OF THE CONFERENCE ROOM, a hand on tall, stocky Jens Brandt's shoulder, lead negotiator for Gloeckner and Associates. Ren led Brandt's three team members, a woman and two men, into the hall behind them.

"And next time, we talk over lunch," said Brandt, his six four frame nearly a head taller than Nate. The dark-haired man had at least ten years on him, too. "Without that swill you Americans call beer. What is it…Bud Light?"

Nate laughed. "Yeah, we'll just serve up the German equivalent for you. Some Warsteiner Light."

Brandt let out a belly laugh. "Point taken."

"Next time you're in town, we'll go for some real beer. Treat you to some great microbrews like Dogfish Head out of Delaware or Bells out of Michigan. Oberon Ale is like tasting summer in a bottle."

Brandt nodded. "I'd like that, Herr Logan. Next time. Auf Wiedersehen."

"Take care, Herr Brandt," said Nate, stopping at the glass doors.

He shook hands with Brandt and three other Gloeckner reps and they departed. Only after they'd disappeared into the elevator did Nate lean against the reception desk, feeling weak in the knees. He glanced at his watch. After ten.

He cast a pained look at Ren who leaned on the desk beside him. "I didn't think that would ever end," said Nate with a groan.

"Me neither. That guy's a killer negotiator." Then he smiled and patted Nate on the back. "But damned if you weren't better. Your dad's going to be so impressed with the terms."

Nate grinned. *Maybe for once, the old man would be impressed by something he'd done?*

"Think so?"

Ren nodded emphatically. "No question. You did an incredible job."

"See," he said, bumping his fist against Ren's shoulder. "Not everybody needs eight hours."

Ren shook his head. "Don't get cocky, Logan. You can't go without sleep forever and even you know it."

The front desk phone rang and Marina the receptionist answered it. "Good Morning, Logan Financial Group. Oh, hello, Corrina. Just a moment and I'll see if he's available."

Nate cringed. *God, please don't let it be another engagement party.*

Marina looked up, her black hair pulled back with a gold barrette. "Mr. Logan, are you available?"

He hesitated, casting an uncertain look at Ren, and then straightened to his full six-foot height.

"Send it back to my office," he said to Marina and hurried down the hall.

The phone was ringing when he stepped inside. He let it ring two more times, steeling himself for more of Corrina's wild social outings, and picked up the phone.

"Hey, doll," he said into the receiver.

"Hi, Nate," she said in her baby talk voice. This morning, he wasn't in the mood for it. Okay, he was never in the mood for it. Corrina wasn't dumb and he hated when she pretended to be. "Whatcha doin'?"

"Working." Something that always fascinated Corrina who'd never worked a day in her life. "What's up?"

"Darling, there's a wonderful party in our honor tonight. Can I send my driver around at six thirty to collect you?"

Nate gripped the bridge of his nose, smashing his dry eyes closed. The thought of another one of Corrina's all-nighters made his chest ache.

"Tonight?" he said.

"Yes, tonight. You're available, aren't you? We *are* getting married in three months."

Nate did his best to hold in a sigh. All he wanted tonight was takeout on the couch and an early night.

"I'm really tired tonight, Corrina," he replied.

"No wonder," Corrina snapped. "Daddy said you were at the Four Seasons all last night and most of the morning."

*How'd Judge Coleridge know his whereabouts?* He felt the slow burn of anger. *Was the good Judge having him followed, hoping to turn up some dirt on his soon-to-be son-in-law?*

"That was business, Corrina. And I'd have much rather been home asleep than out all night."

"And I'm not important enough to warrant a couple hours of your time? Your own widdle fiancée?" He gritted his teeth. More baby voice.

Nate rubbed his forehead, the caffeine spiraling away.

"It's not that. I was…hoping for an early night."

"It'll be only a couple of hours, Nate. And you'll have a positively wonderful time. I promise, baby. Pweeese."

"Fine." Anything to stop the baby talk.

Corrina squealed with delight. "Lovely! Harold will pick you up at your place—six thirty sharp."

"No, just give me the address and I'll meet you there," said Nate, unable to even fake enthusiasm.

"But Nate—"

"The address, Corrina," he said in a tired voice and fumbled for a pen.

"All right," she said, the pout evident in her tone. She gave him the address. He held in a groan. It was in D.C.—another long night.

"Okay, got it. I'll be there by seven."

"What do you say?" she said in that squeaky, baby talk voice.

"What?" He frowned.

"I wuv you..." she said.

Nate did his best to hold back a sigh. "Love you, Corrina," he said and hung up the phone.

"Wuv you," Ren mocked from the doorway.

"Don't start," Nate said as he dropped into his desk chair, hands against his temples, trying to rub away the pounding headache that was starting to form there.

"So, you're going?" Ren asked, arms crossed against his chest.

"It's my engagement duty," he said, trying not to snarl as he said it.

"It's always about what Corrina wants, Nate. Why do you put up with it?"

Dad loved Judge Coleridge's waifish, flamboyant daughter, thought she was perfect for his only son. More duty, he supposed. But she was sweet and bubbly. Never a dull moment with Corrina. Never a quiet moment either, but he'd gotten used to it. She got him out of the house and into the social scene. He played the extrovert well. As Senator Logan's only son, it was expected of him.

"The party's just a couple of hours," he replied.

His desk phone rang again.

"Nate Logan."

"Nate! So, how'd things go last night?"

Dad's exuberant voice filled his ear, no doubt wanting an update on the Gloeckner meeting. And the impromptu with Huffman. He put the phone on speaker.

"No problems," said Nate. "I got Huffman to move his company's entire portfolio over to us. He'll be in on Friday to review the plan and file the paperwork."

"What? Really?"

"Yeah," said Nate, leaning back in his chair. "I had everything laid out for him and when he saw the return on his investment, he was all in."

"Good work, Nate. You did a terrific job."

"Thanks, Dad."

"What about Gloeckner?"

Nate smiled, casting a proud look at Ren who sat down on the edge of Nate's desk, arms crossed.

"Ren and I knocked them dead. Closed the deal this morning. They'll be back next Monday to sign the papers."

"Outstanding! Give Ren my regards."

A smile finally appeared on Ren's angular face.

"Let me know what time on Monday and I'll drop by."

Nate smiled. It'd be good to see his dad. The man was only thirty minutes away and he hadn't seen him in months.

"Maybe we can have dinner afterward? I can catch you up on the details with Gloeckner and Huffman."

"That would be great, son. Maybe you'll bring that cute little fiancée of yours along?"

Nate hesitated. He took the phone off speaker. "I was thinking about a guys' night out," he said in a slow, careful voice.

The line went quiet for a moment or two. "Are you two having problems? Nate, I hope you haven't blown things with Corrina Coleridge. This is a wonderful opportunity and—"

"No, Corrina and I are fine," he said, raising his voice above his Dad's panicked words. "It's just that…well—hadn't seen you in a while and—"

"Great! Bring the little lady along and we'll have a wonderful evening together. I'll call Evan and invite him, too. Make it a family affair. Gotta run, son. See you, Monday."

The line went dead.

"Bye, Dad," he said in a quiet voice and hung up the phone.

"Everything okay?" Ren asked, frowning.

Nate let the surprised look fade from his face as he pasted on that Logan *everything's great* smile.

"Everything's fine. Just planning a family dinner for Monday night."

"Guess I'll get to work on the Gloeckner paperwork. Let me know if you want to get lunch later," said Ren, leaving the room.

"Sure," said Nate, moving to the laptop computer on his desk.

He opened the spreadsheet he'd prepared for Huffman and stared through it. *Why hadn't he insisted that he and his dad have dinner alone? Would that have been so selfish?*

Nate worked through lunch, consulting with investors and his staff until well past six o'clock. Ren left a half hour ago, poking his head into the office to nag Nate about driving carefully tonight. With a wave, Nate sent Ren on his way while he wrapped up the last emails of the day. By then it was nearly six thirty.

Nate combed his hair and swished some minty mouthwash in the men's room before locking up the office and hurrying into the elevator. His SUV was the only one left on the floor as he drove out onto Wilson, heading northeast for Washington D.C. and the party at the Hay-Adams Hotel.

---

THE HAY-ADAMS WINDSOR ROOM WAS FILLED WITH MIDDLE-AGED WOMEN and a handful of men that Nate didn't know. Friends of Corrina's family, he realized, feeling uncomfortable when he entered the room. It was all white trim and white wainscoting, extensive crown molding, gold scones and chandeliers, and a gold damask wallpaper that matched the gold carpeting. An ornate white fireplace with a gold framed mirror reflected the room and all its light throughout the crowded space. The room smelled like lemons.

A dark-haired woman in a charcoal vest and white shirt met him at the door with a silver tray of champagne flutes. He gratefully accepted the champagne and walked through the groups of people in search of Corrina.

At a quarter to eight, after three glasses of champagne, Corrina waltzed into the room, all smiles. Making her typical grand—and very late—entrance. Corrina took fashionably late to epic levels, showing up whenever she felt like it. Her friend Bradley Wilcox, hung on her arm as usual, looking like he'd just come from a tennis match. He wore titanium Oakley's indoors, white shorts, and a white polo shirt over a green one, both collars popped like it was the 80s, a green sweater tied around his shoulders. His white leather tennis shoes sparkled, no blade of grass daring to touch the expensive leather.

Man…what a douchebag.

Bradley whispered something into Corrina's ear, kissed her cheek, and rushed away, to go count his trust fund or something. Nate frowned. She spent more time with that douchebag than she did him.

Corrina wore a slinky silver dress that shimmered with every step, her white-blond hair bobbed at her chin. She was about five foot seven and much too thin, looking more like Daisy Buchanan from the Great Gatsby than the Honorable Evan Coleridge's only child. But he was certainly no Jay Gatsby. He was practical, even plain, and this always disappointed Corrina who craved the spotlight as much as she craved expensive clothes and jewelry. She was statuesque, lithe, and graceful, almost like a butterfly. From a distance, that had mesmerized him. Up close, she was outgoing and playful, constantly pushing him toward a life and a personality that just weren't him.

She wanted him to be all polish and perfection, all Wall Street daring, dazzling her friends with his wit and charisma. Real life bored her. She wanted Hollywood illusions. At times, he did his best, playing the persona for her in public, at her favorite restaurants, and around her friends, but he wasn't any of those things. And he didn't enjoy the pretense either. Like the persona he played for his father.

"Nate, my darling Nate," she squealed from across the room, making a grand production as she flitted toward him, arms folding around his neck, pale lips dramatically finding his in an empty kiss.

"Wuv you," she cooed, the sound like crumpling metal against his ears.

"Hi, honey," he replied, sliding his arms around her waist, pulling her close. "You're more than fashionably late," he whispered in her ear. "Leaving me to flail in a roomful of strangers for nearly an hour."

She giggled then pressed thin fingers to his lips. "I'm sure you charmed everyone."

"Only the woman passing out champagne," he said with a smile. "What kept you?"

"Bradley and I just lost track of the time, baby," she said, tugging on his arm. "But I got a delicious Chanel dress for next week's bash. Can't wait to model it for you. Now, come and let me show you off to Mommy's friends. They'll love you!"

He gripped her hand, allowing her to lead him through the room toward the first group of women.

---

It was well after one a.m. before Nate convinced Corrina that he had to go home. She pouted, but kissed him goodbye and rushed to hang on Bradley's arm, who'd come back to the party. Guess he'd ran out of currency to count. Gangly and awkward looking, Bradley linked his arm in hers, pulling her close, his almost spiky dark hair poking her in the eye as he whispered in her ear. They both laughed and melted into the crowded Windsor Room.

Fighting back yawns, Nate said his goodbyes and hurried out to pick up his SUV from the valet. The day caught up to him as he collapsed into the driver's seat and drove west toward Arlington.

His eyelids drooped. He turned on the radio, finding some hard rock to keep him awake. He was a good thirty minutes from home and the hiss of tires and drone of traffic already made him sleepy.

He was near Highway 120 and North Glebe Road when he realized the first microseconds of sleep had closed his eyes. His body jolted and he struggled.

If he could just get across the Potomac, he'd be fine. Just get across.

Then he'd be home. In his own bed. He gritted his teeth, concentrating on the road.

He wouldn't let his eyes close again. He'd keep them open.

The shriek of metal gouging metal snapped his eyes open, the impact slamming him into the air bag then the window. Air squeezed out of his lungs, the pain raw and sharp in his rib cage as his face smashed into the air bag. The SUV's hood twisted around the streetlight as the vehicle came to a sudden stop.

Nate struggled to free himself from the air bag's jellyfish-like hold and finally pulled free, his face burning. But he couldn't get out of the car. He pushed hard against the door, but the dull pain in his left side sharpened. He struggled for breath as a distant siren echoed somewhere behind him.

Everything descended into cool darkness again until the driver-side door was wrenched open. A fiftyish man in a Redskins t-shirt and jeans peered in at him. "You okay, buddy?"

Nate tried to respond, but he couldn't get enough air to speak. His chest hurt, his left side aching. He closed his eyes, so tired he couldn't keep them open any longer.

When he opened his eyes again, paramedics had him on a gurney, loading him into the back of an ambulance. It was late—he needed to get home.

In green scrubs, a dark-haired guy hovered beside him, glasses, hair pulled back in a ponytail, faint smell of pepperoni hanging above the antiseptic scent.

"Easy, Mr. Logan. We're gonna take good care of you."

"Need to get home," Nate muttered through clenched teeth, struggling against the restraints to climb off the gurney.

"We'll get you home after someone checks you out, okay?"

Nate nodded as his whole body jolted against a wave of searing pain that tore through his side.

"Possible ruptured spleen," the paramedic said to the blond woman beside him wearing pale blue scrubs.

Not even the screeching siren kept Nate from sliding into unconsciousness.

# THREE

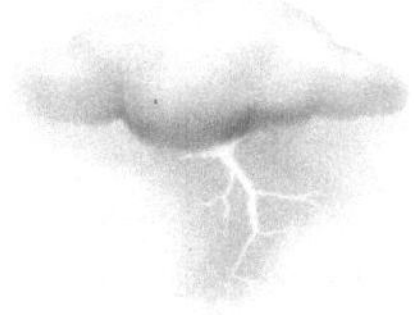

*Monday, August 29, 2005 —*

FIVE DAYS LATER, NATE AWOKE IN SIBLEY MEMORIAL HOSPITAL. A THICK bandage on his left side. The private room, all beige, was dim lit and shadowed, several vases of flowers on the shelf across from him. The sweet smell of roses and Asiatic lilies was faint against the scents of rewarmed food and germicide.

The pain was a raw ache as he struggled to raise the bed enough to sit up, but couldn't. When he saw the red call button, he poked it, hoping someone could tell him something about last night.

A thick-bodied nurse in a flowered scrub shirt and navy scrub pants entered the room, smiling at him. She pressed her gold-wire glasses against the bridge of her nose and stepped over to him.

"Mr. Logan," she said through a grin. "Glad you're with us again. I'm Sara, your nurse."

She patted his left shoulder gently.

"What happened last night? I don't remember much."

She squeezed his arm. "Do you remember the accident?"

He shrugged. "Parts of it. I remember driving west toward

Arlington." He frowned, struggling against the fog in his brain to call back an image, a detail—anything. But it was too fuzzy. "I remember the airbags deploying and somebody asking if I was okay." He smashed his eyes closed, searching. "A paramedic said he'd get me home after he checked me out."

Sara's hand was comforting against his shoulder.

"You were in a one-car accident, Mr. Logan. You ruptured your spleen and cracked some ribs. It's been five days since the accident, but you're going to be fine."

"What? Five days? Are you sure?"

She nodded. "Today is Monday, August 29th."

His eyes widened. "Monday? Are you sure?"

She chuckled. "Quite sure."

"Five days...but I've missed clients, appointments, portfolios to transfer," he said, panicked, pulling himself into a sitting position. He swung his legs off the edge of the bed as the room began spinning. "I've got to get to the office."

Sara pressed her hands against his shoulders. At the moment, she was much stronger than he was and even though he struggled, he couldn't dislodge her from his path.

"Mr. Logan, please—you'll break open your stitches. Lie still now. Dr. Stillwell will be in to check on you in a half hour. Okay?"

Her grip on his shoulders didn't let up and Nate felt too weak to keep struggling. Finally, he nodded and slumped against the hospital bed.

"I need to make some calls," he said. "Let people know where I am."

Sara chuckled. "I think they already know, Mr. Logan," she said, pointing to the rows of flowers. "Would you like me to read off the names to you?"

"Please," he said and she moved to the first vase: roses, daisies, and carnations. She tilted a card toward the light.

"Get Better Soon. We miss you. Staff of Logan Financial."

Okay, the office knew where he was. Ren probably had everything covered. Probably didn't even need him.

The next vase: yellow Chrysanthemums. "Sorry to hear about the accident. Get well soon." Gloeckner and Associates.

The next six vases of flowers were from clients. She read off the card from a bright bunch of purple flowers that included lilac roses.

"Nate, you're in my prayers, buddy. Get better and get back to the office where you're needed. Ren and Meredith."

Nate smiled. Nobody could have a better friend than Ren Stewart.

The largest bouquet that included orchids, anthuriums, and bird of paradise sat on a side table by itself.

"All my love. Dad."

The last bunch was a tall vase of red roses and baby's breath. He knew before Sara read the card who had sent them.

"Wuv you, honey. Get better soon. Corrina."

"Thanks for taking time to read those," said Nate. "I appreciate it."

"No problem. Do you still need to make those calls?"

"Just one quick one to the office," he said.

Sara moved toward the white nightstand beside his bed and lifted the beige phone off it. She sat it beside him on the bed.

"Thanks," said Nate. He called his work number, amazed by how weak he felt.

Sara left him to talk in private.

"Logan Financial," said Marina, the professional tone almost cool.

"Marina. It's Nate."

"Nate!" she cried. "Oh my God, how are you? We were all terrified when we heard the news. Are you doing okay?"

"Yeah, I'll be fine."

"It's so good to hear your voice."

Nate smiled. "Thanks. Is Ren in yet? I need to talk to him."

Marina laughed. "Not yet. I imagine he's on his way to the hospital to check on you. He's been there every day since he got the call." Her voice fell quiet for a moment. "He's been so worried, Nate."

"Thanks, Marina. Tell everyone thanks for the flowers."

"Take care, Nate. You get better, you hear?" she said and hung up the phone.

Nate laid the phone back in its cradle and let his arm fall to his side. He closed his eyes a moment and settled against the thin pillow. He must have drifted off to sleep for a few minutes, but the sound of Ren's voice shook him awake.

"Ren?" he asked, opening his eyes. "That you?"

Ren, dressed in a navy suit and white shirt, dropped down in the light blue recliner beside his bed, leaning forward, a hand on Nate's shoulder. He grinned, relief shining in his dark eyes.

"Nate! They said you woke up this morning, but I didn't believe them. How you doing?"

"I'm okay," said Nate. He studied his best friend's haggard face, the tired look in his eyes. He hadn't slept much, Nate realized. "But you look like hell."

Ren waved him off. "Better than you look. Your face is still pretty bruised from the accident."

Nate squinted at him. "What can you tell me about it?"

"Don't you remember?" Ren asked, a look of surprise widening his eyes.

"Not so much," he replied. "Just bits and pieces."

"That describes your SUV, buddy."

Nate winced. "Was there a lot of damage?"

Ren sucked in a pained breath. "It's totaled, Nate. You wrapped it around a pole on North Glebe. What happened? Did you fall asleep?"

Sighing, Nate ran a hand across his chin, feeling the bruised, swollen flesh. He'd fallen asleep. That's what caused the accident. He remembered now.

"I think so," said Nate. "Corrina kept me there until late. I should have left earlier, but I didn't want to disappoint her."

Ren crossed his arms, an almost sullen look on his face. "She was in rare form the day after your accident. Throwing herself at the doctors, sobbing, and carrying on—making herself the center of attention while you were in surgery. Didn't stop her from going out shopping with her friends later that night. And she hasn't even been back to see you."

That stung. Sitting around a hospital for hours on end was far too boring for Corrina. He was glad he'd been unconscious and didn't have to listen to the whining. Corrina knew how to whine when it suited her purposes.

"Marina said you'd been here since the accident."

Ren swallowed hard and looked down at his hands. "Just wanted to make sure you didn't need blood or anything. Had to make sure you'd be okay."

Nate reached out and patted Ren's arm. "I appreciate it, man. I'm sure Meredith wasn't happy to be without you all that time."

He smiled. "She understood."

Ren was lucky to have someone like Meredith. Always patient and understanding, outgoing and fun. Except with Corrina. They were cordial and polite to one another, but Nate knew she didn't care for Corrina. Ren said Meredith thought Corrina was selfish and narcissistic.

"Doesn't surprise me. You'd better not let that one go."

"I don't plan to," Ren replied. "So how you feeling?"

"Sore. Weak. What kind of surgery did I have?"

Ren chuckled. "Boy, you've really been out of it, haven't you?"

Nate nodded.

"You ruptured your spleen, so they removed it. It almost killed you, too. But they got to it in time. Thank God you were so close to Sibley. That probably saved your life. You're a very lucky man, Nate."

"I don't feel so lucky," said Nate, groaning as a wave of pain pulsed through his side. He laid his hand against the bandage, rubbing the tender skin.

"If you saw your SUV, you wouldn't say that."

Nate fell quiet, contemplating his near-death experience. The whole accident had been surreal, but it scared him. He couldn't control the exhaustion that had crept up on him with its soft, deadly silence. He'd never even felt the first microsecond that he'd fallen asleep at the wheel. A momentary blink, he'd told himself. Just an instant of closing his eyes and then opening them again.

*What if he'd hit another car? Or worse. What if he'd killed someone?*

The thought ached through him now, making him feel sick and stupid. He'd endangered so many people that night, including himself. And it hadn't even been about drinking and driving. Falling asleep at the wheel was just as bad, maybe worse.

"Hey, you okay?" Ren asked.

Nate nodded.

"Like I believe that?"

He sighed. "I was just thinking about how stupid I was that night."

"You almost died, Nate," said Ren, carefully avoiding an agreement with that statement.

"I fell asleep at the wheel, Ren," he said, looking Ren square in the eyes, unblinking. "It was a stupid thing to let happen."

"No argument from me on that. I hated like hell having to call your dad and tell him about your accident."

Nate frowned, struggling to sit up a little straighter in bed. "You called my dad?"

Ren nodded. "Tracked him down at the airport."

"Airport?"

"Yes, he had a trip to New Orleans scheduled, but it was canceled because of *Hurricane Katrina*?"

"What hurricane?" Nate asked.

Ren patted him on the shoulder. "While you were here, buddy, a category five hurricane formed in the Gulf. It landed as a category three in New Orleans. Parts of the city are under several feet of water."

*Several feet?* The thought made his blood chill. He had friends in that area. He hoped they'd gotten out all right. "That's horrible."

"It's chaos down there. Hundreds are dead or missing."

"Dear God—hundreds?"

Ren nodded. He leaned back in the recliner. "Your dad's in Georgia now, trying to organize some fund-raising efforts. He was here at the hospital when they took you into surgery and stayed until the doctors said you'd be okay."

*So, the old man had been here.* Nate settled back against the pillow.

"What can our firm do to help the hurricane victims? Donations? Matching? We could hire our own freight company. Truck in supplies ourselves."

Ren pushed back in the recliner until his feet elevated. "I've been thinking about that, Nate."

"I'm scared already," said Nate with a smirk.

"We can swing a fifty-grand donation, no problem, but I want to do more."

Ren always wanted to go that extra mile. That's one of the things Nate liked best about him.

"I'm in. What's your plan?"

Ren grinned, laying a hand to his chin. "A charity auction to raise money."

Nate squinted at him, noting that his grin hadn't faded. It wasn't just an auction, Nate realized.

"Okay, a charity auction. Keep going."

"There's this auction site on the web. Auctionanza. They auction off unique items and services. Lots of charities use it."

"And..." Nate said, motioning at Ren to get to the point.

"So, I was thinking we organize an executive auction right here in D.C."

"You mean get senators and representatives to auction off personal items, something like that?" Nate squinted at him, trying to judge how close he'd come to Ren's plan.

But that unflinching grin remained.

"Not exactly. We auction off executives."

Nate forced himself to sit up, despite the ache in his side. "Executives? You can't auction people!"

But Ren was nodding, that smug, *wanna bet* look unwavering.

"I never pegged you for a slave trader, Ren."

Ren laughed. "Buy an executive for a month. All proceeds go to a *Katrina* fund to be distributed to local agencies that provide direct help to the victims."

"No one will agree to that."

"Ten people already have."

"Actual senators?" Nate replied, shaking his head.

"No," he said, glancing down at his hands. "But some corporate folks have agreed to the proposal, including myself."

Nate couldn't hold back his laugh. "You're crazy, Ren. You're actually going to auction yourself off to the highest bidder?"

He nodded. "Meredith will probably be my high bidder, but yeah, I'm going to do it." He patted Nate's arm. "And I was hoping you'd volunteer, too."

"Me?" He held onto his side, the laughter bubbling out. "Ren, you're crazy. No way! I'm happy to match your high bid, but –"

"Why not, Nate? You're single, you're successful—"

"Engaged."

Ren rolled his eyes. "Whatever. Get Corrina to bid on you."

Nate shook his head. "Sorry, buddy. That's a crazy idea."

"It'd be good for you to get away from things for a while. Let your body heal from this accident. You need a break, Nate, whether you'll admit to it or not. This way, you could be doing some charity work. Maybe help someone get their business back on track with that expensive MBA of yours?"

"No way."

"Well, Corrina liked the idea when I told her about it."

Nate felt the anger burn in his face. "You told Corrina about this before you talked to me?"

"I told you, too. In this very room, but you were unconscious."

"That's an underhanded trick, Stewart," Nate said with a growl.

"But was it successful, that's what I want to know?" Ren replied.

With stiff movements, Nate crossed his arms against his chest. If he'd already blabbed this whole scheme to Corrina, the decision was already made. Or she'd nag him to death until he gave in—her usual M.O. In his condition, trapped in a hospital bed like he was, he had no desire to test Corrina's nagging skills. If he gave in now, he might get to dictate the terms of his surrender. Besides, if Corrina had the highest bid, he could just donate the money.

"If I wasn't flat on my back, I'd deck you for this little stunt, Ren."

"My evil plot is all going according to plan," said Ren. He rubbed his hands together with an evil laugh.

"So, what do I have to do after you've sold me into slavery?"

"Stay with the buyer for a month, developing a financial plan for them or clean out closets and bake cookies. Maybe put out a shingle at the shelters and help *Katrina* survivors develop financial plans to get back on their feet. You won't be scrubbing toilets or anything."

Nate sighed. "All right. I give in."

Ren pumped the air with his fist. "Yes! I knew the Corrina nag card would seal the deal."

"Ren!"

"Come on, everybody knows that, including you, so don't bother arguing to the contrary." Suddenly, Ren looked serious, the smirk fading from his face. "It'll give you a solid rest before you return to the job. You've been under too much stress lately, Nate. I'm just relieved that you've got a second chance. When I saw that SUV, I was sure you were dead."

"Maybe you're right? This whole accident's been a wake-up call."

Ren patted him on the shoulder as he rose from the chair. "I've gotta get back to the office. Need to start promoting our charity auctions. I have a few more executives to guilt into participating, too." He stopped in the doorway. "I'll be back tonight and bring you some real food."

"I'll take you up on that. Thanks for everything, Ren."

With a wave, Ren disappeared into the hallway. Nate tilted his head back against the pillow. *Maybe this auction thing wouldn't be so bad? Maybe it would even help some people who had probably lost everything?* Like he'd nearly lost everything a few nights ago. The thought chilled him to the bone. *What would it feel like to auction himself off to the highest bidder?* He was about to find out.

# FOUR

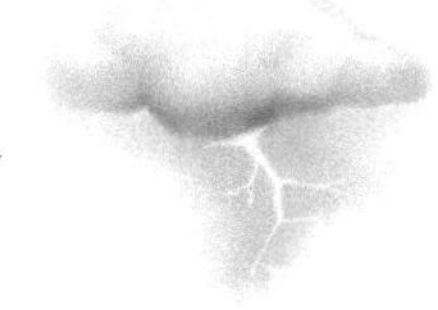

*Thursday, September 1, 2005—*

IT WAS TWILIGHT WHEN KADENCE DROVE UP TO HER BUTTER-YELLOW, BRICK farmhouse south of Lake Charles. Just outside the small town of Hackberry. They had to stay the night in a hotel because Elsie had been too exhausted to travel and needed to eat a good meal and sleep.

Bushy blue hydrangeas clustered around the edge of her white wraparound porch, the rusty red earth pale beneath the Live Oak shadows creeping across the yard. The air smelled warm, sweet with fresh-cut grass. Cicadas buzzed and chirred in the lazy calm, the red gravel popping underneath her tires as she rolled to a stop in the car port beside the house.

"It's a lovely place, Kadence," said Elsie.

Kadence turned off the car and pushed open the car door, letting the heat rush inside and the exhaustion coil around her shoulders. She wanted a long soak and a chilled glass of chardonnay. She gazed at Elsie as she climbed out of the car. She could only imagine how Elsie must feel.

Forcing herself to rise, Kadence climbed out of the car and

opened the back door. She slid the cat carriers out of the car. These exhausted felines slept all the way after eating a full can of tuna apiece. She and Elsie had stopped at a diner for meatloaf and mashed potatoes before heading for Lake Charles. With plenty of coffee. Tomorrow, she'd take Elsie shopping for clothes and anything else she needed.

She hefted the cat carriers onto the porch, setting them by a weathered, old yellow porch swing that hung in front of the picture window. Her favorite place to sit after work. McNeese State University, where she usually taught criminal justice, was only thirty minutes away. But after struggling through last year, she'd taken a leave of absence this semester, to clear her head. They tried to get her to take a sabbatical, but she wasn't ready to dive into her research just yet. Then she'd gotten the call from the Lake Charles Fire Department, asking all first responders to assist in New Orleans. She'd left immediately. That was nearly a week ago.

As soon as she'd gotten Elsie settled, she'd return to New Orleans and continue to search for survivors—human and animal.

She opened the green screen door that squeaked in protest, holding it open with one hip as she slid her key into the old lock, rattling the doorknob until the door rasped open. She motioned Elsie inside then picked up the cat carriers.

She set them down on the old, worn maple floor in the family room, the air smelling like fresh apples. A blue and purple area rug covered the sitting area in front of the river rock fireplace that stretched up to the ceiling. The pale aqua walls made the place feel cool as she turned on the ceiling fan that whupped whupped overhead.

The overstuffed couches, striped blue, green, and lavender, flanked a large square, walnut coffee table strewn with tattered issues of *Glamour*, *Taste of Home*, and *Scientific American*. A flat wicker basket filled with catalogs sat at the end of one couch. A library table sat behind the other couch, balancing two ceramic table lamps, a small vase of flowers, and some white votive candles.

After depositing the cats safely inside, Kadence returned to the car, popping the trunk to grab her duffle bag which she slung across one shoulder and two bags of groceries. She tucked the new cat litter pan under her arm and carried everything inside. She'd come back for the box of cat litter in the back seat.

"Make yourself at home, Elsie," Kadence called to her from the sunny yellow kitchen with its new maple cabinets and warm granite countertops the color of peaches and cream.

Elsie sat down on one of the couches, sinking into the soft, striped fabrics. Her eyelids drooped. Poor woman had been through a lot.

Kadence ran back to get the box of cat litter and brought it inside. Then she hurried to put away the groceries. She set a bag of Meow Mix on the counter and filled a cake pan with it. She filled another cake pan with fresh water and set them both at the end where the counter rounded out into an overhang with two barstools.

The litter box, she filled and sat in the hallway where both cats could see it. She'd move it to someplace more permanent tomorrow. When everything was in place, doors closed, she opened the carriers. Percy and Diva slinked out of their carriers, the assault of strange smells overwhelming the poor creatures. Both cats found the litter box first thing and began to clump up the box. When they'd finished their business, they immediately found the dry cat food. Both cats pressed their faces into the pan, gobbling dry food.

"Elsie, why don't I show you to your room? You must be exhausted."

Elsie nodded, her salt and pepper curls looking droopy, the bags under her eyes more prominent than they had been only an hour ago.

"I'd love to sleep in a nice soft bed."

With an arm around Elsie's shoulder, Kadence led her down the hallway past the parlor to a back bedroom. An old oak sleigh bed sat in the center of the room, flanked on either side by walnut nightstands. A blue and yellow patchwork quilt served as the bedspread, hiding a soft navy blanket beneath its old squares. Made by her grandmother. The pale blue sheets were crisp and smelled like lavender as Kadence turned them down. She turned on the brass lamp beside the bed.

"Bathroom's just outside your door. I'll leave out a toothbrush for you. Help yourself to whatever's in the cabinets."

Elsie sat down on the bed, her eyes welling with tears. "I don't even have a pair of underwear," she said in a quiet voice.

Kadence sat down beside her and hugged her. "We'll take care of that tomorrow."

Kadence opened the top drawer of the chest of drawers that stood against the far wall and rummaged until she found a long cotton night-shirt, this one lavender. She laid it and a pair of white socks on the bed for Elsie.

"I hope this will do for tonight."

"It sure will, honey," said Elsie, patting her arm. "Thank you."

Elsie slid off her battered black shoes, probably still wet from the flood waters, and reached for the nightshirt.

"Sleep well, Elsie. Tomorrow, things will look much better, I promise."

"Good night, Kadence," said Elsie.

Percy and Diva flitted into the bedroom. Percy jumped onto the bed and curled up, but Diva dived under the bed. Kadence patted the tabby cat and stepped out of the room. She walked down the hallway to the stairway that rose from the battered maple floor. Upstairs, there were three bedrooms, one of them her office. The room was soft with sage greens, buttery yellows and deep blue accents. Her old wooden desk sat in front of the lace curtains, facing out toward the mossy Live Oaks and vacant fields.

Her computer was still on from days ago when she'd hurried out of the house bound for New Orleans. Microsoft Word was still open, cursor flashing on a blank white page. She'd just sat down to work on a paper when the phone rang.

Her mail program was open, too, the barrage of new messages overwhelming as she sat down and paged through them. Lots of university email, colleagues, and committee members needing infor-mation, more meeting invitations. Always more meetings, but she was on leave so it felt good to delete these invitations. Not tonight though. She pinched the bridge of her nose between thumb and forefinger, unable to deal with all of it. Tomorrow, she told herself and closed her mail.

She launched a browser window and googled relief efforts for *Katrina*. They were already cropping up everywhere. Fundraisers. Donations. Telethons. The usual assortment of attempts to gather money for the victims, and the scammers, but Kadence doubted the authenticity of many of these so-called charities. A newsfeed ran in another window above her browser as Kadence scanned back and forth between Google and the news feed.

One of the human-interest stories caught her attention. The headline read: East Coast Firm Auctioning off Executives for Katrina Relief. And there was a link: http://www.auctionanza.com/LoganAuctions. She clicked on the link and another browser window opened, displaying the online auction site.

Ever needed a financial planner or high-priced MBA, but couldn't afford one? Now, you can own one for a month. To raise money for Katrina victims, Logan Financial is auctioning off the finest talent from Arlington and the D.C. area to the highest bidder. At your service for a month, bid on the executive of your choice. He or she will be flown to your location for a month of assistance. Need help balancing your checkbook or advice on managing your business? Help is just a click away.

Kadence laughed as she paged through the executives and their bios and photos until she stared into Nate Logan's smiling face, light green eyes, and tousled blond curls.

*Nice eyes*, she thought, studying the kind green eyes. *Definitely eye candy*. But the name rang a bell. Where had she heard it before?

She googled Nate Logan and as the hit list appeared on her screen, she saw Senator Lee Logan's name pop up.

"A Senator's son," she said out loud. Bet there was plenty of media coverage on this guy, she thought with a smirk as she closed the search window, returning to the Auctionanza site and the handsome face staring back at her. She was too tired to look at all those links.

The idea hit her like a speeding truck. It was crazy. Her colleagues would think she'd lost her mind. Maybe she had, but these poor people needed lots of help...and the more publicity the better. She glanced out at the dim-lit hallway. She had one extra bedroom left—there was plenty of room.

The red Bid button flashed at her as she slid her mouse over it. Two bids so far. He was already up to $750 with one day left to bid.

Bringing Nate Logan to Louisiana would also bring more cameras and coverage to the devastation. As if they weren't already clogging the roads and hotels. But with her calling the shots and renting Senator Logan's son, she could focus that attention where it was needed. On people like Elsie.

She clicked on the link and bid $2000 on Nate Logan. *Maybe if Senator Logan heard these people's stories from his own son, he'd push harder to help them in Washington?* Long after that first sympathetic wave of giving ebbed and the rest of the country moved on to other causes and other disasters. *Katrina* would stay with the public a long time, she knew that, but aid disappeared quickly. If she could help keep the relief efforts alive, it was worth it.

Kadence rose from her chair and walked back downstairs. She poured a glass of chardonnay from the refrigerator and carried it outside to the porch swing. Cicadas scritched in the gathering night, heat still blanketing the air. She shook loose her rusty red hair from its clip and ponytail holder, letting it tumble onto her shoulders as she rocked the swing gently. Chains creaked, boards whined as her bare feet scuffed across the wooden porch. The air smelled sweet with freshly mown grass, the chardonnay cold against her fingertips.

She let the crisp, lemony wine slide over her tongue and warm her belly as she studied the stately oaks strewn with lacey moss. She loved nights like this, the world feeling soft and safe, its hard-edged realities far away if only for a few hours.

*What would someone like Nate Logan do in a place like this?* Trapped in the country, away from double shot lattes and designer martinis. *Would he feel lost in the cattails and cicadas? What had she been thinking to bid on him?* It was a dumb idea. She should have slept on that decision before rushing ahead and plopping down a bid.

*Like he was a floor lamp.*

Her stomach twisted into a knot of regret. She couldn't retract her bid. She knew that. Most likely, this was just a publicity stunt and one of his friends would outbid her. They'd raise a few dollars, tell some fun stories, and go on with their lives.

Besides, he probably had no idea what it meant to give something back anyway, beyond opening his checkbook for a donation. Someone like that probably had a perfect life and wanted it to stay that way. She couldn't fault him for that. She'd had a shot at that perfect life once, but it slipped through her fingers one night on a rainy highway.

Being a first responder brought her to so many fires and car accidents. She'd never dreamed it'd place her first on the scene of her fiancé's fatal car crash. Those fleeting moments of confusion and pain in his eyes, unable to even speak to her as his life ebbed out onto the pavement. The crushing mass of metal twisted around the remnants of the driver's cage. Punctured his ephemeral artery. He bled out in a matter of minutes and she could do nothing to stop it. She couldn't even reach the wound to put pressure on it. Instead, she'd held his hand, hers trembling against his bloodied face while those wild eyes fought to communicate with her, to say something without words.

"I love you, too," she'd told him and that seemed to soften the pain in his eyes. She felt his lips press against her palm and then fall still. The life trickled out of his eyes then, his body limp as his spirit left him.

Out of pain, she knew as the tears rushed down her face, sitting there on the double yellow with his blood all over her clothes, persistent click of the Mustang's left turn signal flashing against the asphalt. It took two firefighters from her station to lead her away from the car. Even as she moved toward the shoulder and the wet grass beyond, she felt the emptiness spread through her chest with the mounting distance.

She couldn't cry for Tom after that. The pain and sorrow just sort of scattered through her instead of balling up into a knot that pressed for release. She hadn't felt much since that night and even now, she wasn't sure she ever wanted that kind of intensity back in her life. It was exhausting and when it was gone, it left nothing else in its wake. Nothing to fill all the holes.

She went on with her life, after that. Next month was the first anniversary of his death. That raw ache had dulled to a mixture of numbness and half-feeling. It was survivable, she knew, but it wasn't much fun.

Kadence took another sip of the cool chardonnay, watching the huge moths beat their powdery wings around the porch light. With the cicadas' steady presence and the wine warming her belly, Kadence let that awful night fade into the dusty corners of memory. Tomorrow, she and Elsie needed to go into Lake Charles and get her some clothes. She'd focus on someone else for a change, see if she could make a difference even for one person.

She'd call LaWanda's cell tomorrow and find out when they needed her back to the rescue efforts. It would also give her time to pick up food and water—and anything else—for the shelters. With the first anniversary of Tom's death fast approaching, she needed to be as busy as possible. After all, forgetting was easier when she was busy.

# FIVE

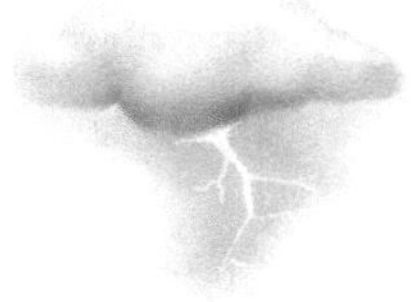

*Tuesday, August 30, 2005 —*

NATE SAT ON THE END OF HIS HOSPITAL BED, DRESSED IN KHAKI CARGO shorts and a red sweatshirt as he waited for Ren to arrive. He was going home today, the ache in his left side better, but still tender. They told him he'd need another four weeks of rest before he could go back to the office. With Ren his only ride until he replaced his SUV, he wouldn't have much say in when he went back to the office. He could always borrow Corrina's driver, he thought with a chuckle.

In about ten minutes, Ren walked into the hospital room, a strange look on his face. He looked pale, nervous, Nate realized. He was dressed in faded jeans and a Navy polo shirt.

"What's wrong?" Nate asked. "Get a speeding ticket or something? Somebody hit your Land Rover?"

Ren sank down on the bed beside him, looking…Nate squinted at his best friend…looking scared.

"How you feeling?" Ren asked, not looking at him, instead playing with the ring of keys in his hands. "You doin' okay?"

"Why?" Nate snapped, studying Ren. *What was going on with him?*

*Had something happened at the office? Did they lose the Gloeckner account?* Tomorrow was the last day of the month and the long Labor Day weekend was almost here. *What could be wrong?*

Ren licked his dry lips, still fiddling with the keys.

"Spill it, Ren," he said finally, irritated by the stall tactics. If it was bad news, he wanted it right now. Not later to blindside him.

Ren cast a quick glance at him and returned his gaze to the jingling keys. Still silent.

Nate reached over and snatched the keys out of his hands, tossing them into the recliner.

"What's the matter with you?"

"Remember that auction thing? Rent an Executive for Katrina Relief?" He looked pale, almost sick.

Nate frowned. "Of course."

"We made a hundred and fifty thousand dollars."

"What?" Nate's eyes widened. "Are you serious?" He clapped Ren on the shoulder. "Great job, Ren! You should be proud of yourself."

Ren sucked in a breath. "Yeah, we raised a lot of money. But—well...some things turned out a little differently than we'd uh, planned."

Nate felt his stomach sink. "Like what?" he asked, his tone wary. Ren should have been ecstatic over raising that kind of money. *Why was he stalling like this?* "Ren! Out with it—you're making me crazy."

"Well, see—Corrina was supposed to be your highest bidder."

"Supposed to be?" Nate's mouth fell open, a bad feeling quivering through his stomach.

"Yeah," said Ren, a nervous laugh escaping through his grin. "Marina and I showed her how to bid and everything. She said she understood."

Ren rose from the bed and began to pace, driving Nate's heart into his throat.

"Just what are you trying to say?"

"Corrina wasn't the high bidder, Nate," he said, stopping in front of him, his face taut with dread. It was bad, Nate realized. Ren had gotten him into a bad situation and he had no way out.

"So, who was...buddy?" he said with a snarl.

"A—a college professor."

That didn't sound so bad. He raised an eyebrow. "Georgetown?"

Ren shook his head. "No…it's a little farther south, I'm afraid."

Nate felt the heat rise in his temples. "How far south are we talking, Ren?"

"Louisiana," he said in a small voice.

"Louisiana!"

Ren held up both hands, backing away as Nate jumped up from the sick bed. He'd tear Ren limb from limb!

"It doesn't get any farther south! Unless somebody from Cuba bid on me." He balled his hands into fists, but fought down the urge to deck Ren. "I could just kill you, Ren!"

Ren took two steps backward until he was standing in the hallway, but Nate grabbed him by the shirt and slammed him against the door jamb.

"You're sending me to freakin' Katrina-ravaged Louisiana for a month, Ren! I can't believe you got me into this mess."

The ache in his side radiated and he gasped, letting go of Ren to clutch his left side. Ren grabbed hold of him as he began to sink and steered him back to the bed.

"I'm so sorry, Nate. Corrina screwed up the bid, didn't get it posted until the auction expired."

"Remind me to send her a thank-you note," he said with a groan. "Dammit, Ren, what am I supposed to do now?"

"I don't know, but I'll think of something. Maybe if I contact Professor Harlowe and explain about your accident, she'd accept a refund?"

Nate sighed. Then he'd look like a fool. Not man enough to live up to his obligations. It was a binding contract, he realized that. *But Louisiana?* He'd never been south of Louisville and had no desire to either.

"Where'd you get sent?" Nate asked. "I hope it was New Jersey. That's the only place worse than Louisiana."

"Nowhere. Got bought by a local."

Nate cast a sour look at him. "By Meredith no less. But you let me

—your best buddy, still in the hospital—get sent to hurricane-ravaged Louisiana after losing a spleen. Thanks for watching my back."

"I can't begin to tell you how sorry I am. But damn, Nate— Professor Harlowe paid three grand for you. The least you could do is show up and help her out."

Now, he was playing the guilt card.

"You are *so* going to owe me, Stewart. I'm going to get a lot of mileage out of this guilt trip, I promise you that."

A woman in beige scrubs appeared at his doorway with a wheelchair.

"Your taxi's here, Mr. Logan," she said with a grin and motioned him toward the chair.

Ren helped Nate stand up. He slid his arm around Nate's waist and helped him over to the chair where he collapsed into it, his eyes opened to slits. He felt weak and shaky, not to mention the steady ache in his side.

"Louisiana," Nate said with a sigh. "I could just kill you, Ren."

***

IN A COUPLE OF DAYS, NATE WAS READY TO GO BACK TO WORK, WHETHER or not the doctors agreed. Dozens of times, Ren offered to contact Professor Harlowe and negotiate a prisoner release, but Nate refused. Even Ren seemed surprised that the Professor expected him to actually show up in Lake Charles.

Only two other executives had to leave the area, Nate thought with a sigh. He was one of the lucky ones.

He sat on the sofa in his bathrobe, a steaming cup of coffee balanced in his hands as he watched Ren pace in front of the white leather bar separating the sitting area from the kitchen. He hadn't slept well at all last night, flashes of the accident invading his dreams.

"You're doing it on purpose now!" Ren shouted, slapping his arms against his side. His grey suit looked a little more wrinkled than normal.

"No, I'm not," said Nate, sitting up on the couch. "I've just reached a grim acceptance of my fate. I'd rather just get it over with now and get it behind me."

Ren scowled, shoving his hands in his pants pocket, key ring jangling.

"Are you all packed?" he asked, that look of remorse returning to his face.

Nate shrugged and pointed to the large suitcase at the front door.

"When's your flight?"

"Ten forty-six. Corrina and her driver will be here any minute to drive me to Dulles." Nate studied his best friend a moment. "Oh, I'm going to get so much guilt mileage out of this when I get back."

Ren glared at him, but didn't say a word as Nate rose from the couch. He took a long sip of his coffee and set it on the table. He walked toward the hallway that led to a den and two bedrooms. His bedroom—all greens and burgundies—was the first door on the left. He tossed his bathrobe onto the bed he'd already made and dressed in jeans and a pale blue t-shirt. He slid his feet into brown Merrell's and snagged his sunglasses, cell phone, and wallet off the dresser.

He shoved his wallet into his back pocket, clipped his cell to his front pocket, and took one last look at his bedroom. He'd be gone a month, staying God-knew-where. *Had Dad heard about this yet?* He'd visited a couple of days ago before flying out to San Antonio. Another *Katrina* relief effort. Not quite like the one Nate was about undertake.

Nate grabbed his plane ticket and returned to the sitting room. He pulled his leather jacket off the coat rack beside the door and laid it over his suitcase before grabbing his cup of coffee again.

"All right, say it. Call me a jerk. Scream at me! Anything but this silent treatment." Ren rubbed his hand across his brown eyes, looking genuinely upset now. "I feel terrible about this, okay, Nate? You're not even well enough to be at work yet and because of me, you're being shipped off the Louisiana. Meredith and I feel terrible!"

"What's done is done, Ren," he said, standing in front of his best friend. "Let it go, all right?"

Ren nodded finally, but he still looked distraught. Nate knew it hadn't been intentional. Corrina's computer skills were limited to mouse clicks and shutting down the computer. It was nobody's fault.

Besides, maybe Professor Harlowe really did need some help? Maybe he could even do some good? Regardless, he'd make the best of it.

A loud buzz resounded and Nate moved to the intercom.

"Nate, my wuv—we're here." Another contrite voice.

"I'll be right down," he replied, holding in the button.

Nate slammed the rest of the coffee and set the empty cup on the coffee table.

"Take care of that for me," he said, draping his jacket over his arm. He grabbed hold of his blue suitcase's telescoping handle and opened the front door. "Seeya in a month, Ren."

"Take care of yourself, Nate. And if you need anything—a ride home—I'll be there in a heartbeat."

Nate chuckled. Yeah, he could mine Ren's guilt for a long time. He opened the door, pulling his suitcase into the hall, and waved at Ren before closing the door.

"Call me when you get there. So, Meredith and I know you're okay."

"Yes, mother," he shouted and started down the hallway to the elevator.

---

Corrina draped herself across Nate in the limo's backseat. She smelled like Coco Chanel and salty tears that still leaked down her heart-shaped face.

"Oh, Nate—will you ever forgive me? I feel so terrible!"

He grabbed a tissue from the seat pocket and pressed it to her face, dabbing away her tears.

"It's not your fault, Corrina. It was a crazy idea and you were outbid. It's okay."

It *was* her fault, but he wouldn't make her feel worse. She just wasn't good with computers and Ren knew that.

"But I won't see you for a whole month," she wailed.

He wrapped his arms around her and kissed her on the lips, tasting coconut lip gloss.

"Everything's gonna be fine," he replied. "You'll have all your friends and the weekly mall outings to keep you busy."

"Oh, Nate, it's just not the same!"

Her elbow jabbed him in the left side and he gasped, pain snaking across his torso. He let her go, his hands falling to his side as he tried to ease the sharp pain that radiated now.

"What's the matter?" she asked, her face pale, eyes wide.

He couldn't talk for a moment, the pain choking him. He let the seconds tick past, unable to speak as he rubbed his side.

"It's okay," he said finally, his voice thin. "Just a little pain—it'll pass."

They remained quiet the rest of the ride to Dulles International. The limo pulled up to the curb of the Continental Airlines terminal and Nate stepped out. His suitcase was waiting for him on the curb.

Corrina wrapped her arms around his neck, pressing her lips against his in an urgent kiss.

"Nate, promise me you'll call and let me know how you are."

He smiled and held up his hand. "I promise."

"I wuv you," she said, grinning, and kissed him one last time.

"Love you, too," he replied.

The tears started to fall again, her face twisting with sorrow. "You didn't say it right," she said.

"I wuv you, too," he said in a quiet voice, trying hard not to cringe as he said it, hoping no one heard him.

Smiling now, she waved at him then climbed into the limo. It surged away from the curb as Nate wheeled his suitcase into the terminal.

*Louisiana*, he thought with a groan. *Maybe if he was lucky, he'd been eaten in his sleep by an alligator?*

# SIX

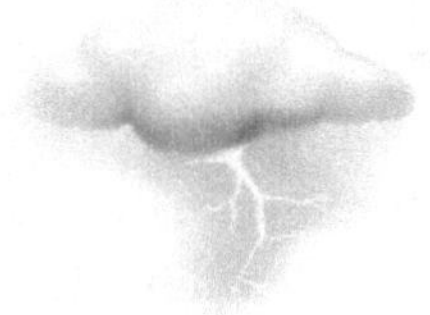

*Saturday, September 3, 2005 —*

KADENCE WAITED JUST OUTSIDE SECURITY, ON THE WAY TO BAGGAGE CLAIM, a cardboard sign displaying *Mr. Nate Logan* in purple Sharpie. The over-cooled air gave her goose bumps, but it was her fault for wearing cut-offs and a tank top. Three Lake Charles reporters and a cameraman meandered around behind her, waiting to snap photographs of the senator's son, won in an online auction.

She wanted to laugh, the idea so absurd she still couldn't believe she'd actually bid on the man. She even upped her bid another grand to snag him. But she'd see it through if it brought more relief dollars into the region where they were most needed.

His plane had been on the ground only a few minutes and she watched the stream of people shuffling toward baggage claim. The air smelled like ground coffee and fresh baked cinnamon muffins from the Creole Coffee House. She leaned against the wall, drinking in the intoxicating smells, and held up her sign to the line of passengers. She'd seen his picture online. Curly blonde hair, nice smile, light green eyes—expensive suit and tie. *Probably a glamour shot,* she mused.

In a few minutes, a tall, blond man in faded jeans and a t-shirt approached, moving slowly and looking a little haggard. He carried a leather jacket over one arm. *Wouldn't get much chance to use that jacket,* she thought with a grin.

She moved away from the wall, holding up the sign. He scanned the walkway, left then right until his gaze met hers. She smiled and pointed to the sign.

Nodding, he returned her smile and walked toward her.

"Mr. Logan? I'm Professor Harlowe." She extended her hand to him. "Nice to meet you."

"I'd much prefer Nate, Professor." His smile widened as he shook her hand. Firm grip. Strong, squared hands. "I'm betting Professor isn't your first choice either."

She shook her head. "Please, call me Kadence. With a K."

His eyes widened. "Kadence? What a pretty name."

She smiled.

Two Channel 7 reporters moved toward him, cameras flashing. Ted Arbaugh, the newspaper reporter, also from Lake Charles, moved beside Nate. A sallow man with more liver spots than hair and a deft hand with the written word, he wrote notes on a steno pad with thick, shaking fingers. Startled, Nate Logan turned a confused gaze toward them then back at Kadence.

She almost felt badly about ambushing him with media before he'd even hit baggage claim, but it was for a good cause.

"Apparently your arrival here is news, Mr. Logan. I mean, Nate."

"My arrival? Why?" His forehead scrunched, a slight furrow beginning between his eyebrows.

She laughed. "It's not every day a guy gets bought off Auctionanza. A senator's son at that."

His face brightened into a smile again. "You've got a point there. My first time on the auction block, so I'm a little new at this."

"Hello, I'm Rhonda Reed from KLPC, Channel 7 news. Could we ask you both a few questions?" asked a black woman with a thick, smooth bob and a pleasant smile. She wore an ivory linen blazer and navy pants and carried a tape recorder. Her nails were long and painted a rich burgundy.

"While we walk," said Kadence. "I'm sure Nate's had a long day and would like to rest a little before facing a barrage of press."

He nodded at her and she noticed a slight grimace as he laid a hand against his side, his steps a little slower now.

"I'd be happy to talk you as long as you'd like tomorrow," Nate replied. "But can we keep it short today?"

He looked very tired, Kadence had to admit. It hadn't been that long of a flight from Virginia, but the man looked beat.

The woman nodded and motioned for the cameraman to stop filming.

"Just a few questions and we can talk more in a day or two," said Rhonda, microphone at her side.

"Would you care to make a statement for the print media?" Arbaugh asked, standing beside Rhonda.

Nate squinted, halting his slowed walk toward baggage claim. "And you are?"

The man smiled, revealing teeth yellowed from nicotine. "Ted Arbaugh. What in God's name made you auction yourself off for charity, Mr. Logan?"

Rhonda held back a laugh. The cameraman snickered, the red light lit on his camera. He was filming.

Arbaugh pulled out a greying handkerchief and pressed it to his mouth as he coughed.

"An objective account, aye?" said Nate, smiling at Kadence then Rhonda. "It was just a crazy idea to help *Katrina* victims. My partner came up with the idea. Although he managed to remain in Arlington while I got shipped out here."

"You're not gay, are you?" Arbaugh barked out, handkerchief against his mouth again.

Kadence couldn't hold in her laugh this time. Nate's mouth fell open, his eyes unable to hide his shock at this man's bluntness. Ted Arbaugh was part of Lake Charles' local color. Most people put up with his off-kilter approach because he was an excellent reporter. Regardless of the attitude he gave off and the baffling lack of objective viewpoint, Arbaugh always seemed to capture the essence of a story. And he had a nose for unusual stories.

"Not that it matters," Nate said with a chuckle, "but no, I'm not gay. Ren is my business partner. Together, we manage Logan Financial Group."

Arbaugh scribbled a few more notes in his shaky scrawl. "You're Senator Lee Logan's boy, aren't you? He voted against raising funding for the Lake Pontchartrain levee project this Spring, didn't he?"

Nate's face turned a little pale, his jaw tightening. "I wouldn't know how he voted on that issue or what information he examined to reach his decision."

"You sound like a politician's boy," said Arbaugh.

Kadence watched Nate's entire demeanor change, the relaxed state stiffening, hands propped on his hips, eyes darkening.

"Maybe I do, but I refuse to comment on a decision he made when I have no facts to analyze. Other than the obvious. The levee broke. It was a bad idea to cut the funding. Or would you like to hear the standard political response: I fully support my father's Senate record." He shrugged and walked away toward baggage claim again. "Either way, you'll turn my comments around to suit your purposes. If you want a real answer, you'll have to leave that chip on your shoulder at home, Mr. Arbaugh."

Rhonda exchanged a *well said* look with Kadence who smiled politely at her then rushed after Nate who'd already gotten to the stairs. He was halfway down before Kadence managed to touch his elbow.

"Nate, slow down," she replied.

"Why?" he asked, anger burning in his eyes as he cast a glare at her. "What other surprise attacks do you have planned, Professor Harlowe?"

"I'm sorry about that," she replied, following him toward the baggage claim conveyors trundling black and green suitcases in a half-circle.

Nate stopped beside the belt, studying the bags as they trudged past.

"Really," she said, forcing him to turn and look at her. "I never intended for that to happen. I thought it would be some nice publicity for your firm and one more spotlight on the plight of the *Katrina* victims."

He sighed, his gaze falling to the ground a moment. Finally, he looked up at her and managed a brief smile. "Okay. It's forgotten."

"It will be," she said, "when I cook up some jambalaya and dirty rice for you."

"That's a start," he said. His blue suitcase lurched past and he reached out to grab it. The suitcase thunked against the floor and he winced, sweat threading his upper lip. His jacket fell into the floor. He stood there motionless for a moment or two until Kadence realized he was in pain.

"Are you all right?" she asked, studying his face.

He closed his eyes, sucked in a quick breath, and then opened them again. "I'm fine," he said with a nod and extended the luggage handle. "Where are you parked?"

Kadence grabbed his jacket from the ground. It smelled new, a hint of Lagerfeld clinging to it. Warm and inviting.

"Just outside in the lot. It's a small airport."

She motioned him toward the automatic doors that slid open as she approached. Kadence braced herself for the heat that hit her hard and heavy as she stepped outside. She wondered how hot it got in Arlington. And humid? Nate didn't seem to be bothered by the heat or humidity as she led him down the long sidewalk toward the nearby car lot. Her Accord was parked toward the back. She popped the trunk and with a grunt, Nate hefted his suitcase inside and moved toward the passenger side door.

Kadence laid the jacket on top of his suitcase and closed the trunk. She unlocked the doors and they climbed inside at the same time. He struggled a little with the heavy door, sweating profusely.

"I'd better get the AC going," she said, starting the car. "You're probably not used to Louisiana heat."

He reached out a warm hand to hers. "No, don't crank it. I'm fine." His gaze met hers a moment, two, then flicked away. His hand left hers a moment or two later.

The car dinged at her, reminding her that the belts weren't fastened.

"I'll just put it on low, okay?"

He nodded as he clicked his seatbelt in place. She fastened hers, silencing the annoying dinging and pulled out of her space.

She drove out of the airport and onto the highway in silence, headed south until finally, Nate broke it.

"So why did you bid on me? Out of all the others? And want me to actually show up down here?" he asked, squinting at her.

*Boy, he was direct. A little more tactful than Arbaugh, but definitely to the point.*

"You want a political answer," she asked with a grin, "or the truth?"

"The truth would make my stay here much easier." He propped his right arm against the door and turned to stare at her. She felt the weight of those green eyes on her, patient but unyielding.

"It's not an exciting answer, but I bid on you to draw more attention to the *Katrina* victims. You're Senator Logan's son, so you're newsworthy."

He frowned.

"You may not believe that, but Ted Arbaugh knows a good story when it crosses his desk. He wouldn't have shown up at the airport if he didn't think you were newsworthy."

"So, you're hoping to get to my father through me?"

"No, I'm hoping the media will follow your story while you're down here, raising awareness and increasing donations—which helps victims of the hurricane."

"So, I'll be helping the victims?" he said, his voice softer, accepting, sounding almost pleased.

Kadence nodded. "I'm a first responder. I volunteer at the fire department and when the call for help went out, we went to New Orleans. I just got back a week ago from there. I'll be going back in a few days. And you're going with me."

When she glanced back at him, he was smiling.

"What?"

"You're really trying to help these people, aren't you?"

"Of course," she replied. "But you're surprised by that."

He laid his hand against his mouth, rubbing his smooth chin. "I am. But more than anything, I'm relieved. When I saw the press, I thought

I'd walked into a three-ring circus or some other nightmare. I'm glad the goal isn't greed."

Kadence smiled at him. "And I'm glad you followed through. When I read your profile, I thought you were some cushy executive who had no interest in helping anyone except from the convenience of your wallet. Throw a little money at the problem and forget about it."

His gaze stayed on her until she finally looked away, making sure she wasn't about to run over a few cars or wildlife.

"So, we're both pleasantly surprised," he replied.

"I guess we are," she replied, casting another look at Nate, who looked more like a grad student than the head of an investment group.

She felt comfortable with him. He seemed straightforward and didn't tint things in pretty colors, so she saw what she wanted to see.

"So, is there going to be any wine with this jambalaya tonight?"

"I've got some killer chardonnay. Crisp, cold, and Californian."

"Looking forward to it," he said, closing his eyes and leaning back in the seat. "Do you live close to Lake Charles?"

She shook her head. "About an hour drive and that's close enough for me. "I drive this three times a week or more."

"Where do you teach?" he asked, his voice softer now, sounding sleepy.

"McNeese State University. I teach criminal justice." She glanced over at him as he stretched out his legs and folded his arms against his chest, eyes still closed.

He yawned. "I took a few criminal justice classes at Georgetown."

"What was your bachelor's in?" Kadence asked, glancing at him before she changed lanes and turned off 210 and onto Highway 10.

"Finance," he said, pressing his hand to his mouth to hide another yawn.

"MBA from Harvard, right?" she replied, glancing at him again.

He nodded, his head pressed against the window, eyes closed, mouth slightly open as he began to snore quietly. She smiled. He'd been fighting it, she realized, trying to be polite. She'd wake him up when they were in Hackberry.

Almost an hour later, she pulled up in front of her rural home surrounded by the lazy trill of frogs and the steady scritch of cicadas. The air smelled warm with dried grass from a nearby field, the ruddy gravel popping under her tires. She stopped the car, a cloud of dust rising as she shut off the motor and opened the car door. Nate was hunched in his seat, head turned toward her, but sound asleep.

Elsie sat on the front porch, the swing squeaking. A breeze brushed across Kadence's face and long hair that clung in wisps to her face. Elsie waved, dressed in blue shorts and thin white blouse. A pair of flip flops sat on the wooden planks beside the swing.

"He don't look like much," Elsie called to her. "Seeing as how you paid three thousand for him."

Kadence burst out laughing. "Elsie! Give the man a chance."

Looking embarrassed, Elsie waved her away.

"I know you were kidding," Kadence replied.

She went around to the passenger door and opened it. It squeaked a bit, but Nate didn't even rouse.

"Nate?" she said. "Nate?" When he didn't respond, Kadence gently shook his shoulder until finally, he lifted his head, staring bleary-eyed at her, a look of confusion on his face.

"Kadence—remember?"

He nodded finally and sat up. "I remember. Sorry, the flight took more out of me than I realized."

"Don't MBAs travel all over the place?" she asked as he stretched and rose stiffly from the seat.

"Not this one," he replied. "I joined my father's firm right out of school so he could run for office."

Kadence nodded at him, doing her best to hold back her frown. Everything arranged from financing to courses to careers. *How would someone with such an obviously charmed life be of any use down here? Could he even understand these people?*

"Look, I know I was lucky, okay?"

"I didn't say anything—"

His jaw tightened. "Your face said it all."

"I'm sorry," she said. "I'm being a reverse snob."

"It's okay," said Nate, the tension in his jaw dissipating. "My folks had money and paid my way through Georgetown. But I paid for Harvard myself. I took out the loans and worked nights, the whole bit. Did I have to? No. I wanted to earn that degree. To show that I could do the job on my own."

She smiled. He'd do just fine. He had integrity; she saw it in his face. And conviction. She admired that in a man. Tom had always insisted on doing the right thing. To him, that mattered.

"Let's get your things inside and I'll show you where you'll be sleeping."

Kadence hurried to the trunk and opened it. She lifted his bag, but he took it from her hands, easing it onto the grass. He carried it to the porch, setting it down when he saw Elsie.

"I'm Nate Logan," he said, extending his hand to her.

Elsie grinned and held out her hand for him to shake.

"I'm Elsie Paige, child."

Kadence stepped onto the porch. "Elsie survived *Hurricane Katrina*. Her house was submerged in several feet of water."

Nate's face turned pale as he stared at her with admiration.

"We had to cut a hole in the roof to free her from the flood waters. They were nearly up to her chin."

"I'm so sorry about what you went through. It's a miracle you got out alive."

Elsie nodded, letting go of his hand. "Lost everythin' I had but the clothes on my back—and my two kitty cats."

"She wouldn't let us pull her up until we took the cats out."

A smile lit his face.

"I knowed if I got out of there afore they did, they'd drown."

Nate patted her on the shoulder. "You're a very brave woman, Elsie. Good to know you."

He hefted his suitcase onto the porch and followed Kadence into the house. He gazed around the sitting room and the kitchen.

"Nice place. Very homey."

Kadence moved toward the stairs and started up as Nate picked up the suitcase and followed. He was winded by the time he got to the top, pausing to lean against his luggage as he struggled to catch his breath. A thin sheen of sweat glistened on his face as he closed his eyes a moment, chest heaving.

It had only been about fourteen steps. Kadence squinted at him. He looked lean and muscular, easily able to handle those steps.

"Are you all right?"

"Fine," he said in a half-whisper, still catching his breath. "Just a little winded."

"You don't look like someone who gets worn out by one flight of stairs."

He exhaled. "I was a little under the weather recently," he replied, straightening up to stare at her. "But I'm fine. Just a little slow on the rebound."

"Let me show you to your room so you can rest for a bit." She smiled. "Before you have to tackle some spicy jambalaya."

He chuckled as he extended the handle of his luggage. "Lead the way."

She moved toward a deep blue bedroom. A hall bathroom separated it from Kadence's bedroom. Her office was diagonal to the guest room. Tom used to keep his clothes in here. Probably a dress shirt or two still hung in that closet, she realized.

"This will be your room, Nate," she replied, holding out a hand to usher him inside.

An antique oak chest-of-drawers hugged the medium blue walls, the pale maple floor and white trim giving the room brightness. A pale peach and blue quilt covered the bed, three goose down pillows hunched against the headboard. Beside the plain oak bed were two marble top nightstands, one with a lamp and digital clock, the other with a glass blue and green carafe. The room smelled faintly of lavender from the sachets Kadence had tucked in each room. In the corner stood the walk-in closet with its bare light bulb and long string.

"Feel free to use the dresser and closet, Nate. Bathroom's to your left. Get settled in and we'll see you for supper."

Percy leaped onto the bed, meowing as he turned circles, his thick paws kneading the old quilt.

"I hope you're not allergic to cats," said Kadence, moving toward the bed to scoop up Percy.

He shook his head as he reached out to pet the brown tabby's head. "No, it's okay. He's fine."

Kadence moved toward the door, but paused in the threshold.

"Thanks for being such a good sport about all this."

He grinned. "Glad to do it. Just hope I'll be worth the three grand you shelled out."

It was a nice smile. His features were chiseled, but just slightly angular, his jaw line strong and well-defined. He looked content, not restless or annoyed or angry. He seemed laid back and patient, thoughtful. Not at all what she'd expected.

Percy rolled onto his back, paws and feet splayed as Nate rubbed his belly.

"See you later," she said and closed the door.

Nate was a pleasant surprise and definitely nice to look at, too. She hoped he'd still be like that at the end of the thirty days. Even so, it was a quick trip to the airport. That's exactly where she intended to end this contract at the end of September. If he brought any attention at all to the right people to do the right things, then it was worth bringing him down here. And the three grand she paid would help a few more victims.

As she walked down the stairs, she paused halfway down to listen to the noises in the house. The footsteps creaking on the faded floorboards, rustle of quilts, rasp of drawers, the low rumble of a male voice that sounded so strange now. That sound had been absent from this house for nearly a year.

She closed her eyes a moment, remembering the sound of Tom's laugh echoing through the house. She could almost feel the shuddering thuds as he bounded down these stairs two at a time, calling for her, asking where his work boots were or his car keys. Or the sound of him singing in the shower above the rush of water. God, she missed those sounds. The feel of him in the bed beside her, the warmth of his breath against her neck as she slept in his arms.

Her eyes stung with tears as she folded her arms against her stomach, remembering his arms around her, her back pressed against the wall, the rough brush of his stubbled cheek against hers. The weight of his body against hers, the substance and realness of him. His warm lips exploring her mouth and neck, whispering that he loved her as they brushed across her ear, nibbled her earlobe. That he'd see her in the morning.

She gritted her teeth, willing away the tears. Morning never came. He died that night on Highway 27.

At first, she'd felt his presence like a warm touch against her heart, in the house, on the stairs. But as the days passed, she felt it less and less. Sometimes, late in the afternoon or in the early hours of the night. She'd miss him forever, but she'd learned to go on without him. It was still hard, especially with the first anniversary approaching. She wished it would have fallen later—after Nate left for Virginia. Unfortunately, he'd still be here on the seventeenth, but she'd deal with it. The pain of losing Tom had convinced her she never wanted to feel that razor sharp agony ever again. Once was enough.

She couldn't imagine that pain a second time.

Kadence glanced up the stairs when she heard Nate's voice echo from the upstairs bedroom. His strong voice carried. On his cell, calling the people who cared about him. He'd be back with them soon enough. His voice filling the house was nice, but she would be glad when he returned to Virginia where he belonged.

# SEVEN

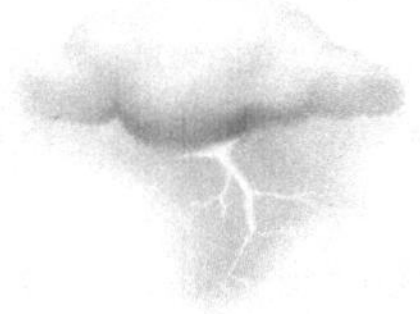

Nate sat down on the bed as he rubbed the cat's belly. *Goofy little guy,* he thought as the cat lolled his head back, looking more like a throw rug than an animal. He'd had a dog growing up and preferred them, but he liked cats well enough.

His whole body shook with exhaustion and after a moment, he stopped petting the cat. He hadn't realized how unsteady he'd felt after the flight. Granted, he'd only been out of the hospital a few days and his side still ached from the spleen's removal, but he'd expected to feel stronger today. The doctor had told him to take things slowly and to be careful about infections—as if he could control the people around him.

He pulled his cell phone clip off his jeans pocket and glanced at the display. He groaned. Four voice messages. Ren and Corrina. His head ached at the thought of listening to Corrina's high-speed chatter tonight. He'd call her in the morning when he felt better, he decided as he speed dialed Ren. He got Ren's voice mail.

"Ren, it's me. I'm in Louisiana. Near a town called Hackberry. It's laid back and quiet down here, very peaceful. Kadence is cool. She's really trying to help the hurricane victims, so I look forward to helping her with that. In fact, I haven't had the urge to kill you even once yet.

I'm going to crash for a while and then eat authentic Cajun jambalaya. Call you tomorrow. Bye."

Feeling guilty, he ended up speed dialing Corrina. She answered on the second ring.

"Nate? Where are you? I've been calling and calling."

"Hey, babe," he said, trying not to sound so tired. "This was the first chance I had to call."

"How was your flight?" Corrina asked. "Is she pretty?"

Nate stumbled over her two questions, trying to find the politically correct answer. "Flight was fine. Kadence is nice."

"She *is* pretty. I knew it!"

"And I'm down here because you forgot to bid, remember."

"Oh, so, now it's *my* fault."

Nate groaned. "Well, it's certainly not my fault."

"Now, you hate me, too." Her voice turned teary and Nate cringed, too tired to soothe Corrina's insecurities.

"I don't hate you, Corrina. There are a lot of people that need help down here. I'm glad I've got the chance to try and help—"

"I've got a splitting headache," Corrina announced, cutting him off in mid-sentence. "I'll call you tomorrow when I feel better, okay?"

"Sure," said Nate, relieved. "I'm sorry about your headache. Leave me a voice mail and I'll call you back tomorrow."

"Wuv you, sweetie," she said, suddenly cheerful again.

"Love you," he replied.

"Won't you say it our special way, Nate?"

Nate hesitated. He hated Corrina's baby talk, but it always made her happy. And it was easier than fighting it.

"Wuv you," he said finally, trying not to grit his teeth.

"Bye," she said, a grin in her voice as she hung up.

He laid his phone on the nightstand as he kicked off his Merrell's and climbed onto the bed beside Percy. Yawning, he stretched out, careful not to disturb the stretched-out cat. His head hit the goose down pillow that smelled cool like rain and something else he didn't recognize. Sort of flowery, but strong. Was it lavender?

The house was quiet except for the occasional creak of wooden floors or mumbled voice downstairs. No barrage of ringing phones. No interruptions or last-minute do-or-die tasks. Just calm. Peaceful, he realized with a yawn. A state he'd missed for a long time. He was ready to slow things down for a while.

For seven months, ever since he'd given Corrina the engagement ring (which made his father so happy), things had been crazy, out of control. Corrina had become this nervous, clingy person, obsessed with her wedding being the social event of the season. Lately, she hadn't been the alluring fireball-of-a-woman he remembered dating, instead becoming someone he barely recognized at times.

He'd wanted a quiet, civilized ceremony, but Corrina wanted a paparazzi extravaganza. His head ached as he remembered the constant barrage of choices, decisions, appointments, and setbacks: guest list, wine list, bridal registry. Filet mignon or salmon (how about both?), cream or ecru invitations (as if he could tell the difference), chocolate or white cake (he liked either). He just wanted to buy two tickets for Hawaii and elope. But Corrina would be heartbroken. He'd let her have her fantasy wedding—even if it killed him.

And on top of that, Dad had sent a record number of new clients to the office, expecting Nate to wine, dine, and dazzle them with investment opportunities. He'd done it all, the late hours, the appointments, everything that had been asked of him and more. Right up to the moment he'd fallen asleep at the wheel and wrapped his SUV around a pole.

He was ready for things to slow down.

His eyes closed, unable to hold back his weariness any longer. His side ached, a dull throb that had begun when he'd stepped off the plane. It would be fine in a few days.

He'd just sleep for a few minutes.

---

A FEW MINUTES STRETCHED INTO OVER THREE HOURS. HE OPENED HIS EYES, stretched, and glanced at the clock. Eight oh six. He sat up, his head hurting as he perched on the edge of the bed and rubbed his forehead. The warm smells of garlic and cayenne wafted through the room and his stomach rumbled.

God, what bewitching scents!

He rose unsteadily from the bed and stood motionless for a moment or two to gain his balance. His suitcase sat untouched at the foot of the bed. He'd need to hang up his clothes. After dinner, he decided.

He groaned when he saw his leather jacket draped across the suitcase. Brilliant idea to bring a leather coat to southern Louisiana. He picked up the jacket and opened the closet door. Inside, he found a white dress shirt and green and burgundy flannel shirt. On the floor were some old work boots.

*Decoration or left behind by someone? Had these items been worn by a father? A boyfriend? Husband?* He draped his coat on a thick wooden hanger and closed the door.

His bangs were damp with sweat as he stepped into the hall and found the white and blue bathroom next door. A white claw foot tub and pedestal sink made the room look a hundred years old. But he was only interested in a cold washcloth against his face.

He turned on the water and grabbed a pale green washcloth off the towel rack, submerging it in cool water. Squeezing out the water, he laid the cloth against his face. Slowly, the heat seeped out of him, the coolness soothing. He laid the cloth across the back of his neck and hunched there a moment before he glanced into the mirror.

Shadows clung to his eyes, his cheeks looking a little more hollowed out than normal. The bruises had all healed from the accident, including the cut above his left eye. A few days rest would do wonders, he thought as he rinsed the washcloth once more and scrubbed his face before hanging it on the edge of the tub. Then he walked down the stairs, the full force of those Cajun spices warming the air like a sultry August night. He approached the kitchen as twilight settled outside, washing the sky in pale indigo, the bright green grass and trees fading to grey.

Kadence hummed as she stirred three pans on her stainless-steel stove. Barefoot and wearing cut offs and a navy tank top, her pale red hair curled around her shoulders from the heat. She was thin, probably about five six to his six feet, and nicely proportioned with those long legs. He'd never seen a redhead with brown eyes before and hers were large and round, kind but playful. He pulled in a long, satisfied breath as he watched her cook, occasionally stopping for a sip of wine.

"It smells delicious in here," he said, leaning against the doorframe, arms folded against his chest.

She turned, wine glass in her hand, all smiles.

"I was about ready to come up and check on you," she said, laying a wooden spoon on the edge of a pan. "To see if Percy had smothered you with affection." She moved toward him. "Are you feeling better?"

He nodded. "Yeah, much better. Guess I really needed to sleep."

Smiling, Kadence held up her glass of wine. "Thirsty?"

"Point me to the glasses and I'll handle the rest."

Smiling, she pointed to a long, thin cabinet by the refrigerator. "Wine glasses are there."

He moved toward the cabinet and pulled out a long-stemmed glass. The refrigerator was well-stocked with fresh bunches of carrots, broccoli, chicken, and ham. Lots of lidded containers stacked on the bottom shelf beside a case of Pepsi. Jars of jam, pickles—even beets—sat beside a cellophaned head of iceberg lettuce. A pitcher of iced tea and a jug of milk sat on the top shelf, a carton of orange juice beside it. Tucked between the orange juice and the milk was a nearly full magnum of Mondavi Chardonnay, the cork pressed halfway in.

Nate filled his glass and returned the bottle to the refrigerator. He took a sip as he straddled a rattan bar stool beside the kitchen counter. From the barstool, he noticed Elsie still out on the porch, rocking in the swing.

"Elsie's still out there?"

Kadence nodded. "She spends a lot of time out there."

"I'm sure things have been hard for her, losing her home, nearly drowning. She must feel like she's lost everything."

"She has," said Kadence without turning around. "Everything's gone. She has to try and rebuild her life now."

She stirred a bubbling pot full of chicken and shrimp, the smell of tomatoes, garlic and cayenne making his eyes glaze with hunger.

"And I'm sure there are thousands more like her," said Nate. "Makes me feel terrible what some people have to go through."

This time, she turned to stare at him, those brown eyes narrowing.

"But what will you do about that? Will you just reach for a few dollars from your wallet, send them off, and feel better about yourself?"

He bristled. She was judging him. Before she knew anything about him.

"No, that's why I auctioned myself off on Auctionanza," he replied with a smile, hoping to diffuse her accusation.

Kadence laughed, the sound musical, and bowed her head, staring into the boiling pot of jambalaya. "You're right. I'm sorry. I'm just so tired of people turning a blind eye to others in need."

Nate took a sip of his wine. "Until we're personally tested, we usually just open our wallets. Even so, what's so wrong with that? What if no one even wanted to help at all? Where would we be then?"

She turned the heat down on the stove, letting the jambalaya cool as she stirred it with a long wooden spoon. Her red hair looked so vibrant, the soft ringlets clinging to her oval face, brushing long chestnut lashes and full lips. She had a beautiful bow-shaped mouth and pale freckles dotted her nose and cheeks, her shoulders, and forearms.

She pressed the back of her hand to her forehead. "You're right, of course. Forgive me. I sound like a parrot. I just want to do more for these people, people like Elsie. That's why I became a first responder. I wanted to reach more people than just those who could afford tuition to college."

She slid out three square black plates from an overhead cabinet and set them on the counter in front of Nate. After turning off the burners, Kadence dished dirty rice onto all three plates. Steam rose from the plates as the rice sizzled. Over the rice, she spooned out jambalaya in heaping spoonfuls.

"Could you set these on the table please while I get the glasses and silverware?"

"Sure," said Nate, rising from his barstool.

He carried two steaming plates to the table then grabbed the third. It was a small square table, old and worn. Kadence followed behind him with three metal tumblers and a pitcher of sweet tea. He grabbed his wine glass and sat down as Kadence handed him knife and fork and set down a paper napkin holder beside the salt and pepper shaker on the table. She laid silverware beside the two remaining plates and grabbed her half full wine glass.

"I'll get Elsie," said Nate.

He hurried to the front door, opening it into the chirring night. Elsie sat on the swing, a shawl around her shoulders.

"Elsie, think you could eat some jambalaya?" he asked.

She smiled at him and rose stiffly off the swing. "I been smelling it all night. It smells delicious."

He studied her a moment then laid his hand on her arm as she paused in front of him.

"Making your peace with what happened?" he asked.

Elsie stared at him, her dark brow furrowing, a look of surprise in her brown eyes.

"Why do you ask me that, young fella?"

He shrugged, glancing down at his stocking feet. "It just seems like you're spending all this time in your head, trying to figure out how you could have done things differently. Going over those what ifs when the whole situation was simply out of your control."

She bowed her head.

"There was nothing you could have done differently, Elsie, except maybe evacuate. But even if you had, the house would still be gone." He squeezed her thin shoulder. "It's not your fault, Elsie. You have nothing to blame yourself over."

She smiled at him, her eyes brimming with tears. "Thank you, Nate. I don't know how you understand that at your age—and given how short a time you been down here. But thank you. I appreciate that."

He understood her turmoil only in little bits and snippets, but nothing on the scale she was facing. The best he could do for her was to let her know she wasn't to blame and that she could go on with her life. It was okay.

"When your heart understands that, you'll be able to move on, Elsie. It's okay if you go on with your life, you know."

Elsie patted his hand and stepped inside. Nate paused to glance out across the yard at the tall oak trees with their trailing moss and the flutter of moths around the porch light. The air smelled dry but sweet, the clicking of insects steady in the descending nightfall.

He let the screen door bang shut as he returned to the kitchen just as Elsie and Kadence exchanged a look he couldn't quite interpret. But the jambalaya smelled spicy with its cayenne and garlic, the shrimp pink against the bits of tomato and celery. He dug a fork into the jambalaya, spearing a shrimp. He slid it into his mouth, the shrimp hot with heat and spice. Just the way he liked it. He followed the shrimp with a forkful of dirty rice.

"This is delicious. Best food I've had in some time." Okay, he'd eaten mostly hospital food lately, but it was the best meal he remembered.

"Welcome to Louisiana, Nate. Hope you can tolerate the spice and the heat because there's more of that than you can imagine down this way." She set down her wine glass. "Lots more. Especially when we go to New Orleans on Sunday for more rescue work."

He ate another bite, tasting chicken and shrimp this time, along with the bite of pepper. His face flushed.

"I'm glad to do it. You just tell me what to do and I'll do it."

Kadence grinned. "You'll regret that statement before the week's over."

He chuckled. "Most likely, but since you're only renting me, I'll probably exercise my own judgment." He took a sip of cold wine that cooled the cayenne burning his throat. "By the way, is it okay to move the clothes in the upstairs closet?"

Kadence's face turned pale, all traces of warmth leaving her face as the smile fled.

"What do you mean?"

He shrugged. "There's a couple of shirts and some work boots. Is it okay if I move them someplace else?"

"No," she snapped, "leave them alone."

The edge in her voice surprised Nate a little. He'd wanted to know about the clothes, but it looked like Kadence wasn't ready to talk about them.

"I just wanted to put them in the—"

"I said leave them. I'll take care of them after dinner."

Elsie's eyes widened a bit as she stared from Nate to Kadence.

"Sorry," Nate said finally. "I meant no offense or harm."

"None taken," she said, staring down at her plate. "I'll just go up and move them now. Excuse me."

"Kadence, no—finish your food."

Her face flushed as she rose from the table and rushed up the stairs.

Nate stared down at his plate, feeling like a jerk. He hadn't meant to stir up bad memories for her. He wasn't even sure why he wanted to know about the clothes. What did it matter to him? When he looked up, he found Elsie staring at him.

"I didn't mean to upset her," he said in a soft voice, knowing it could carry.

Elsie nodded. "I know you didn't. It was just a question, but you gotta be prepared for the answer whenever you ask one."

He cringed. She was right. He should have kept his mouth shut and left the clothes alone.

"I didn't even think they could have belonged to someone she lost. And I should have. That was stupid." He pushed back from the table, no longer hungry, and rose from his chair.

"Finish your supper, Nate," Elsie called as he opened the front door.

Night had settled like a warm blanket in the darkness, moths and bugs flitting around the porch light, casting shadows across the wood porch as he sat down on the swing. He gripped the chain and rocked the swing in motion, the sweet air infused with garlic and cayenne from the evening meal. Upstairs, he saw Kadence's silhouette against the curtains in her bedroom, flitting back and forth like the moths.

He hadn't even been here one night and he'd already offended the hostess and portrayed himself as a callous jerk. He couldn't wait to see what he'd trash tomorrow. His stocking feet brushed across the wooden planks, the humidity still hanging like wool in the air. His body felt sticky against his shirt.

A muffled voice from somewhere inside called his name, but he let the sound go, focusing on the chirring insects and the occasional cool breeze that feathered across the porch. He laid his hand against his forehead, mopping at the sweat beading there.

"Nate?" the voice called again from inside.

The front door opened, but he kept his gaze toward the field and dark sky.

"Nate?"

Kadence, he realized.

"My apologies," he said, staring at the tall oak trees. The distant sound of tires on gravel echoed through the stillness. "I didn't mean to stir up bad memories."

"It wasn't your fault," she said, padding across the porch. She stepped in front of him and sat down on the other end of the swing. "To you, they're just clothes."

She smelled like fresh washed linen, like something cool and clean. Real.

"But not to you," he said, casting a quick gaze at her, at the pale red hair pulled into a wavy pony tail. Skin smooth and milk-pale except for the warm freckles dotting her features. She shook her head and folded her arms against her tank top as she gazed across the yard.

"And I completely bulldozed right over the possibility that they were. I'm sorry."

She laughed, the sound like wind chimes. "They're just clothes, Nate. But the man who wore them is gone. After nearly a year, they should be just clothes."

He stared at her, afraid to say anything. She was at least talking to him again. He didn't want to stick his other foot in his mouth and strangle himself. He laced his fingers together, laying them in his lap, and hoped she'd keep talking.

The buzz of insects and clink of moths against the glass light fixture seemed suddenly loud, but Nate kept quiet.

"I put them away, so the closet is all yours now," she said finally.

Avoided the explanation of who wore those clothes, but he wouldn't press. After all, it was none of his business. If she'd wanted him to know, she'd have told him.

*What did he expect? He barely knew the woman. Why should he expect her to divulge her deepest secrets to a guy she bought off Auctionanza?*

"Are you happy, Nate?"

He sucked in a breath. "That came out of nowhere," he replied.

"Isn't that the kind of question you ask your buddies over a few beers?"

*Not people you'd just met that afternoon.*

She shrugged. "It was just a question. Most people aren't, you know." Her foot brushed across the wood as she set the swing in motion. "They're either sad because they lost something, missed something, or they're anxious because they're looking for something. Or tired and angry because they found it and don't know what to do with it. I think happy is something you have to make for yourself. Out of those searches and losses. That's what I'm trying to do."

As he watched a dark cloud slide across the darker horizon, not even a sliver of moonlight, Nate knew she was right. His life had been just a series of negotiations as he tried so hard to prove himself worthy to his successful father and independent mother. To prove himself savvy in business and in Dad's high order social circles. Where he'd met Judge Coleridge and his debutante daughter, Corrina.

Corrina had been all nubile grace and raw sexual power wrapped into a lithe body and ambitious but narrow mind. She'd captivated him from the start, like a sip of a 1963 Laffite-Rothschild Bordeaux. One sip wasn't enough, of course, and he'd wanted to consume the whole bottle. Until he discovered she was just a box wine poured into a rare bottle. He had no problem with box wine, only when it was pretending to be something unique. He'd known Corrina nearly two years and as their wedding date approached, he felt the planning had changed her. And him.

*Had it all torn back the layers to reveal the truth in both of them?*

Even now, he wondered who she'd really be after the spotlight fell away and the parties faded. *Was it him or the social fiction she wanted?*

*Was* he happy? He wasn't sure anymore.

"It's the best you can do sometimes," said Nate. "Even when you know you have to move on and you're too scared. Besides, being happy isn't a state or a destination. It's the series of moments we string together and choose to remember. Moments beyond the bad ones."

She turned her head, gazing at him through long chestnut lashes, a smile playing on her lips.

"You're right," she said and let her gaze wander across the dark landscape.

They sat in silence as the heat cooled, the wind rising. It was September, almost autumn now. Even the Louisiana heat would begin to soften. But sitting here looking out at the countryside alive with the night made him feel alive, too. All his senses felt heightened. He was aware of his own breathing, Kadence's presence beside him. The solitude and the peace were attractive. And so was Kadence. This place was so different from the big cities.

"Aren't you going to ask me about Sunday's rescue efforts?" she asked finally, her voice warm, a little raspy, a little playful.

He turned to her, swiveling his body in the swing and drawing one leg up onto it.

"Okay, tell me about Sunday," he said with a smile.

"I'm taking you with me to New Orleans, so you can see the devastation first hand." Her eyes met his in an unwavering stare. "I'm trained as a first responder, so I'll be going out with other rescue personnel. You'll stay behind and help at the shelter."

He frowned. "All right. But I'm willing to help with the rescues, too."

"We'll see. I brought you down here to help, not get you killed."

He wouldn't tell her about the car accident. He was fine, so she didn't need to know that.

"I'm also bringing Arbaugh along for the ride. He'll put the right kind of spotlight on the victims."

Nate nodded. He had nothing to hide.

"Ready to finish the rest of that jambalaya?" she asked, tapping him on the arm.

"Why not."

She rose from the swing and he followed, wondering what Sunday would bring. He didn't see how his presence would help anyone, but Kadence thought it would, so he'd go along with it.

# EIGHT

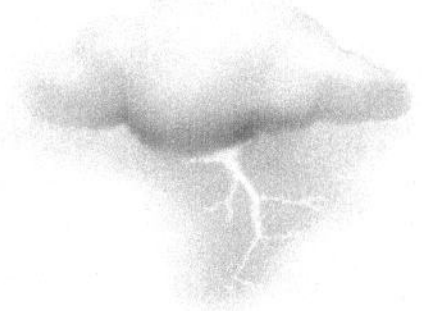

Kadence felt a little queasy about bringing Nate into Katrina's devastation as they set out in Jim Hawkins' Go-Devil boat into the flood waters. Jim had picked them up in his truck and drove them as far as he could before he put the boat in the murky waters.

New Orleans looked like a strange combination of Venice and the bayous, many of the old parishes underwater. The levees had finally been repaired and the water was starting to dissipate, leaving dirty water lines across buildings and houses as it receded. In its wake were piles of debris and dead animals, trees and bushes broken and skeletal.

The heat was oppressive today as they made a quick pass through St. Charles parish to gain their bearings, where they'd investigate structures, locate survivors (human and animal). Once Nate and Arbaugh saw what the city was facing, she'd take them back to the truck.

The stench of the warm, stagnant water with its rainbow, oily sheen, still six feet deep or more in parts of the city, was hard to take. She'd already come to terms with the sight of bloated animal carcasses and the molasses-like murk, but she had no idea how Nate would handle it. Much like she had on her first time out, she imagined, shocked and deeply moved by the damage.

Arbaugh already seemed distressed. He pressed a wrinkled white handkerchief across his nose. His thin blue shirt hung limp against his hunched shoulders, plaid shorts showing bony white legs and scuffed black dress shoes. Nate didn't look green around the gills, but he looked openly shocked by the pervasive water. Stunned silent, he stared out at the buildings underwater, parts of Highway 10 submerged, some of the green interstate signs partially visible.

"It's surreal, isn't it?" Kadence replied, shifting her legs, the army green hip waders squeaking.

"It's horrific," said Arbaugh, his voice thin as he kept that handkerchief in place.

Nate shook his head and pointed at the tops of street signs and floating cars. "And eerie. I could have never imagined this scene. It doesn't even seem possible. The loss of life is beyond belief."

He wore an old pair of jeans, paint-spattered Nikes, and a Saints t-shirt. Not her image of the high-powered MBA from D.C., the son of a senator. Still, he looked at home in the boat and ready to pitch in, and that surprised her.

"Had enough, Arbaugh?" she asked, casting a sideways glance at him as she shifted a pet carrier off her foot, leaning it against a box of bottled water.

He nodded. "More than enough. If you'd be so kind, I'd prefer dry land."

Jim turned the boat around, heading back toward his truck parked near a curb that disappeared into silt-heavy water only a foot from the tires. They weren't more than ten minutes away. Marty would be waiting there for them, ready to trade places with Nate and Arbaugh, ready to respond to the need in this area. Shortly, they'd go out to search houses on the street her unit had been assigned. There were reports of looters and survivors who refused to leave.

If nothing else, she and Jim would deliver food, water, and flashlights to folks still riding out the flooding.

In a short while, the truck came into view as Marty waved at them. He wore his fireman's gear, looking a little warm. Jim cut the motor and ran the boat aground as Marty thrust the plank across to the boat.

"You look a lot more rested, Kadence," said Marty, smiling as he helped Arbaugh walk across the plank to dry land.

"I am."

"How's Elsie doing?" he asked, reaching a hand toward Nate as he walked across the plank without even a bobble and stepped off.

"It's been hard on her," said Kadence, standing up. "But she's going to be okay. She's a fighter."

Marty grinned, his moustache a little bushier than it had been a week ago. "That she is. Glad she's doing good."

"You ready, Kadence?" Jim asked as Marty stepped into the boat, carrying gloves and two more pet carriers.

Nate stared at them a moment. "You sure I can't be of more help?"

"He wanna come along?" Jim asked.

Kadence started to respond, but Jim turned toward Nate, a hand over his eyes. "If you're a friend of Kadence's, you're welcome on my boat."

She frowned as a smile arched across Nate's face. It wasn't a good idea. He wasn't trained in rescue. He probably didn't even know CPR."

"I'd love to do more," said Nate. Finally, his gaze met hers. "Unless Kadence doesn't want me aboard."

She didn't. It wasn't personal. He was a liability. She wanted him where he would draw the most publicity. But not the wrong kind. She could just see the headlines. *Crazy Louisiana Professor Drowns Senator's Son.*

"He has no experience in land rescue—much less water rescue," said Kadence in a low voice to Jim.

Nate held up a hand. "You have my word that I won't be a problem."

Jim squinted at Kadence again who just shrugged. *Did he even know how to swim?* He studied Nate a moment.

"You can swim, right?"

"Of course," Nate said with a frown. "Four years on the swim team count?"

Jim nodded. "That counts." He waved Nate onto the plank. "All right, you're hired. An extra hand may be a big help."

Nate grinned as he scrambled across the plank and back into the boat.

"I'll leave you younger folk to this work," said Arbaugh, fanning himself with his handkerchief. "I'll be at the shelter, interviewing survivors."

He turned and started up the hill toward the cluster of houses that had been spared most of the flooding. The white Victorian had become a makeshift shelter for those plucked out of the flood waters. Kadence knew that Arbaugh would sniff out the stories and give them delicate coverage as only an old school journalist could. She was certain of it. She watched as Nate sat down beside her.

"You need to be careful out here," she said. "Really careful. It's still extremely dangerous." She laid a hand against her green tank top. "As a first responder, I've only been trained in the basics, so if Jim or Marty tells you do something, do it. They're Lake Charles firemen."

"I won't do anything crazy," he replied with a frown, holding out his hands as Marty laid the plank inside the boat. "At least treat me like an adult, Kadence."

"Sorry," she said finally. "I don't mean to be insulting. I just—well —I'd feel responsible if anything happened to you, okay?"

He nodded. "Fair enough. No offense taken."

Jim started up the boat engine and the flat, aluminum Go-Devil boat lurched toward a row of partially submerged homes.

---

FOR HOURS, THEY FLOATED PAST HOUSES WHERE THE WATER HAD RECEDED, but these houses were cut off—little islands in the inland sea. Anyone who'd stayed with their house desperately needed supplies. She and Nate handed out bottles of water and dry goods to exhausted, haggard residents. Their eyes were glazed with the struggle, but she saw—and admired—their resolve to hold onto what was theirs. The National Guard would come through soon and probably carry many of them out. But the stubborn few would remain regardless.

As they passed a once-white house, the silt-strewn water line halfway up the now-grey siding, a dog's desperate bark echoed across the stillness. Kadence caught the movement from the corner of her eye and turned to see a fluffy, brindle tail in the gaping doorway of the dark building.

"Jim, there's a dog," she called, pointing toward the house.

Jim turned the boat around, gently running it aground in the mud in front of the house. Marty set out the plank and Kadence ran down it toward the house, Jim behind her. Nate followed, hanging back a little with Marty, but she noticed he'd grabbed the largest pet carrier.

The old house with its once ornate trim, spandrels, and high ceilings was dark, covered in mud and piles of debris. Kadence slid a flashlight out of her pocket and shined it into the half-darkness, catching the red-gold gleam of canine eyes. The air smelled like rotting fish and raw sewage and she nearly gagged.

"Here, boy," she called, whistling for him.

The dog, a mixed breed, was maybe thirty pounds, its longish fur matted with mud and twigs. He whined, backing away as she approached. She could see the little dog's ribs. He needed food in a hurry.

"Marty, back me up," she said, her hip waders squeaking across the ruined wood floor as she moved slowly toward the thin dog. He stared at them with wary brown eyes, ears slightly back. Poor thing probably hadn't eaten in days. He had on a thin red collar, two silver tags still attached.

"You got it, Kadence," he said, moving slowly toward the dog's left side. He tossed a thick pair of gloves to her and she quickly slid them on.

The other rooms were blocked by broken furniture and debris. The only way out of the house was past her.

"Jim, Nate, watch the front door, in case he bolts."

Nate and Jim took up positions in front of the door. Nate set the carrier beside him and crouched.

"Com'ere, boy. We've got some kibble and water in the boat. I'll bet your starving."

The dog backed up two steps, barked then whined as he turned toward Marty then her. He turned in a quick circle and paced again to the right then left, watching her and Marty's every step. Kadence stepped closer with slow deliberate movements as she tried not to stare directly at the dog.

Even when she was within arm's reach, Marty approaching to the left, she knew the dog would bolt past her.

And he did, careening right toward Nate and Jim. Jim moved left, but the dog pitched to the right, slipping past Jim. Nate lunged forward, low, grabbing the dog with both arms.

The dog yelped, growled, and snapped at Nate, its body wriggling to escape, but Nate held him tight as he lifted the struggling animal into his arms. Jim grabbed the pet carrier, fumbling with the door as the dog's back legs kicked and clawed, trying to free itself, but Nate didn't let go. When the pet carrier door sprang open, Nate thrust the dog inside and slammed the door shut.

He bent over, his chest heaving.

"Got him," he said, out of breath.

"Wow, good work, Nate," said Marty as he hurried over to the carrier.

"Thanks," said Nate as he stood up. "High school football," he said with a smile. "Hit 'em low and hard. Easy when I outweigh him by at least a hundred pounds."

Jim laughed and patted him on the back. "We'll make a first responder out of you yet."

"I'm impressed," said Kadence, laying a hand on Nate's arm.

He shrugged, glancing down at the ground. "Beginner's luck."

"Since Nate's such a good wide receiver," said Jim. "Let's see if we can find any other pets in the area before we move on." He motioned them outside and around the back of the house.

Kadence and Marty searched under broken door frames, soggy mattresses, and smashed books, searching behind dead brush that had once been shrubs, but they didn't find any other animals.

After about fifteen minutes or so, she heard a hoarse meow off in the distance.

"Off to the left, Marty," she whispered, motioning him toward a busted fence.

On the other side, Nate and Jim hunched against the water-logged fence. Nate had a hand on a grey cat, stroking its ears as he coaxed it out with a bit of cheese. The cat licked his fingers as he held out the cheese. The skinny little cat gobbled at the morsel, allowing Nate to pick it up. He stroked its back and held the cat against his shirt, his curly blond hair disheveled, a pale shadow of stubble beginning across his face.

*A man who liked animals. That was very sexy.*

She watched him carry the cat toward the open carrier Jim had set out. His jeans were mud-spattered, a smudge or two on his face as he slid the cat inside the carrier and closed it. That's when she saw the bloody bite mark on his left forearm.

"Nate?" she called, moving toward him. "What happened?"

He turned as she reached out for his arm. He tried to pull away, but she refused to let go.

"Let me see that," she said.

Finally, he gave in and let her turn his forearm to see the puffy bite.

"Dog got me. It'll be okay. You're not going to bench me over a little bite mark, are you?"

She shook her head. "You'll need to get something on that as soon as possible."

He nodded. "I already rinsed it once with bottled water."

"Good," she said, letting go. "Rinse it again, but keep an eye on it, okay?"

"Sure."

---

Across the street, separated by flood waters, Kadence stepped onto the squishy brown grass and walked toward a line of houses. Six or seven people sat outside in lawn chairs, fanning themselves in the growing heat. They looked dazed, exhausted. *Heart sick,* she realized.

An old black man, his white hair cut close to his scalp, rose from his chair, wearing mud-encrusted olive shorts and a white undershirt.

"You got any water?" he asked.

Kadence pressed a cold bottle in his hands. "Here, start on that while I get more."

He nodded, his eyes glazed as he unscrewed the cap and drank the cold water. A younger woman moved up beside him, followed by two twenty-somethings, both white. She looked about six months pregnant, her brown hair scraggly. The young man's face, with days of chestnut beard, looked shell-shocked.

"You got more of dat water?" the young man asked. "My wife . . ." His voice trailed off. "She need it."

Nate was beside her, the case of bottled water in his arms. He set it down and pulled out bottles, handing them off to the couple and the old man.

Marty and Jim set a carton of canned foods on the ground and passed out the cans and can openers to grateful hands.

"You the first people we seen in four days," said the old man.

With no power and no water, these people couldn't stay here much longer. Kadence knew she was wasting her breath in trying to convince them to leave their homes now, but she had to try.

"Do any of you want a ride out?" she asked, a hand over her eyes to block out the sun boring down on them.

"You could take my Sarah and me out," said the old man.

Kadence laid her hand on his arm. "Where's your Sarah?"

He motioned toward a one-story blue house and Kadence followed. Then Nate was beside her again.

The old man stepped inside the dark house filled with antique furniture of heavy dark wood set against warm gold walls. Lace doilies covered the tables and olive curtains hung in the windows. There on the floor, wrapped in a purple and gold patchwork quilt was an old woman, her eyes fixed and staring up at the dark ceiling. Her mouth hung open, body stiff and bloating. She'd been dead for days.

"I been watching over her best I could," said the old man, tears funneling down his ebony face. "But I'm tired now."

Nate winced at sight of the body. Abruptly, he turned away, reaching out to slide his arm around the man's shoulders. "What's your name?"

"Bill. Bill Simon. That there's my wife, Sarah. We been married forty-one years this Saturday."

"You took very good care of her, Bill," said Kadence. "We'll take good care of her for you."

Kadence stuck her head outside and motioned for Jim.

"We've got a body," she said to him a low voice.

His gaze traveled past her to the woman wrapped in a quilt on the floor. "Boat's big enough," he said and moved past her to examine the woman. "Get Marty in here."

She went over to Marty who had passed out the last of the food and water they carried.

"Marty, we've got a body to bring back."

He nodded and ran toward the boat. In a moment, he returned, carrying a black folded piece of nylon. With a nod, she led him into the hot, dark house where Jim knelt beside the woman. Nate sat down beside Bill on the couch, who watched Jim and Marty slide his wife into the body bag. They zipped the bag and lifted it from the floor as Bill Simon watched with an exhausted, detached demeanor that she'd only seen in the face of a disaster.

Her heart wrenched at the man's shell-shocked behavior, knowing the pain he'd gone through. The dark nights here with his wife dead beside him. He'd probably sat with her for days, grieving and in shock.

Kadence followed Nate outside as he led the exhausted man behind his wife toward the boat. With an arm around his waist, Nate helped the old man into the boat and seated him beside the body of his wife. The pregnant woman and her guy followed. They all climbed aboard the boat, silent as Jim started the motor and slowly pushed off into the dark waters. Bill watched the view of his house recede, the tears flowing down his face again as he cast another look at the body bag.

Nate reached out and put an arm around Bill's shoulder. "I wish I could say something that would help."

"She was a good woman, you know," said Bill, his gaze still on the dark bag. "But the water got deeper and she couldn't hold on." A shudder ran through him. "I held her as best I could…but I couldn't hold on no longer. I lost her in the darkness."

"I'm so sorry," said Nate, his voice quiet.

"Yes sir, she was a good woman," said Bill, nodding toward her.

He let go of Bill and pulled out his wallet. From it, he slid out a business card. He pressed it into Bill's hand. "If I can help you in any way at all, you call me. If you need help making arrangements, a place to go—necessities—please don't hesitate to call me."

"You a good man," said Bill, holding the card in both hands as he read it slowly. "Nathaniel Logan, MBA. Vice President, Logan Financial Services. Arlington, Virginia. You a Vice President, huh?"

He shrugged. "My friends call me Nate," he said, smiling at the exhausted man as he extended his right hand.

Bill shook his hand with a meaty right. "Nice to meet you, Nate."

"Do you have anybody you can contact, Bill?" Kadence asked, leaning toward him.

Bill nodded. "Got a son and daughter in Texas."

Nate patted him on the shoulder as the young man and his pregnant wife shifted beside him, their backs pressed against his. The young woman, her dishwater blonde hair tied back in a ponytail, huddled against her husband, a bottle of water clutched in her hand. With the dog and cat, the boat was at capacity.

Jim turned the boat in a slow arc and steered away from the parish. The dog barked as Marty opened the door and slid in some food and water. He put food into the cat's carrier, too.

"Terri, you gon' be fine now," the young man said to his pregnant wife who rubbed her belly through the dingy white tank top. "We'll call your Mama up in Baton Rouge. Everything gon' be fine."

She snuffled, laying her head on his shoulder. "How we gon' get by now? How, Andy? There's no jobs, no money comin' in and there ain't gon' be any here for a long time."

Nate turned around until he straddled the boat seat and reached out his hand to the young woman called Terri. He took hold of her hand and pressed something into her palm.

"Take that," said Nate. "Maybe it'll help with the expenses until you get help from FEMA?"

Terri sat up, her mouth open as she stared at the folded bills in her hand.

"Five hundred dollars?" she said with a gasp, her eyes glistening as she stared at him a moment.

"There's my business card, too. If you need more help to get back on your feet, a line on a job, whatever you need, call me and I'll do what I can."

She gripped his hand in hers, the tears slipping down her face.

"It'll give your baby a fighting chance," Nate said with a smile then let go of her hand.

"Thank you, mister," said the young man called Andy. He rubbed a dirty hand across his red t-shirt and shook Nate's hand. "I appreciate that. For my baby."

Nate pointed at the business card in Terri's hand. "I mean it. When you're ready to look for jobs, call me. I do business with a lot of firms. I can make some calls and get you some interviews."

A smile curved across Andy's thin face. "I will. Thank you."

Kadence watched Nate, studying his expression, a little surprised by his generosity. *Was it all an act? Did he mean any of it or was it all for the media? Like he didn't know Arbaugh wouldn't write about it.* Five hundred dollars was probably nothing to Senator Logan's son. But the man was out here in toxic flood waters passing out food and rescuing survivors. Without a reporter in sight. Maybe he did care? Maybe *she* was the snob?

She reached out and laid a hand on Nate's shoulder. "Good work," she said. "Looks like you didn't need any training."

He stared at her for a moment, his light green eyes holding her gaze. He was so attractive just now, his hair disheveled, stubble shadowing his jaw line, dirt smudging his face and arms. He didn't look like the East Coast executive she'd bid on. More like the soft-spoken fireman she'd fallen in love with once, over coconut shrimp and ice-cold Miller Light. A man who'd carried her out of a burning building during a training exercise.

Intelligent, quick-thinking, and needing to help anyone in trouble. That had been her Tom. And she saw shades of that integrity and courage in Nate's face.

"Everything okay?" he asked finally, still smiling at her, his face closer now.

She nodded. "Yes, and you've made them a little better. Thanks."

He patted her hand and turned around when Bill asked him about how he might get his wife to Austin, Texas.

Nate's hand was on Bill's arm now as he leaned closer, his voice rising above the boat's motor. "As soon as we get ashore, I'll make some calls, arrange to fly you and—and your Sarah—to Austin. Then you can contact your kids and have them meet you at the airport. Contact me after you've made the funeral arrangements and I'll take care of the bill. It's the least I can do."

Bill squeezed Nate's arm. "Thank you, son."

IN TWENTY MINUTES, JIM LET EVERYONE OFF NEAR HIS TRUCK. WHILE HE and Marty secured the boat onto its trailer, Kadence helped Terri and Andy into the front seat.

"Looks like the rest of us will have to climb into the bed," she replied and opened the back.

Nate helped Bill climb up and held out his hand to Kadence.

"Thanks," she said, accepting the help and climbing up into the truck bed.

Nate pulled himself into the back and sat down, leaning against wheel well. The dog bite looked swollen and red now. She reached out a hand to his arm, examining the bite.

"That's not looking so good, Nate. You'd better have it looked at."

He nodded. "I will once we've got these folks settled and safe."

Marty lifted the dog and cat carriers into the back of the truck then hefted himself onto the bed. Kadence moved the carriers to the back of the truck then glanced at the little dog. He wagged his tail and panted in the heat. She looked closer at the collar, confirming the little guy had had his rabies shots.

"Good, the dog has its rabies tag."

Nate's head shot up and he stared at her. "I didn't even think about that."

"It's okay. Nothing to worry about now."

Everyone fell silent as Jim started the truck and drove away from the stagnant water toward a passable road that would take them to one of the shelters north of the city.

The drive took nearly thirty minutes, but Jim finally pulled up in front of the old red brick school where she'd first brought Elsie. Andy helped his wife, Terri out of the truck and they hobbled toward the shelter, both wearing battered flip flops. Nate helped Bill out of the truck as Marty climbed out to help Jim with the body bag.

Nate motioned Bill inside the building, cell phone in hand as he disappeared inside.

Marty laid the body bag in the sparse grass beside the building. Four other wrapped bodies lay against the brick.

"They're going to start taking the bodies to St. Gabriel," said Jim who stood beside her, looking tired and sunburned, hands on his hips as he studied the shelter.

Kadence frowned. "Where's that?"

"A little over an hour up north." He let a sigh escape through his gritted teeth. "That's going to make it very hard for people to find their dead."

Marty was beside him now, running a hand through his sweaty hair. "Guess that's the best they can do for now."

Jim nodded and poked at the ground with the toe of his fireman's boot. "Things aren't gonna get much easier for these people, are they?"

Marty shook his head. "Not for a while longer."

Jim sighed then checked his watch. "I'm gonna fuel up the boat and find some more cases of bottled water."

"After I drop off the pets, I'll get some more dry goods from my car," Kadence replied. She saw Nate standing in the doorway of the shelter, cell phone pressed to his ear, a credit card in his hand. And she'd get a bandage for that bite wound.

Marty nodded. "I'll make sure everyone's got a place to stay and meet you at the truck." He motioned toward Nate. "Nate's coming back out with us, ain't he?"

Kadence smiled, doubting she could convince him to stay behind. But he'd done a good job out there. She wanted him to go back out.

"As soon as he makes arrangements to get Bill—and his wife's body—to Texas."

"Okay, meet me at the truck in fifteen minutes," said Jim who hurried toward the truck.

Kadence waved at him and rushed across the street to unload more food they'd collected from the university.

---

Using every scrap of daylight, she and Nate made several trips into the flood waters to rescue pets and trapped homeowners. At the end of the day, when the sun was a pale ball hovering above the dirty water, they climbed out of the boat. Kadence dragged her exhausted body up onto the truck bed beside four dazed *Katrina* survivors and three pet carriers. Nate climbed in beside her, his face shadowed with weariness, those light green eyes hooded and a little dazed. His face was sunburned, lips chapped, and from the way he moved, muscles aching from the overexertion.

Marty climbed in beside them, rubbing his face, a day of beard darkening his chin and jaw line. He leaned back on his elbows, his eyes closing to slits. Nate huddled against the truck bed wall, his eyes closing.

Day one of a three-day assistance effort, Kadence knew. She watched poor Nate struggle to stay awake. But the day was far from over. They had an hour's drive to Jim's campsite and the tent that would sleep five. Then up again at six a.m. to do it all over again.

"Doing okay, Nate?" she asked.

He nodded, his face devoid of emotion. "Fine," he answered. "And you?"

"I'll make it," she replied. "Will you for two more days?"

"Sure," he answered.

His cell phone rang and he flipped it open. "Yeah? Hi, Corrina. I know—I saw the missed calls. No, I couldn't pick up. No, phone service down here is spotty." He turned his body away from Kadence, lowering his voice.

"Because of the hurricane. *Katrina*? God, Corrina—the hurricane. You saw it on the news. That's why we had that auction, for God's sake. Yes, in New Orleans." He held up a hand, a look of exasperation on his face. "Look, I'm way too tired for this right now. I'll call you in a couple of days when I'm back in Lake Charles. The connection's going —call you soon."

He shut the phone abruptly, a touch of anger in his eyes. *Could there actually be someone that clueless running around? Someone who hadn't heard about the hurricane?*

He looked at Kadence with an apologetic gaze and sighed, but he didn't offer any sort of explanation. Of course, what could the man say? He'd just spent twelve hours in putrid water, weathering the stink and the tragedies and the exertion and then to get a phone call like that?

She leaned back against the truck wall, her body sore and aching, as she watched Nate stare out at the Louisiana landscape. This trip had changed him forever; she saw it in his eyes. She couldn't help but wonder how he would relate to this Corrina and Senator Logan when he returned to Virginia.

# NINE

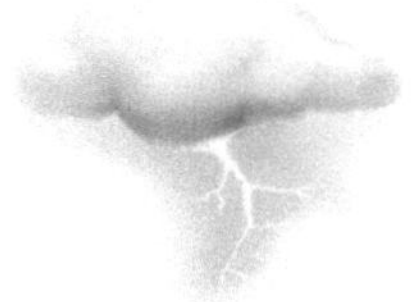

Nate stared at the red-gold sky and the growing darkness, feeling restless despite the weariness that ached in his bones. The heat pressed against him, settling in an oddly comforting way. He liked the heat against his face. It helped clear his head.

Tonight, Corrina's insistent conversation about bridesmaid dresses and the menu at the Four Seasons grated on his last nerve. Right now, he couldn't even wrap his brain around such trivialities. It seemed almost laughable in the face of what he'd seen today. He'd helped carry two dead bodies out of the flood waters and he'd seen countless lives shattered and many destroyed. And Corrina wanted to know if he preferred Steak Au Poivre or Crabmeat Remick as an appetizer?

He felt a mixture of guilt and regret tonight as he stared out at the distant bayou, hearing the almost unbearable quiet and sadness that had descended on this corner of the world. He remembered the night on Kadence's porch and the rich weave of chirring and scritches that made the dark feel alive and vital. Here, everything felt stunned. He could only imagine the terror and death these people had endured, facing storm surge and rising flood waters, so many unable to evacuate.

He wanted to do more to help. So much more.

Tomorrow, when he got time, he'd call Ren and arrange for investments for the funds they'd collected. Something that would bring in more help for these people.

God, he felt tired tonight. Tired of the suffering and devastation. Tired of the commonplace sight of bodies stacked in shelters beside the living (there weren't places for the dead yet). The image of Bill Simon seated beside his dead wife, wrapped in a family quilt, would stay with him forever. All day yesterday, he'd seen death and anguish. He felt torn up inside over it and a feeling of helplessness that made him angry. There was so little he could do to help.

He shifted his arms onto his knees and the right one ached with red hot pain. Where the little pooch had bitten him. He'd managed to rinse it once or twice between runs and he even intended to get a bandage for it at the shelter. But there hadn't been time. Tomorrow, he'd get something on it.

The fire pit burned to embers in front of Jim Hawkins' olive green tent and the smell of canned soup reminded his stomach he hadn't eaten since breakfast. Marty slid down on the grass beside Kadence and laid a foil wrapped package onto the wood, shifting it with a stick that lay near.

"What do you have there?" Kadence asked, stirring the pot of Campbell's Minestrone with a metal spoon.

"Some barbequed pork." He laid a package of hamburger buns beside him in the grass as Jim carried over a cooler. "Picked it up at a roadside stand just east of here."

"Can I give you some money for the food?" Nate asked.

Marty waved him off. "I'll let you buy tomorrow night."

"Deal," said Nate with a nod.

Jim set down a battered, blue cooler and flipped open the top. Iced bottles of Samuel Adams poked out the top.

"Help yourselves," said Jim, sliding out a bottle. He twisted off the cap.

"I'll buy the beer tomorrow," said Kadence as she patted Marty on the back.

Marty stood up, stretched, then moved over to the cooler for a beer.

"Come on, Nate," said Marty, sliding out a bottle. "You earned a few of these today."

Nate smiled as he hefted himself to his feet and plodded over to the cooler. He was glad they'd found him useful today, instead of a nuisance. He'd never been trained for this sort of thing, but neither had anyone else. Nobody had ever seen a disaster like this on American shores before—especially down here. Even so, how did anyone prepare—or train—for something like this?

"I'm all over that," he replied. He took out a bottle and held it out to Kadence. "Thirsty?"

"Yes, thanks," she said, taking the cold bottle from his hands.

Her hands felt soft against his, fingers long and tapered, fingernails short and squared. The light from the fire deepened the light red cast of her hair. It gleamed like a halo around her. Long legs crossed in front of her, thin hips snug in her Levi's cut-offs. The tank top was covered by a jean shirt now. She was lovely in the firelight, looking strong and confident—comfortable, he realized. He liked a woman comfortable in her own skin. Very different from Corrina, who seemed to need approval—and praise—for every decision, every action. And designer everything.

He picked up a bottle of Samuel Adams and twisted off the cap, tossing it into the cooler. The icy cold beer soothed his throat and the ache in his shoulders as he sat back in front of the fire.

Jim knelt beside him and set down a bag of potato chips, some paper plates, four coffee mugs, and a roll of paper towels.

"Now, you can't have barbeque without hot sauce," said Marty with a grin as he slid a bottle of Frank's Red Hot out of his shirt pocket.

Kadence laughed, poking Marty in the shoulder. "I was wondering how you were going to eat without that stuff."

"He always carries a bottle of hot sauce," said Jim with a chuckle as Marty set it beside the paper plates.

Nate slid closer to the fire, taking another pull off his beer. Using a dingy green towel, Kadence slid the pan out of the fire, giving it another quick stir before setting it beside the paper plates.

"All we've got are some coffee mugs," she said, motioning toward the pan.

"Works for me," said Nate, watching her fluid movements as she picked up the spoon and started filling mugs, setting them beside Marty then Jim.

She filled a mug and handed it to Nate, their gazes holding a moment. Then two. He loved looking into those warm brown eyes. His fingers brushed hers again as he took the mug and thanked her.

Grabbing a stick, Marty maneuvered the foil out of the fire and onto the grass. With quick pulls on the foil, he opened the wrapped packet, letting a trail of steam rise into the air as Jim opened the package of buns.

"Damn, that smells good," said Jim.

There was enough smoked meat to make two sandwiches each. Good. He was hungry. Marty even shared his Red Hot, passing it over to Nate as he laid a bun on his plate and filled it with pork. The beer and hot, smoky meat reminded him of Sunday cookouts, but the warm soup made him sleepy. And the beer numbed the ache in his forearm and the knotted muscles in his shoulders.

"So, Nate," said Marty through a bite of barbeque. "Where exactly you from anyway?" He laughed, his voice raspy. "Because you obviously ain't from around here."

"I flew down from Arlington, Virginia," he said, leaning back in the grass.

"So, what brought you all the way down here?" he asked, licking sauce off his fingers.

Nate gazed at Kadence for a cue, but she chuckled, tossing back that bright red hair, beer in one hand. "I did," she said. "I bought him off the internet."

Everyone laughed, including Nate.

"Seriously," said Jim. He laid a handful of potato chips on his plate then passed the bag to Nate. "How do you and Kadence know each other?"

"Auctionanza," Nate said with a grin. "She really did buy me off the internet. Or at least rented me for the month."

Marty and Jim exchanged confused looks. "Is that some electronic dating service?"

Kadence gave Jim a hard look, her eyelids hooding in a bored, *oh, please* kind of look.

"It was a charity auction," said Nate. He took a quick swig of his beer. "You know, rent an executive for charity? My investment firm set up the auction to raise money for *Katrina* victims."

They laughed.

"No joke," said Jim, a smile on his long face.

Kadence nodded. "I wanted to bring more attention to the people who lost everything and thought the media might eat up this story."

"Have they?" Marty asked.

Kadence shrugged, her gaze falling to the ground. "Too early to tell. We've gotten some local coverage—Channel Seven, the paper." She winked at Marty. "We'll see what CNN has to say in a few days."

"Is that why you brought Arbaugh down here?" Jim asked.

She nodded. "He has friends in Baton Rouge, so he's up there tonight. They'll bring him down again tomorrow. I'm sure he'll overwhelm Nate with questions on the way back to Hackberry."

Marty turned back to Nate, the beer in his hand almost empty. "So, you're an investment banker or something?"

"More like the *or something*," Nate replied with a shrug. "My father got into politics, so I'm running his firm."

"Virginia Senator Lee Logan," said Kadence.

Both men stared at him, their eyes widening. They'd heard of his father. He was so tired of being Lee Logan's son. Nothing he'd ever do in this life would ever be of his own volition. It would always be attributed to his father's influence.

"Must be some big bucks there," said Jim.

"It has a range of clients," he said with a shrug and set down his beer for the mug of minestrone. He sipped the hot soup carefully, trying not to burn his tongue.

Marty stared at him a moment. "You look more like a college kid than a financial whiz."

"Did that, too. And I'm probably more college kid than financial whiz. My strength is in reading people, knowing what they want." Too bad he wasn't worth a damn about reading himself. "Investing is a stressful job in some ways, but nothing like what you guys deal with."

He took another sip of soup and set down the mug. "How'd you get into firefighting?"

"By accident," said Marty with a grin. "Set my stove on fire one night. I had the fire out by the time the crew arrived, but I was hooked. I asked about volunteering and before I knew it, I was full time."

Nate turned his gaze to Jim who lay with half-closed eyes in the grass.

"What about you, Jim?"

"I'm a third-generation firefighter," said Jim, pulling at the soggy label on his beer. "It's all I know. It's all I ever wanted to do."

He admired people who knew exactly what they wanted out of life. He'd spent a lot of time drifting, trying things on his own to differentiate himself from his father.

Kadence rested her elbows on her knees, beer in one hand, a sweet smile on her oval face. "I didn't know I'd be a professor when I grew up. I wasn't sure really what I wanted to do, but I was good at teaching people things. And I liked helping people. So, being a professor just sort of fit. That's also what drew me to volunteer with the fire department."

"That and Tom Bujeau," said Marty with a wink.

Her smile spilled into a grin, her brown eyes turning a little misty as she tilted her head down to stare at her beer bottle. *The work boots,* Nate realized. *A former boyfriend.*

"Tom was a good man, Kadence," said Jim, bowing his head. "We miss him every day."

She swallowed a breath, her gaze drifting to the popping embers. She poked at them with a stick. "So do I," she said in a quiet voice.

Nate cringed. *The clothes. The work boats—the guy was dead. That's why she'd reacted so strangely about the clothes. He felt terrible.*

"I'm sorry about your loss," said Nate. "God, the clothes, I didn't—"

She held up a hand, the stick falling into the fire pit. "It's okay, Nate. You didn't know."

"I didn't mean to treat them like they weren't important."

"They're just clothes now," she said, at last fixing him with her gaze. "Tom's been gone nearly a year. It's okay."

He cast an uncertain look at Marty who offered him a supportive nod.

"What about you, Nate?" Jim asked, thankfully changing the subject. "Did you always want to be an investment banker?"

He laughed, staring down at his half-empty beer bottle as he lifted it from the grass. "I'm not a banker. To tell the truth, I never even thought about finance as a career. Not until I got my MBA. It wasn't something I'd even considered until my Dad got elected to the senate. Then suddenly, he needed someone to manage his firm—and I was available. That was four years ago."

"What do you want to do, Nate?" Kadence asked, swiveling around to stare at him with one of those soul-searching looks she had a way with, he'd noticed.

He settled back on his elbows in the grass, the beer bottle clutched in his left hand. "Until today, I was okay enough where I was, but seeing all these people—lost, broken, their lives destroyed...I want to help those kinds of people, not the already well-off. Give them a chance at financial stability they wouldn't otherwise have."

"Any plans in that area?" Jim asked, eyebrows raised. He took a swig of beer, finishing off the bottle.

Suddenly, Nate had all of them watching him in contemplative silence.

"I'm just starting to turn some ideas around in my head. But what if I could arrange some investment opportunities for these people, help them to safely regrow a little financial security and return some comfort. Take the donations we've already raised and create a community trust for these people, to help them rebuild. Get major corporations to kick in more, match these monies."

Kadence's eyes smoldered as her unwavering gaze encompassed him.

"You'd be doing a good thing for a lot of people," said Marty.

"That's amazing, Nate," said Kadence finally.

"It's my hope anyway." He sighed, running a hand through his hair. "I just can't imagine walking out of here and forgetting these people, turning my back on them after all they've been through."

Marty reached over and slapped him on the shoulder.

"You're good people, Nate," said Marty as he twisted open another beer. He glanced at Kadence. "God, woman, do you know how to shop or what?"

She laughed, laying a hand to her mouth, but her gaze returned to Nate's face and he saw something new in those soft eyes. *A little bit of that distance melting away.*

"Nate, if you can pull this off, we'd all be so grateful," she said as she rose from the grass, brushing the dust off her Levi's.

"I'm going to work hard on it. Get my business partner on it, too."

"Corrina?" she asked, unblinking.

He laughed. "Definitely not Corrina. No, my business partner, Ren Stewart. He and I manage Logan Financial."

Marty's expression changed slightly as he cast an uncertain glance at Jim. "Partner, huh?"

Nate sighed. *What was it about that word that made people assume stupid things?*

"Yeah, partner. That's how I introduce him anyway, so people don't figure out he's my lover right away."

The silence around the firepit was deadly. Marty and Jim looked stunned, looking at each other with uncomfortable glances. Kadence looked, well…he watched her eyes…disappointed. That was it. Genuinely disappointed. Finally, he couldn't hold in the laughter any longer and let out a belly laugh.

"It was a joke, okay? I'm not gay and he's not my lover, so get over it," he said with a snort.

Jim and Marty laughed, a look of relief on their faces. But Kadence howled with laughter, slapping her leg as she nearly toppled her beer into the fire pit. *Was that a hint of relief on her face, too, he wondered. A look of possibilities?*

"No, Ren is my best friend in the world and he's engaged to Meredith Hudson, his college sweetheart. Sorry, I'm just tired of that look when I say Ren is my partner."

He finished off his beer and rose to grab another one as silence took over the conversation again.

"Do I know how to kill a conversation or what?" he asked, taking a swig of cold beer. He picked up his sandwich and took a big bite.

Jim and Marty laughed again. Marty reached out and lightly punched him in the shoulder.

"It's okay, Nate. It's just that, well—you just didn't look light in the loafers to me, so I was a little surprised is all."

"Marty!" Kadence said with a gasp. "It was a joke."

"Yeah, a joke," said Nate, rising up on his knees with a groan. Marty really thought he was gay now. "Apparently, a bad one. I'm straight, see?" He grabbed hold of Kadence, pulling her against his chest, and kissed her hard on the lips.

The burn of her lips against his shot through him like a hot poker, gouging his chest and sliding right to his groin like a wild fire. He tasted beer and lavender and all he wanted at that moment was to gorge himself on her full lips, slide his hands across those supple shoulders, up those slender legs.

She pulled back, a mixture of shock and desire in those wide brown eyes, a hand against her lips. She'd felt it, too. He saw the burn in her eyes. For a moment, she laid her emotions bare right there on her face, but the distance quickly swallowed up that need, anger narrowing her eyes.

And then the fiery sting of her palm slammed against his face as she pulled away to cackles from Jim and Marty.

Nate laid his hand against his face, rubbing at the sting, but the fire that burned in his gut was rising, blotting out the pain. God, he wanted to press his lips against hers again, feel the heat of her skin against his, the weight of her body, that soft red hair tangled in his fingers.

The jolt of reality smacked him in the back of the head like a fist. *What the hell was he thinking? He was engaged!*

"Kadence, I...I'm so, so sorry." He rubbed a hand across his face, his dry burning eyes. "I don't know what I was thinking," he said, his voice clipped. "I'm really sorry."

Jim and Marty were still laughing, Marty pounding the ground with his palm, Jim biting back a full tilt belly laugh.

"Serves you right, Kay," said Jim with a snicker.

Nate frowned at him. *What did that mean?*

Jim pointed a thumb at Kadence. "I watched her corner Tom like that one night and plant one right on him in the station. Burned him right out of his boots, she did. A four-alarm fire if I ever saw one."

Kadence turned back to them, her face burning with embarrassment. She stared at her hands.

A smile curled across Nate's face as he studied her eyes, the flustered movement of her fingers, and blush of her cheeks as she twisted the hem of her jean shirt.

"It's not funny, Jim," she said finally.

"Kadence, I mean it," said Nate, holding out his hands. He bit back a snicker. "I'm really sorry. But if I'd kissed Marty, I'd have just proved his point."

Marty let out another belly laugh. "No, after seeing that kiss, you convinced me ol' Ren is history." Grinning, he pointed at Kadence's flushed face and wide eyes. "Y'know, I've never seen Kadence that flustered in a long time."

"Oh, shut up, Marty," Kadence snapped and flounced up from the grass, beer in hand. She walked away from the fire.

"Kadence has had a rough time this year," said Jim, suddenly serious as he watched her walk through a stand of tall grass and stare out at the gravel road.

"Losing Tom?" Nate asked, the smile slipping from his face.

He nodded. "She found him, you know. First one on the scene."

His heart twisted into a knot as he watched her stand there, shoulders hunched, arms folded against her stomach as she poked the gravel with her old Reeboks.

"Oh, God—how'd it happen?"

"Car accident," said Marty. "Lost control on wet pavement when he swerved to miss a motorcycle. Plowed head first into a telephone pole."

Nate lurched, remembering his own recent accident. The broken bits of his memory that night on North Glebe Road flashed in his head. Horrible crunch and twist of metal. Smothering air bag that kept him from dying. And the fiery pain. He'd had another dream last night, bits of the accident rising through his dreams.

"She was first to respond to the accident call that night," said Jim.

"She had no idea it was Tom. No idea at all. She thought he was still at the station, not out on a call."

Marty's eyes turned glassy as he glanced from his beer bottle to Nate. "He bled out in her arms. Ephemeral artery. He was gone by the time the ambulance hit the scene five minutes later."

Nate bowed his head, feeling like a bastard. If he'd known about Tom's death, he wouldn't have forced that kiss on her. He hadn't exactly planned it, but knowing that might have stopped him from doing something so stupid. He sighed. He had a habit of doing stupid things around her.

"That's horrible," he said in a quiet voice. "I had no idea. Now, I feel like a total jerk."

Jim patted him on the arm. "'Course not. How could you? Kadence is so tight-lipped about her personal life. You'd have never pried that out of her willingly. Marty and I were both at the scene that night, otherwise we'd have never known all the details."

"The first anniversary of his death's comin' up soon," said Marty, his voice low enough that Kadence couldn't hear.

"September seventeenth," Jim replied. He pressed his beer bottle to his lips and drank. "Gonna be a bad day for her."

Nate nodded, trying to remember that date.

"I'd better go apologize," he said, rising to his feet.

He set down the beer bottle and brushed the dust off his jeans as he walked with measured steps toward her, hands pressed into his jean's pockets. She stood at the edge of the firelight, arms folded against her chest as she looked out into the darkness.

"Kadence?" he called, letting her know he was behind her.

"It's okay, Nate," she said with a weary voice. "Really. It's okay."

"No, it's not," he said. He stood behind her, wanting to squeeze her shoulder, touch her hand, offer some gesture of comfort, but from her stance, that was the last thing she wanted from him. "That was totally rude and uncalled for—especially knowing that Tom—"

"Died?" she snapped, whirling around to glare at him, hands on her hips.

He pulled back a little. "Yes," he said with a nod.

"You give yourself far too much credit, Nate Logan," she replied.

"You assume that kiss had some great effect on me." She crossed her arms. "Well, it didn't, so get over yourself. I barely know you. It was just a joke, remember?"

He held up his hands, taking a step back. "I meant no offense. I just wanted to apologize for being rude, that's all."

"Fine," she snapped. "Apology accepted. Now, I'd like to be alone, please."

Not a problem, he thought and walked away. Glad that was all settled. It was going to be a long month.

He dropped down by the fire and snatched up his beer, taking a long drink. When he glanced up, Jim and Marty were snickering at him.

"What?" he said finally.

Marty nudged him with his elbow and nodded toward Kadence. "That meant somethin' all right," he said with a smile. "She wouldn't be that mad if it hadn't meant anything. She'd have just laughed it off."

"Marty's right," said Jim, glancing over at Kadence. "That meant more than she's willin' to admit."

"How many execs could she have bought, Nate? I mean, how many could she have chosen from?"

He shrugged. "Couple dozen, I'd guess. I didn't see the actual listings." No, he'd been flat on his back in the hospital and hadn't a clue.

"They have pictures, this website? Pictures of the executives, I mean?" Jim asked, glancing at Kadence who stepped farther from the firelight until only her silhouette was visible now.

Ren had mentioned putting up pictures of all the executives along with a bio.

"Yeah, there were bios and pictures of all the executives," he replied.

Marty grinned and poked Jim in the shoulder. "Maybe our Kadence was doing a little shopping along with her fundraising?"

Nate laid back in the grass and stared up at the stars beginning to scatter across the darkness. He smiled, but felt the bitter taste of guilt rise in his throat. He'd have to have a long conversation with Corrina about this.

He would never cheat on her and he wouldn't keep this from her either. He sighed. No matter how painful the result. She'd be furious. She'd cry and scream then pitch one of her tantrums. Followed by days of not speaking to him. Her typical reaction whenever she got angry. But Dad loved her and her father the Judge, so Nate had learned to avoid making Corrina angry.

*She's good for your career, Nate,* Dad had said. *She puts color in your life.*

But many times, that color bled into self-absorption and selfishness, something he hadn't realized until her earlier phone call. Like she'd never even heard of Hurricane Katrina and how indifferent she sounded about people who'd just lost everything. As long as it didn't affect her, she ignored such tragedies.

Even when he'd been in the hospital, she hadn't acted concerned about him or his nearly fatal accident. No, she'd concentrated only on her weekly shopping trips with Bradley and her friends. She'd made her appearance at the hospital (like it was some droll party she was forced to attend) and gone on with her life. *Being with him, the engagement, the wedding plans—maybe it was all about appearances and he'd been too concerned about pleasing his dad to notice?*

*He wasn't happy with Corrina. He hadn't even realized it until now.*

He'd hid that fact in his good son routine, dating a high maintenance woman that pleased his father, allowing those social circles to arrange his life. *Why hadn't that ever bothered him until now?*

But the memory of that kiss still resonated through him. Kadence was so different from Corrina: unassuming, confident—independent. She cared about others, wanted to help and make a difference. He hadn't seen one designer handbag or sweater in her house, much to his relief. And if that kiss had meant to her even a glimmer of what he'd felt, they were both in big trouble.

# TEN

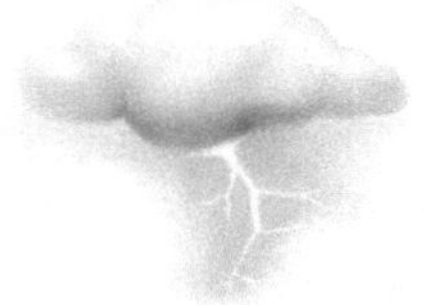

Kadence hugged her arms around her waist, the heat from Nate's kiss throbbing through her in ways she couldn't even fathom.

The smell of woodsmoke rose in the cooling night air, the smell of him still clinging to her face, a soft clean scent like soap mixing with the husky smell of charcoal. She hadn't been that close to a man in nearly a year, felt that kind of proximity. Hadn't wanted it, couldn't imagine it. She'd avoided any contact that might bring the pain of Tom's death into full, razor sharp focus.

But the memory of Nate's touch lingered, trembling through her in raw waves of need and ache and her body had reacted, betraying her attempts at distance. Sure, she'd seen his picture, knew he was attractive (she'd have to be blind not to notice), but until he'd stood in front of her with that gentle smile, laugh lines curving across his cheeks, framing that quirky mouth, she hadn't been affected by those good looks. And nice, tight body—she hadn't expected to feel any inkling of attraction to him.

He was Senator Logan's son. Guaranteed media attention. That's why she'd chosen Nate over the other executives. He'd been the best media opportunity for these people overlooked in the disaster.

But his selflessness today had been so attractive, so inspiring.

Nothing like what she'd expected. No, she hadn't expected his incredibly giving nature. She'd expected an out-of-touch, awkward executive who only had rudimentary people skills. And the way he'd just emptied his wallet into those people's hands without even a shadow of second thought—that was so unexpected. And so very attractive. The way he'd pushed himself a hundred and ten percent today, not even a whimper of complaint, even when that dog had bitten him.

And the glow of the firelight had been so warm, his face haunting. And that smile lit with those dancing flames, the infectious laugh that had filled the silence, warming her emptiness. She felt a fever burning through her now, an awakening that hurt as much as Tom's memory and her inability to have saved him. She missed him desperately and she felt terrible because, dammit, she'd enjoyed Nate's kiss. And she'd wanted more. A lot more.

She felt like she was cheating on Tom. And she hated that sick feeling quivering in the pit of her stomach. But more than that, she hated how that kiss had made her feel.

*Because it had been a joke.*

Just a silly joke on Nate's part. That's all it had been to him. And she was stupid to think it meant any more than that to him. Besides, she barely knew the man. He could be married for all she knew. And here she was trying to see something that wasn't there. Something she had no right to feel, no right to imagine.

*For God's sake, what did she expect? She bought him on the internet!*

In a month, he'd be back in Virginia, going on with the life he put on hold. And she'd be here, still missing Tom, still struggling through the days one at a time with no real thought to what they'd add up to— the term *future* so foreign.

*Suck it up, Kadence. It was just a joke. Don't make it into something it wasn't. Something it had never been meant to convey. A joke. Laugh it off and let it go.*

She stood in the darkness and wiped away the cold tears until her eyes had dried, her sniffles fading. Only when she could summon up that distance again did she return to the firelight. She sat down in the grass and picked up her beer, taking a quick drink as Marty launched into the full story of setting his stove on fire.

Nate's attention was focused on Marty, but his gaze instantly flicked toward her, a look of contrition on his face. He looked a little sad, almost confused, but she looked away, toward the mug of soup she'd left. She wasn't ready for this. She set down the beer and cradled the mug in both hands, sipping the soup.

She sat in silence, listening to Jim tell stories about fighting wildfires in Arizona and his days as a smokejumper.

Nate listened with an unwavering stare, a look of fascination on his face. Jim had done a lot of dangerous work in his life and had gratefully left it behind when he moved to Louisiana. He and Tom had been good friends, so she really appreciated his friendship now. He was her last link to Tom, the one man who knew them both well. Besides, Jim looked out for her, making sure she was okay on those long holiday weekends, that first Christmas—even Valentine's Day.

"How you doin', Kadence?" Jim asked, smiling at her.

"Fine, Jim. Getting tired. I think I'll rinse out these mugs and turn in now."

Marty stood up and stretched as she gathered up the four coffee mugs. "Good plan." He picked up a rusted Folger's coffee can that sat near the fire and poured sand onto the fire pit. Embers scattered like fireflies into the darkness, the warm glow changing to indigo.

Nate rose stiffly from the ground, looking a little lost, a little tired.

Jim poked a thumb toward the tent. "Got four sleeping bags inside. Grab your favorite."

Marty tossed his empty beer bottle into the cooler, Nate following his example. Kadence grabbed a plastic tub out of the truck and set the cups inside. She opened a jug of water that sat in the back and poured it over the cups, letting them soak.

"G'night, Kadence," said Marty as he walked toward the tent, its flap peeled back.

"Good night and thanks, everyone," said Nate, following Marty into the tent.

Using paper towel, Kadence rinsed the cups and dried them. It was a good distraction. She set them upside down on sheets of paper towels and returned to the tent. Jim stood beside the flap, watching her with watery eyes.

"He didn't know how Tom died," said Jim in a low voice.

She nodded. "I know. It just took me off guard."

Jim laid a hand on her shoulder, squeezing. "Tom wouldn't want you still mournin' him, y'know."

He'd be furious, she knew, insisting that she move on, keep her life moving. But it wasn't that easy. She didn't have an on and off switch. If she had, she'd have already turned off the guilt and the remorse. Truth was, she didn't want to turn it off. She needed more time to work through it.

"Like you're not?" she said, staring at him with an unblinking gaze. "He was your best friend, Jim." *Hers too*, she realized. "How do you move on from a loss like that?"

He bowed his head, kicking at the grass. "Every time you hit the ground chin first, you pick yourself up and go on." His gaze finally met hers again. "My chin's awful sore, Kadence, but I'm still on my feet."

She put her arms around him, standing on her toes to hug him. She rubbed his chin, feeling the rough beard growth.

He laughed.

"Good night, Jim," she said, letting him go. She slipped past him into the tent.

Inside, Marty had already slid off his boots and had crawled into the farthest sleeping bag. Hunter orange. His head was down, eyes closed. Nate had grabbed the sleeping bag closest to the flap, his boots setting beside the dark green sleeping bag. He lay with arms folded behind his head, staring up at the tent's ceiling. He didn't look toward her when she walked past him. Deep in thought about something. Hopefully the investment opportunities for the *Katrina* victims.

The faint scent of mildew clung to the rough tent fabric as she took the left-hand sleeping bag, a faded red one with plaid interior. It was the farthest one from Nate and that suited her fine. He'd shaken her up enough for one night. A battery powered lantern stood in the center of the tent, giving Kadence just enough light to see the sleeping bags.

She slid off her tennis shoes, setting them against the tent wall and shimmied into the zipped sleeping bag.

Jim stepped inside, closing the flap, and veered around Nate to grab the right-hand sleeping bag. Light brown with deer on the lining. With a groan, he slid off his heavy, clunky boots and crawled into the sleeping bag.

By now, Marty's loud snores reverberated through the tent. Jim glanced over at him, giving him a dirty look before he reached out and turned off the lantern.

Kadence turned onto her side, gazing across the dark tent at the outline of Jim across from her. She glanced toward the flap, at Nate's silhouette as Jim's breaths grew heavier, deeper, more even as he quickly drifted off to sleep. Nate was still awake and she wondered what was going through his mind. But if he'd wanted to talk about it, he'd have spoken up. It was better to leave him alone.

She yawned, her eyelids growing heavy until she fell into an exhausted sleep. Dreaming of water and floating houses.

***

THE HOARSE SHOUT STARTLED HER AWAKE. KADENCE JOLTED UP FROM THE sleeping bag when she heard someone moan in pain.

"No—no!"

She listened in the darkness above the resounding snores.

Another moan. Somewhere in front of her. Nate, she realized. It was Nate.

Unintelligible murmurs echoed as she crawled out of her sleeping bag, moving toward the tent flap. She knelt beside him as he tossed back and forth in his sleeping bag, mumbling the word *no* over and over.

"It's late," he muttered. "Gotta leave." He moaned again as she crouched at the foot of his sleeping bag. "Get across the Potomac."

He shouted again, a frightened sound and Kadence knew she had to wake him. Gently, she laid her hand against his bare shoulder. His skin felt over-warm as she shook him.

"Nate? Wake up. Nate!"

He jolted up from the sleeping bag, grabbing hold of her arms, his eyes wide, his chest heaving.

"Ren?" he gasped, glancing around the darkness.

"No, it's Kadence," she said. She laid her hands against his forearms. Knots of muscles and tension. He was shaking. "You're all right. Just a bad dream or something."

He shuddered and even she felt the tremor run through his body as he collapsed against the sleeping bag, a hand brushing away damp curls from his forehead.

"Sorry," he said, struggling to catch his breath. "Didn't—didn't mean to wake you."

"Everything okay?"

He nodded, closing his eyes as he held his breath a moment. "Yeah, fine. It's okay. Go back to sleep."

"Sleep well, Nate," she whispered and gave his shoulder a quick pat before she moved back to her sleeping bag.

Nate groaned once more and then fell back into a heavy sleep. Kadence lay awake, listening to make sure, still a little surprised. Everybody had bad dreams once in a while. She knew that as well as anyone. But his had been so intense.

*Maybe he'd seen too much death yesterday? Maybe it was Marty's hot sauce or too much beer,* she thought with a yawn, her eyelids growing heavy. *She hoped so.*

---

MORNING CAME GREY AND SULTRY, THE LAZY BUZZ OF INSECTS STRANGELY absent. Once, a bird fluttered overhead, but even today, the world had fallen silent. She slid out of the sleeping bag, still hearing Marty's steady snores. Jim was on his side, sleeping peacefully. Near the tent flap, Nate's sleeping bag lay in a tangle, the edge thrown back to show the plaid lining. His boots were gone.

She moved through the tent flap, tennis shoes in hand when the smell of hot coffee hit her. He sat in front of the firepit, bare back to the tent, and sipped coffee. Jim's coffee pot was nestled into wood embers, a thin trail of heady coffee scent filling the air.

"Coffee smells good," she said in a quiet voice.

Startled, he jolted, turning around. He still looked tense when he saw her, those curly locks disheveled, green eyes red and bleary, muscles looking taut. He'd barely slept.

"Help yourself," he replied, motioning toward the coffee pot. "I made plenty."

"Everything okay?" she asked as she grabbed one of the mugs she'd washed out last night.

She picked up the coffee pot with a towel and tipped it to her cup, filling it with hot coffee.

He nodded, kneeling in the grass. He pressed a coffee mug to his lips, staring past her, obviously troubled about something.

"Nightmares?" she asked finally.

He shrugged, his gaze falling to the ground.

"It's normal, you know."

"What's normal?" he asked, squinting at her.

"Having nightmares after seeing that kind of devastation. Many rescuers go through that." She took a sip of coffee, studying his troubled expression. "It's nothing to be ashamed of."

"I'm not ashamed," he replied in a quiet voice and rose to his feet as he paced around the firepit, staring off into the brush. "I'm just tired. That's all."

Didn't like to admit weakness. It was okay. Most people didn't, herself included. But somehow that didn't quite fit Nate; it seemed more than that. Almost like he didn't want to trouble her about it, like it was secondary to the rest of the world. Like his troubles didn't matter.

She felt a twinge in her stomach as she watched him, wanting to help. How ironic that he was the distant one today and she wanted to reach out to him.

Already the heat was gathering in the daylight. Another humid day in Jim's boat. She tried to turn her thoughts to the day's rescue route, (Jim had cleared all their routes two days ago) but the change in Nate's demeanor unsettled her.

*Would he get out there and freeze up at the sight of another dead body?*

She let him pace a little more while she finished her coffee. "Nate, maybe you should stay here today? Get some rest and be ready for tomorrow's route."

He turned around, anger in those green eyes. "I said I was fine," he replied still polite, but there was almost an edge to his voice. More like icy professionalism. "I'm just a little tired this morning. Probably no more than you or Jim or Marty."

She nodded at him. He looked almost embarrassed that she was singling him out. "Okay, but if this is getting to you, Nate, you need to let us know."

His eyes narrowed. "I'm fine," he insisted and slung the remains of his coffee onto the ground. "If I think I'm dragging down the rescue efforts, I'll stay at the shelter," he said and moved toward Jim's truck.

Jim stepped out of the tent wearing only his jeans. He moved toward Kadence, his gaze following Nate as he grabbed a bottle of water out of the truck bed.

"What was that about?" Jim asked, staring at her.

She shrugged. "Not sure yet. He didn't sleep so well, so keep an eye on him today."

Jim nodded, hands on hips as he watched Nate another moment then turned his attention to the hot coffee.

By 8:30 A.M., they'd driven back to New Orleans, checked in with the Coast Guard, and put the boat in the water. Lower Ninth Ward, one of the parishes closest to Lake Pontchartrain—where the levee had broken. She'd already called Elsie to make sure she was fine and checked in with Arbaugh. He was still touring shelters and interviewing survivors, but he promised to meet her at the campsite tomorrow evening.

Marty jabbered away, telling stories, and chattering at Jim while Nate stared out into the stink of swirling flood waters as they approached another drowned parish. The flood waters had movement here, the area more dangerous than yesterday. They'd have to be more careful today.

Nate seemed disconnected from everyone today, not at all like the man who'd been here yesterday. He wore his hip waders, a faded red polo shirt the hem frayed, and old jeans. He hadn't shaved either, giving him a more relaxed appearance. The beard shadow was attractive, she admitted.

The faint sound of a desperate voice rose above the motor's buzz as Jim steered the craft toward a street sign. The once quiet intersection flowed with water that was still as high as the street sign.

The voice shouted again, drawing Nate's attention.

"Jim, over there," Nate said, pointing. "By that little hill...and all that debris."

A tiny island of land struggled against the flood waters, surrounded on three sides by piles of ruined furniture, parts of a boat, and tree limbs, aluminum siding wrapped like twist ties around them. The air smelled like rotting fish, crude oil, and brine.

Jim maneuvered the boat out of a swirl of current toward one of the debris piles. Half a walnut sideboard, the husk of an old television, an old tire. None of it looked sturdy enough to step on, much less climb across. But it was the best they had right now.

As soon as Marty extended the plank, Nate was on his feet, thundering down the shaky stretch of wood, hip waders squeaking as he ran toward the hand waving at them from a pile of debris.

"Nate, wait!" Jim shouted, casting an unnerved glance at Marty. "Marty, get over there."

Kadence scrambled out behind Marty as Jim shut off the motor and stepped out of the boat, tying it to one of many fence posts, the boards they'd once held up long gone. The line of poles wound around the debris piles and the little island of brown grass.

"Careful, Nate!" Marty called out as he entered the unstable wash of debris that shifted in the water from the nearby current.

Tangles of insulation and siding twisted around broken trees and wire bundles.

A little black girl, no more than eight years old, huddled beside the remains of a cardboard box, wearing a lime green t-shirt and yellow shorts. She clung to a white plastic lawn chair that had lodged between the sideboard and the television set, water rushing over it. Beyond that rubble was a stream of current from draining waters. The drainage systems were pumping again, but creating currents and eddies.

Kadence felt her stomach clench. If the little girl got swept into that, she'd drown.

Nate was nearly beside the girl now, balancing on top of a submerged red car that bobbed in the water, shifting with his every movement. He reached out to the little girl, surprising calm on his face.

"Can you grab my hand?" he asked in a steady, soothing voice.

The little girl nodded slowly, but made no move to take hold of him.

"I'll move closer," he said, stepping over splintered two-by-fours as he tried to get closer.

Kadence sucked in a breath. He had no idea where that car ended. If he moved too far, he'd plunge into the water and risk being pulled into the current.

"Nate, careful!" Jim called.

Nate stepped left onto a hunk of wood that sank with his weight. He pitched forward.

"Nate!" Kadence shouted, her body lurching helplessly, knowing she'd never get to him in time.

But he grabbed hold of a fence post, the only thing that kept him from pitching head first into the swift moving water beyond the little girl.

Relieved, she let out the breath she'd been holding as he steadied himself and reached out again for the little girl. She stared past him; she no longer seemed to realize he was there as she huddled closer to the lawn chair. Nate kept moving, stepping onto broken siding as he steadied himself with arms outstretched.

One slow step after another, he inched toward the terrified little girl.

Kadence felt her heart hammering in her throat with his every step, his progress slow. Marty and Jim stood by, helpless to approach. The whole area was so unstable that if one more of them stepped onto the debris, they might send Nate and the little girl into the current.

Anger rose in her cheeks as she clenched her hands into fists. At his carelessness. His recklessness. He hadn't even thought through his route. He'd just blundered forward like a ...like a total noob. She sighed. That wasn't fair. It was only the man's second day on the job. Of course, he was new at this.

"Move slower, Nate," she called to him.

She held her breath again, watching him wind his way through more tangles of insulation and wire until his hands touched the lawn chair. He bent down and scooped the little girl into his arms. When he stood up, the water was flowing over his feet, washing over the lawn chair.

And it was rising around him.

Marty stepped onto a long wooden plank he'd laid down across the broken furniture and edged his way toward a taller more stable pile of boards and tree limbs. If nothing else, it was higher ground. Higher than the patch of land where Nate stood holding the little girl, land being slowly engulfed by as the debris shifted and water drained.

He had to get out of there. Now.

Kadence stepped onto Marty's plank that angled above Nate as she made her way across.

"Nate, get out of there! Before you can't!"

Nate moved with measured steps toward the taller stand of boards, broken furniture, and tree branches, the little girl clinging to his neck. Finally, Marty was an arm's length from him, kneeling three feet above him.

Nate lifted the thin little girl high, his arms shaking from the effort, teeth gritted as he held her above his head while Marty edged close enough to grab her. His face flushed, arms quivering until finally Marty lifted the girl out of his hands.

The flood waters had risen to Nate's waist, the current pushing against him as he slogged toward the furniture, attempting to climb out.

It was rising too fast. Kadence cringed. He'd never make it.

She rushed down the plank when Marty stepped off it, carrying the little girl to the safety of the boat. When Kadence reached the end, she laid down on her stomach, holding out her hands as Nate lifted himself onto the shifting furniture. That was slowly sinking.

"Nate, grab hold!"

He didn't hesitate, taking hold of her hands as Kadence set herself, pulling hard enough to get him higher onto the debris. Once he had a foot hold, Nate pulled himself up and onto the plank. He shimmied across the plank on his stomach, collapsing against it, his cheek pressed against the wet board as half the debris pile he'd been standing on gave way, swirling away into the dark flood waters.

"Move, Nate!" she shouted, pushing herself up from the plank as it, too began to shift downward.

Nate pulled himself onto his knees then his feet, fumbling his way behind Kadence until they reached the end. Kadence stepped onto the roof of a SUV and Nate followed. He reached out behind him and grabbed the plank, dragging it along as he moved toward the other plank leading back to the boat.

Marty looked relieved, holding the shivering little girl to his chest, but Jim's face was pinched with anger. Nate looked exhausted.

Jim grabbed hold of his arm when he stepped in the boat.

"Nate, what the hell were you thinkin' back there?" Jim shouted. "You could have drowned!"

Kadence gripped his shoulder, still angry at him as she sat down in front of him. But the look on his face made her pause. He looked heart sick and more than a little shaken.

"What is it?"

He sucked in a breath, pointing with a weak hand toward the debris.

"She's been—holding onto her—mother for hours," he said, trying to catch his breath. "Body's still there," he said closing his eyes a moment. "Lodged against the television…and the siding." His voice was barely above a whisper now as he stared at Kadence. "The body kept her from drowning."

Kadence gasped and slid her arms around him, wanting only to ease the pain in his eyes. He held onto her, shaking. His clothes smelled like kerosene and grime as he pressed his face against her shoulder. But she didn't mind. He'd just risked his life for someone he didn't know, not even realizing how close he'd come to dying himself.

Finally, he sucked in a breath and let her go, moving toward Marty and the terrified little girl. When she saw Nate, she reached out to him. He dropped down on the seat and held out his arms. The little girl slid into his arms and he cradled her against his chest, stroking her hair, only partially drawn back in a ponytail now.

She began to cry and he rocked her.

"It's okay. I've got you now."

"Can't leave my momma behind," she said through her sobs.

"We won't, honey, we won't," said Nate, his face contorting. He bit his lip as he laid his head against hers.

Jim clapped Marty on the shoulder. "Come on, let's see if we can recover the body."

Marty was already sliding out a rescue harness from the tackle box under the front seat.

Kadence reached under the seat, grabbing a folded body bag beside the box as Marty and Jim climbed onto the plank. Both men attached rescue lines around their waists and made their way toward the white lawn chair. Nate glanced up, still rocking the little girl, and Kadence pointed toward the lawn chair. He nodded then angled his body so the child's face was turned away.

———

It took an hour and some luck, but Jim and Marty managed to recover the little girl's mother from the flood waters. They laid the body in the front of the boat, trying their best to shield the sight from the child. The whole way back Nate kept the little girl's face turned to the back of the boat.

When Jim had tied off the boat, Marty set out the plank. Nate carried the little girl onto safe ground and knelt in front of her.

"What's your name, honey?" he asked, a hand against her cheek.

"Shawna Martin," she answered, her hands still clutching his arms.

"Do you have any relatives we can call?"

She nodded. "Aunt Annette."

"Where's she live?" he asked.

"Mobile."

"What's her last name?"

The little girl's long face scrunched, dark eyes glancing away from him a moment, brows pressing into a frown. "Gates," she said at last.

"We'll find her," he said, taking the little girl's hand as he led her to Jim's truck.

"What's your name?" Shawna asked, the hint of a smile on her face.

"Nate Logan," he replied and lifted her up into the front seat.

"Will you sit with me?" she asked, a hand on his arm.

Nodding, he climbed up beside her as Jim hopped into the truck. Kadence and Marty climbed into the back after Marty had laid the body in the truck bed.

"Poor kid," said Marty, the sadness unmistakable on his lined face.

"I can't even imagine," said Kadence with a sigh.

Jim drove until he reached St. Gabriel's. He stopped at a shelter in an elementary school.

Nate lifted Shawna out of the truck and onto the sidewalk, the heat thicker inland. The air had lost that briny, oily scent, smelling almost sweet by comparison. With Shawna's hand in his, Nate approached the shelter. Kadence followed.

A heavy-set black woman shuffled out, arms outstretched toward the little girl.

"Where'd you come from?" she asked as the little girl fell into her arms. "You're safe now, baby. Don't you worry now."

Shawna cried. "I miss my momma."

"I know, baby," said the woman, her gaze flicking toward Nate who shook his head. "But we're gonna take real good care of you."

"She's got an aunt in Mobile. Annette Gates."

The woman stood up, an arm still around Shawna as she faced Nate. "Don't you worry, we'll find her."

Nate reached into his back pocket, retrieving his wallet. He slid out a business card and handed it to the woman. "If Shawna needs…" His voice trailed off and he ran a hand across his face, visibly disturbed. "I'll do whatever I can, okay?"

The woman patted him on the shoulder. "Thank you."

He knelt down in front of Shawna and ran a hand across her cheek. "You're safe now, sweetheart."

"Thank you for saving me," she said and wrapped both arms around Nate's neck. He kissed her on the forehead, his eyes glassy, but then the woman led her toward the shelter.

"She'll be fine—" She glanced at the card in her hand. "Nathaniel."

"Nate," he said, the corners of his mouth rising in a brief smile.

"Nate. Don't you worry. We take care of our own in Louisiana."

"But—if I can help—"

She smiled. "You already have. Thank you."

"Come on, Nate," said Kadence, turning him around.

He glanced over his shoulder, watching little Shawna go inside. She paused on the threshold and waved at him.

"Bye, Nate," she called.

"Take care, Shawna," he replied, waving.

And then she was inside, in the care of the shelter. Nate shoved his hands into his pockets and walked toward the truck to wait for Jim and Marty.

---

It was nearly nine p.m. when they returned to the campsite. Nate had ridden in the back alone while she and Marty climbed into the front. He'd handed Kadence his wallet to buy the evening meal. Chinese takeout. Mu Shu pork, sweet and sour chicken, Mongolian beef, and plenty of sticky white rice. She'd bought the beer, another case of Samuel Adams and some ice, thrown into Jim's cooler.

"He's really messed up," said Marty, glancing in the rearview mirror at Nate who leaned against the wheel well.

"Wouldn't you be if you'd been first on that scene?" Kadence asked, surprised by the edge in her voice.

She opened his wallet to put the change inside when a piece of paper fell out. A florist card, this one a get-well card. It read, "Wuv you, honey. Get well soon. Corrina."

*Girlfriend.* The word burned into her head.

Her stomach sank a little as she slipped it back into the wallet and closed it. *Of course, he has a girlfriend. The good ones are always taken,* she thought with a sigh.

"Didn't want to see that, did you?" Marty replied, pointing at the wallet.

"See what?" Kadence asked with a frown.

"That card."

She shrugged, looking at the wheel ruts Jim followed through the woods toward the camp site.

"Admit it, Kadence," he said with a smirk. "You're a little attracted to the guy."

Jim smiled, his gaze flicking from the road to Kadence.

"That's ridiculous," she said, rolling her eyes. "I barely know him."

"Whatever you say, Kay," said Marty, settling back against the seat as he shifted the box of Chinese food on his lap.

Kadence glanced into the rearview mirror, watching Nate a moment. He looked a little lost and despairing. He must think they were callous, but they'd all seen a lot of death and had learned ways to hide those private moments from others. They each grieved for people lost in fires and other accidents, but it took time and a lot of coping strategies to appear calm in the face of it. But some people never managed that disconnected professionalism.

He'd pulled off the polo shirt he'd worn, replaced it with a clean grey t-shirt.

Jim pulled up beside the tent, angling the boat trailer off the dirt road. He shut off the engine, a look into the rear-view mirror.

"The first ones are always the hardest." He let out a hiss of breath. "The rest aren't any easier either." He turned his gaze to Kadence. "Most people need to come to their own terms with it."

*So, don't press,* she could almost hear him say the words.

"Some time and beer, that's what I always say," said Marty. "And we're here if he wants to talk about it."

"You're right," said Kadence, opening the door. "I won't press him."

She climbed out of the truck, watching as Nate climbed over the tailgate and walked off into the woods.

# ELEVEN

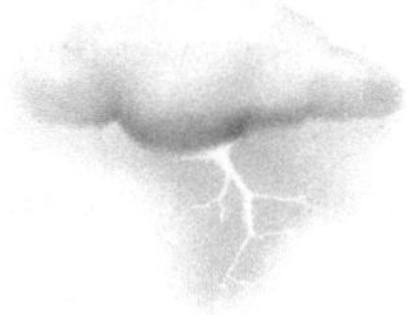

The empty eyes stared back at him, the memory of the dead woman's face burning behind his eyes. Nate squeezed his eyes closed, hoping to blot out the image, but it was too deep, too raw. Too real.

*How long had that poor little girl clung to her dead mother, treading water, trying to climb out of the rising waters?* His chest burned and he clenched his fists, the anger rising above his shock. He wanted to hit something as hard as he could, but he fought down the urge, surrounded only by trees. He shoved his hands into his pockets, kicking at the ground.

He didn't want to go back to the camp and face the others. He didn't want to talk about this. It ran too deep and it wouldn't make him feel better. What he wanted though was enough beer to get him past his dreams.

Night was already softening the world, casting its dark blanket across the horrors of the day. But with the night came the release of those dreams. Slivers of the accident he couldn't remember—didn't want to remember. Memories of the Louisiana dead, of their losses, of things he could never have imagined before.

*Faces. Emotions. Plain old raw pain.*

*Maybe Corrina was smarter than he was after all?* Insulating herself in her designer clothes, chauffeured limos, and exclusive parties—removing herself from the ugly realities that lurked beyond her social circles. He thought he was tough enough to handle the real world, but he wasn't. The face of that little girl clinging to her dead mother haunted him now.

"Nate?"

He froze, his muscles tightening at the sound of Kadence's voice behind him. He didn't answer. What could he say? Her high-priced internet executive was worthless down here. If she needed a nice quiet project managed in some safe place, he was perfect. If it involved anything of worth or importance—like a human life—she'd better ask for a refund.

"You did an amazing thing today," she said. He heard the smile in her voice and the bright tone angered him.

He turned around.

"Which thing? Sitting there like a shell-shocked zombie in the boat or doing absolutely nothing to help that little girl once we got to dry land?"

Her mouth fell open, a look of surprise on her face, in those soft brown eyes. Turning hard now with anger. She stormed across the forest, grabbing his arms. Her left hand was crushing against the angry red dog bite and he winced, finally pulling away. His forearm throbbed now and he gripped it in his left hand.

"Are you totally blind?" she shouted, slapping her hands against her side. "My God, Nate...you threw yourself onto debris that could have collapsed at any moment, sending you into that current to drown! And you pulled that little girl out of the debris with only moments to spare."

Her hands were gentle this time as she gripped his upper arms.

"You saved a life today, Nate—just you. And if you hadn't acted so quickly, that little girl would have died. Don't you understand how difficult that rescue was? How close you came to dying?"

He stared at her, his stomach twisting into a knot. Had he been that close? He hadn't paid attention. His only focus had been the little girl.

"Your foot missed the edge of that car by inches, Nate. You'd have

been sucked away into the current. And when you freed Shawna…
didn't you see the water rushing in to fill the void?"

He shook his head, his knees feeling weak now. He was sinking, his
legs buckling as he felt the ground at his knees. Kadence was kneeling
in front of him, hands still on his arms, her eyes wide. With worry? He
wasn't sure.

"You saved a life today, Nate. You're a hero. Not even Jim would
have attempted that rescue without a life line or harness. You had
nothing."

"Nothing but raw stupidity," he said, gazing into those kind brown
eyes.

She laughed, the sound soothing, like wind chimes, and he smiled,
a chuckle escaping at last.

"There's a fine line between courage and stupidity, Nate," she said,
laying a hand against his face. "You weren't a zombie. And you didn't
just walk away from her. You got her to safety and into the care of
people who will reunite her with family. You went above and beyond. I
wish you could see that."

The feel of her hand against his skin made his face burn with its
softness, its caress.

"I was so impressed," she said in a hushed voice. "You scared me to
death, but you were amazing."

*God, she was so intoxicating.* Her intensity, those large brown eyes—
the concern that echoed from her voice. Her attention was solely on
him. No one else…him.

He laid his hand over top of hers, the warmth soothing against his
fingers. He slid her hand to his mouth, kissing her palm.

Her eyes closed, her head tilting back as she drew in a quick breath.
He leaned toward her as her hand slipped from his face and his mouth
found hers, moist and soft, hungry. He pulled her into his arms, his
kiss deep, his tongue finding hers, the slide of her lips against his
frantic now. She gasped, her hands exploring his face, his neck, under
his shirt.

His hands slid underneath her tank top, under the bra to stroke
those firm breasts pressing against him. His breath was heavy,
matching her frantic gasps as she nibbled his lips.

"Oh, God!" she cried, pulling back from him, her red hair clinging to her flushed face. "What are we doing?"

"Kadence," he said, out of breath as he slid back from her. "I'm so sorry. Please, forgive me. I don't know what came over me."

*What was he doing? He was getting married in November, for God's sake!*

She smoothed her tank top back in place, running her fingers through that rusty red hair, looking upset and flushed.

"Takeout's getting cold," she said, looking embarrassed, her gaze averting his face.

Nodding, he shoved his hands in his pockets and followed her out of the woods, feeling like an ass. She probably thought he was taking advantage of her, knowing she'd lost her boyfriend. Truth was he was painfully attracted to her. Her warmth and concern for others, including him. Her quiet strength and the way she stood up for others. If he was going to survive a month around her, he'd better keep his distance.

Otherwise, he might do something he'd regret.

She was several paces ahead of him as they emerged at the campsite. Marty and Jim sat around the dark fire pit, eating Chinese food from plastic plates and drinking beer out of the open cooler. The air smelled like fried food. Both men looked concerned, but relieved when Nate sat down in the grass.

"How you doin', Nate?" Marty asked, clapping him on the shoulder.

He shrugged. "Okay. How's the takeout?"

Jim sighed. "Edible," he said and tossed a small carton of rice at him.

Nate caught it as Marty set a plastic plate and fork beside him.

"What's your poison?" Marty asked, pointing at the three larger containers spread out in front of him.

"Mongolian beef," said Nate and Marty handed it to him.

"I'll have the sweet and sour," said Kadence.

Jim passed her the carton.

"And a cold beer," Nate said as he dumped rice and beef onto his plate.

Jim reached into the cooler and lobbed a beer at him. He caught it in both hands as he gazed over at Kadence, wanting to run his fingers through that red hair.

*But you're getting married,* the voice screamed in his head.

He looked away, twisting off the bottle cap, and took a long pull from the bottle. The silence around the camp was heavy tonight as he sucked down his beer. He was making a great start on getting numb. He picked at the food, most of it turning his stomach, so he shoved it away. Instead, he finished his first beer and grabbed a second. He'd just taken a cold swig when his cell rang.

"Excuse me," he said, rising to his feet. He slipped the phone out of its clip and flipped it open. He smiled. Ren.

"Hey, how are things?" Nate asked.

"Good. No crises. How are you doing? Hope things aren't too awful." Ren's voice was almost timid. Probably afraid Nate would take his head off.

Nate swallowed a sigh. Ren didn't even have a clue.

"Doing okay," he replied, turning his back to the others as he took a step or two toward the tree line.

"So where are you right now?" Ren asked.

"A little north of New Orleans."

"What? New Orleans?" The phone went deathly silent. "But…the levee broke—everything's flooded."

*No shit,* he wanted to snap, but he didn't. "I've been helping with the rescue efforts."

"You? For God's sake, Nate—are you crazy? You've only been out of the hospital a week! Besides that, you're not trained for that. What if you—"

Nate cringed at Ren's loud voice. "Calm down. I've got three kick butt firefighters handling everything. They're doing all the work. I'm just along for the ride."

"Dammit, Nate, the doctor warned you about being susceptible to infections—just a second…Meredith wants to talk to you."

*Oh, great, one more person yelling at him. Just what he needed.*

"Nate," Meredith said in a soothing voice and he relaxed, still pacing the tree line. "What Ren is so rudely trying to say is that we're worried about you, okay? Please be careful and don't over-exert yourself. He also wants to say that he misses you terribly, but he's too—manly—to say so. He'd rather just shout at you."

Nate laughed. "Thanks for the translation, Meredith."

"No problem. Stay safe. We love you."

"Love you, too, Meredith. Now, put Ren back on."

The line went quiet a moment. "You're my best friend and I'm worried about you, okay? Especially since I feel responsible."

"I'm okay. And incidentally, you should feel responsible. Nobody in their right mind would have put Corrina in charge of anything."

"But Nate, she wuvs you," Ren said with a snicker.

"Like she loves her Louis Vuitton luggage," said Nate through gritted teeth.

"What was that, buddy? A little trouble in paradise?"

"Shut up, will you?"

"Sorry, I'll back off. I know how the baby talk pisses you off. Seriously though, everything okay?"

"I swear if you ask me that one more time, I'm going to heave this phone into the first bayou I see. I'm fine."

"All right. Anything I can do for you? Anything you need taken care of while you're down there?"

The investments! He'd nearly forgotten to call Ren about setting up something.

"Yes, there is something you can do. I want to take a chunk of the relief money we raised and invest it. Give these people more return. And I want a campaign, Ren. I want Logan Financial on the phone to every deep pocket corporation out there, asking for fund matching."

Ren was quiet for a moment.

"Get Meredith working on that. She does a lot of non-profit work. Set her up on the payroll if you have to, but I want this fund to triple by the time I get back there. You got me, Ren?"

"Wow, what's come over you?" Ren asked. "I think it's a great idea and I'm all over it, but...you sound different."

He stared out into the growing darkness. He *was* different. And he could never be the person he was before coming down here. This mattered. More than anything he'd ever done before. And he'd give it his all.

"If you saw what I've already seen…" His voice trailed off, cracking as he sucked in a breath at the memory of that little girl and her dead mother. It tore through his gut.

"Hey…you don't sound so good."

"Just make this happen for me. For these people who've lost every-thing. Okay?"

"You got it, Nate. No worries. Meredith and I'll move it forward."

"Thanks," he said in a quiet voice.

"Your Dad was in the office yesterday."

Nate stiffened, lifting his head high to stare into the dark woods, feeling the urge to run headlong into the cool darkness.

"Did you tell him about Louisiana?" Nate asked.

"Had to. He wanted to see you. He's pissed, Nate—real pissed that you didn't tell him about the auction."

"He'll get over it," said Nate. "I wanted to tell him, but he was out of state again. There wasn't time."

"You could have called," said Ren, his voice without judgment, but it annoyed Nate just the same.

"So, could he. And he was in a much better position to call than I was. Tell him he can dock my pay for the absence."

"Whoa, cool down, buddy," said Ren. "He's pissed because he's worried about you. He didn't think you were well enough for the trip."

Nate had no response to that.

"Call him when you get a chance. So, he won't keep worrying."

"All right, in a few days."

"When will you leave New Orleans?" Ren asked.

"I'll be back in Lake Charles tomorrow night," said Nate.

"Well, you take it easy and don't overextend yourself. Hear me?"

"Yes, mother."

"Talk to you soon."

"Bye, Ren," he said and closed the phone.

He flicked it off and pressed it back into the clip at his waist before he returned to camp. Everyone watched him as he sat back down and grabbed his beer.

Marty smirked at him. "Kick butt firefighters, aye?"

Nate smiled. "You got a problem with my observation?"

"Not me," said Marty. He took a swig of beer.

He glanced over at Kadence. She wasn't smiling. In fact, she looked a little sad.

"Is it always a habit of yours to pass off credit to other people?"

He frowned. "What do you mean?"

"You singlehandedly pulled Shawna Martin out of flood waters and saved her life, Nate. Not me, not Marty, not Jim. You. Yet you told your friends you were just along for the ride. That's incorrect and you know it."

He shrugged. He'd never been one for the spotlight and he wasn't a braggart. Besides, Ren didn't need to know about any of that. It wasn't important.

"Shawna's safety was all that mattered. Not who pulled her into the boat. We all helped."

Kadence shook her head, frowning at him. "No, Nate, it was you. Whether you like it or not, you were a hero today."

He felt his face redden, uncomfortable with that word.

"Kay's right," said Jim with a nod. "You deserve a lot of credit for pulling off that rescue. Don't sell yourself short, Nate. You did a kick butt job today. One any fireman or Coast Guard would have been proud of. So, stop being so damned modest and accept the credit. You earned it. Even though you scared the living hell out of all of us in the process."

Everyone laughed, including Nate. He finished off his beer and reached into the cooler for a third. He didn't want to dwell on the day because it would revisit him in his dreams. Dreams already disturbed by the car accident he was starting to remember. He twisted off the cap and took a long pull off the bottle. He'd need a lot more to get through the night. And then there was tomorrow to worry over.

---

He was on his fifth beer when Marty rose to his feet and stretched.

"G'night everyone. Take it easy."

"Night, Marty," Kadence called, rising from the ground to collect trash.

Nate, feeling a healthy numbness spreading through his veins, got unsteadily to his feet. Jim was on his feet, too, now, tossing his empty beer bottle into the cooler.

"Night, y'all," said Jim. "We're leaving at seven thirty sharp tomorrow morning."

"Sleep well, Jim," Kadence called as she threw plates into a paper grocery bag.

Nate carried his trash over to the bag beside the tent and tossed it inside. He was exhausted, but the thought of sleep made him uneasy. He didn't want to relive last night's nightmares.

Kadence moved toward the tent flap, but paused, turning around to study him a moment. He sat back down beside the dark fire pit, drinking his beer.

"Aren't you going to turn in?" she asked.

He shook his head, the beer bottle against his mouth. He took a quick sip. "Not tired yet."

"Sleep well, Nate," she said and went inside the tent.

"You, too," he answered, leaning against a maple tree near the fire pit.

He watched her lie down in her sleeping bag, the feeble light from the lantern enough to see her silhouette as she turned on her side. He wanted to curl up beside her, feel her warm body against his, those silky red locks soft against his cheek. He wanted to soften the distance in those warm brown eyes, soothe the pain that she carried.

The lantern light winked out and then it was only him and a sliver of moonlight shining pale, the night thick and hot. The cold beer kept him cool, distracted. He was buzzing enough to forget how exhausted he felt, how much his forearm throbbed from the dog bite. How much his chest hurt at the horrors he'd seen today.

He finished his fifth beer and tossed it into the cooler. Two beers floated in the ice water and he plunged his hand in, snatching up a sixth. He twisted off the cap, tossed it into the water, and proceeded to guzzle it.

# TWELVE

Kadence stared out at Nate through the hazy tent window, watching him slam his beer and grab another one. She'd heard enough of his phone conversation to realize that even his friends were worried about him. And they didn't even know what he'd encountered down here. *What had Nate left behind in Virginia before coming here?* She didn't want to pry, but they were obviously concerned about him. She wanted to know why.

Even when Jim turned out the lantern, she knew Nate wouldn't come to bed tonight. He'd be dead on his feet tomorrow, but she'd watch out for him.

She touched her hand to her throat, smiling at the memory of his lips urgently pressed against hers, his hands caressing her breasts. It was an intoxicating mix of gentleness and passion, something she hadn't felt in a long time. If ever, she realized.

Tom's lovemaking had been like a flashpoint, a quick, hard burst that burned wildly then subsided. Nate was a slow burn, building intensity like a flame burning blue then yellow then white hot. She grinned, remembering Nate's lean, muscled chest and tight abs and how her hands felt against his skin. And how much she'd wanted to explore his body. His clean scent, a little husky with woodsmoke, was intoxicating.

A twinge of guilt poked at her. A week from tomorrow was the first anniversary of Tom's death. Until now, the thought of another man in her life hadn't even crossed her mind. It felt strange, looking ahead, wondering about the *what ifs*, the possibilities. She barely knew Nate, nothing about his background, his character—his love life. That florist's card still gnawed at her and she wanted to just come right out and ask him about Corrina.

But honestly, it was none of her business. On October second, Nate Logan would board a plane for Dulles and she'd never see him again.

*Was that what she wanted? A fling?*

No, not her style. She wasn't casual about relationships and it wasn't just play to her. When she felt something for someone, it meant more than a few rolls between the sheets. For her, it had to. But what about Nate? Was that what he thought? That she could be a warm body down south while he was here? She shook her head. No way. Nate didn't seem like that type of guy to her.

No man who'd risk his own life to pull a little girl out of flood waters was into one-night stands. She cringed. No man who carried around a florist card from a woman. She meant something to him. Something special.

She struggled for distance, even though she just wanted to go out there and wrap her arms around him. But she couldn't. On the strength of that card in his wallet, she feared the rejection.

Kadence lay down against her sleeping bag and closed her eyes, blotting out his brooding silhouette.

---

WHEN MORNING CAME, KADENCE AWOKE TO THE SMELL OF HEAT AND coffee. She sat up, stretched, and found an empty tent. Marty, Jim, and Nate were packing up the coolers and the trash. Marty's raucous laugh carried on the early morning air as she rolled up her sleeping bag. She gathered it in her arms, her tennis shoes clutched in one hand, and joined the men. Jim had on a fresh t-shirt against dirty, faded Wrangler jeans. Marty had on yesterday's clothes, but Nate had managed something clean. An olive short-sleeved shirt that bagged over his jeans.

"Hey, Kay—thought you'd sleep all day," Marty said with a smirk, poking her with a forefinger.

"Guess I was tired," she replied and carried the sleeping bag over to Jim's truck.

Jim was up in the bed, shifting around equipment and coolers. She handed him the sleeping bag.

"How's Nate this morning?" she asked, her voice soft enough that Nate hadn't heard her question.

Jim rocked his hand up and down. "So-so. I was the first one up this morning. His sleeping bag didn't even look slept in. The guy probably hasn't been to bed yet."

Kadence sighed. "I was afraid of that." She watched Marty trying to draw Nate into conversation, but Nate seemed a little quiet.

"He'll be okay," said Jim, smiling at her. "You seem awfully concerned about him, Kay. Any reason?"

She shrugged. "I brought him down here, so I guess I feel responsible for him."

Jim squinted, the smile unwavering. "That all?"

"For now," she said and returned his smile.

He crouched at the end of the tailgate and laid a hand on her shoulder. "It's okay, y'know."

Kadence frowned. "What's okay?"

"To have feelings for someone other than Tom. Hell, it's been a year, Kay. You deserve to be happy."

She bowed her head, toeing the grass with her bare foot. "I know that in my head, but my heart's just been a little slow about it."

He squeezed her shoulder. "It's not being disloyal to him."

"Hey, Jim, want us to take down the tent now?" Marty called, Nate beside him.

Jim pulled himself up to his full height and nodded. "Go for it."

Kadence grabbed her small duffle bag from the back of Jim's truck and dug for her toiletries. She found the toothbrush and paste right way, but had to hunt for the deodorant. She couldn't wait to get back to a hot shower and clean clothes.

After the camp site had been torn down, Jim jumped into the driver's seat, starting the motor. Marty motioned Kadence into the front seat as Nate climbed into the back of the truck. Marty piled in and motioned Jim forward.

---

TODAY, IT TOOK NEARLY THREE HOURS TO REACH NEW ORLEANS. THE waters were receding, but places like St. Bernard's Parish were still floating. Much of the city was too dangerous to enter now, mostly from looters and predators. Kadence had heard the horrible stories of rape and murder in the Superdome, at the convention center—in many of the streets.

People were terrified as the police and the National Guard struggled to gain the upper hand, but the looting and violence continued. People who survived *Katrina's* eye wall and her storm surge were being attacked in the streets, some of them murdered. Much of the city was unbridled chaos, emergency management messed up at every turn. Getting survivors out of the city remained difficult, but the staging areas were helping, giving rescuers places to take people where they could be evacuated to safer locations. Texas, Arkansas—Tennessee and beyond.

Most of the day, Jim's boat remained chained and locked down while they ferried evacuees out of the city and to the staging areas. Sometimes, they were just parking lots, but having these gathering places gave people hope that they'd get out. From these places, greyhound busses (and anything else still running) ferried people to neighboring states.

Nate and Marty fell right into step with this change of duties. Nate seemed in his element now, talking to people, managing lists of names and other details so that Jim's ferry ran smoothly. Marty provided comic relief, doing his best to distract the battered survivors for a little while.

They stopped briefly to eat some peanut butter sandwiches Kadence made and hand out more to their hungry passengers.

"Thank you," said a middle-aged man with two young boys beside him. "All we had for four days was saltines." The two boys tore into their sandwiches, devouring them in moments.

Kadence made more, finishing off a jar of peanut butter and two loaves of bread. That was the last of the food they'd brought. But they had plenty of bottled water. Nate passed out bottles to everyone who climbed into the back of Jim's pickup. Right up to the last load of passengers.

"Guess that's it, for this trip," said Marty to her, standing on the truck's running board, one foot on the floorboard. "We're going to drop off this last group at the staging area and head back to Lake Charles with the boat."

Kadence nodded. "I'll call you guys in a few days."

"For a batch of your jambalaya?" Jim called from the driver's seat, grinning at her.

"Sure. You bring the beer and I'll cook."

"Deal!" Jim called. "Y'all be careful going back, ya here?"

"You, too, Jim. Seeya later, Marty."

"Bye guys," said Nate, waving.

Marty closed the cab door and the red truck sputtered away, carrying over a dozen dazed survivors in the back.

"C'mon, Nate," said Kadence, glancing at her watch. "Arbaugh said he'd meet me at my car at five p.m. sharp."

"Lead the way," he answered, looking so tired. She hoped he'd sleep on the way back to Hackberry.

They walked through a group of rescuers who leaned against a brick wall, looking grimy and exhausted, eyes half-closed. The smell of hot oil filled the air as Kadence wound through the tangle of vehicles, at last finding her Accord. Ted Arbaugh, wearing a blue and white Hawaiian shirt and black shorts leaned against the car, scribbling on a green, dog-eared steno pad. His weathered skin looked sun-burned.

"My dear, Kadence," he said, pausing. "You're right on time."

She unlocked the car and Arbaugh climbed into the front passenger seat. She tried to hide her disappointment as she unlocked the back door for Nate, who slid in without a word.

"And tell me, Mr. Logan, sir, how did you fare in this lower circle of hell?" Arbaugh asked, glancing back at Nate.

Nate stared at him a moment, eyes looking distant. "Inconsequential, Mr. Arbaugh compared to the overwhelming need here. Just blows my mind."

Arbaugh raised an eyebrow as he closed the passenger door. Kadence climbed into the car and started the motor, easing her Accord toward a checkpoint for rescue workers. The National Guard would direct her to a route out of the city.

She glanced at the gas gauge. Half full. She hoped they'd have enough to get out on Highway 10 where they had a good shot at refueling.

"I heard about you rescuing little Shawna Martin yesterday, Mr. Logan." Arbaugh asked.

Nate sat with knees spread, elbow against the door, head tilted back against the seat. His eyes were hooded with exhaustion. And something else. Weakness. He laid a hand across his eyes, shielding them from the sunlight streaming through the windows.

"Did Kadence tell you about that?" he asked. It sounded more like small talk than a real question.

Kadence turned onto a side street at the motioning of a National Guardsman, then veered left as a police officer beckoned her forward. She held up the rescuer badge that had been in her front window and was directed into a line of westbound traffic. She groaned. Slow-moving and bumper to bumper.

"Son, please—I am a reporter. I got the story from the source."

Nate pulled his hand away from his eyes, frowning as he sat up to stare at Arbaugh who'd turned around in his seat.

"What do you mean?" he asked, face scrunched.

"Had a long talk with Shawna before she boarded a bus for Alabama."

"Did they get hold of her Aunt Annette?" Nate asked, a smile curving across his face.

Arbaugh nodded. "She's supposed to meet the bus."

"Thank God," said Nate, sinking back into the seat, still smiling. "Hope she's going to be okay. She went through a terrible ordeal."

"Yes sir. That was quite a rescue, young man," said Arbaugh, scribbling on his steno pad again, his gaze still on Nate's face.

Nate shrugged. "Just glad the little girl's safe."

"Also talked to a Bill Simon. At one of the staging areas. Seems he'd met a Nate, too. Said he'd arranged for his flight to Austin, along with the arrangements for his wife's burial."

Nate said nothing, looking almost annoyed.

"And a young couple expecting a baby said they'd met a Nate. Called him an angel, they did, sayin' how he'd handed them five hundred dollars cash to get them to Baton Rouge."

This time, Nate frowned.

"Look, Arbaugh. It was just a little help and not nearly enough. I'm no angel and I didn't do all that much. Talk to that young guy who commandeered a bus and drove all those people to safety. He's your hero."

A smile cracked Arbaugh's leathery expression. "My good man, who said there could only be one hero?"

Nate pointed out the window at the groups of rescuers and relief workers. "These are your heroes, Arbaugh. The people who've been here since *Katrina's* landfall—police officers who stayed in the city despite the risk to protect survivors, shelter workers, the Coast Guard." He looked over at Kadence. "First responders."

"Noted, Mr. Logan," said Arbaugh, still scribbling with a black Bic pen. "I intend to write about them, too."

Nate leaned his head back against the seat, clearly finished with the conversation. But Kadence saw the gleam in Arbaugh's steely eyes as he kept writing on that steno pad. That old pit bull knew a story when he heard it and he'd locked onto something for all he was worth. Whether Nate liked it or not, Arbaugh was crafting a piece about his efforts.

Publicity for relief efforts. That was a good thing and if putting Nate's name out there (as Senator Logan's son) made that happen, then she was comfortable with that. She knew Nate would be, too.

---

The trip home took nearly five hours. She drove Arbaugh to his home outside Lake Charles. A small two-bedroom house in one of

Lake Charles' classic neighborhoods. She shut off the motor and walked Arbaugh to the door.

"Ted, thank you for coming along to capture events," said Kadence as he unlocked the door and set down the black shoulder bag he carried. "With your byline, your accounts should bring even more attention to relief efforts."

He leaned over and kissed her on the cheek. "Thanks, hon. Appreciate the opportunity. I think your rent-an-executive will draw interest." He winked at her. "Especially when they read how he saved that little girl. Although, I don't think our boy's comfortable in the limelight."

Kadence smiled. "Guess he'd better get used to it."

Teddy laughed with a yellow-toothed grin. "Especially when I'm through with him."

"Say, Ted—I wonder if you could do me a favor?"

"For you, hon, anything."

She didn't know quite what she was looking for, but she wanted to know why Nate's friends seemed overly worried about him. Maybe he'd been ill? She wanted to know and she intended to ask, but with Ted's connections, he might get more information.

"Would you say that Nate probably runs in a high-profile crowd? Newsworthy in a social sense?"

Arbaugh nodded. "A senator's son—especially one as popular as Lee Logan? Of course. In D.C., Nate couldn't hide a sneeze without the local press picking it up."

She nodded. Made sense. She didn't want to snoop around in his personal business, but she wanted to know his situation.

"You think somethin's wrong?" Arbaugh asked, squinting at her then back at the car.

"Maybe. I don't know. I just know his friends seemed worried about him, more than I'd expect, I guess." She sighed. "Maybe I'm just being nosy? It's just that he's been running himself ragged and if he's been ill or something…well, I'd like to know. I don't want the guy dying on me while he's here."

Arbaugh laughed, patting her on the arm as he stepped inside his house. He paused, hand on the door.

"I'll dig through the archives for those local rags, make sure he wasn't trampled by bulls or pearl diving beforehand."

She squeezed his arm. "Thanks, Teddy. Appreciate it."

With a wave, Arbaugh closed the door and Kadence returned to the car.

"Okay back there?" she asked as she started the car.

"How about you?" Nate asked.

"Tired. Ready for a hot shower and some cold chardonnay."

"Me, too," he replied.

"Climb up front, will you? I don't like feeling like a chauffeur."

He grinned and popped open the back door. He slid into the front seat and snapped the seatbelt in place. She backed out of the drive and backtracked to Highway 10. It seemed like only minutes until they'd turned onto Highway 27, headed south for Hackberry.

"Jim and Marty really like you, Nate," Kadence replied, casting a glance at him.

"They were great. I learned a lot from them."

"Jim told me that if you ever want a job, he'd find a place for you at the fire department."

Nate grinned. "Thanks, I'll keep that in mind. I know who I'd call if I need someone to watch my back. That includes you, too, Kadence. You saved my butt back there."

She felt excitement quiver in her stomach. Hearing him say that made her feel strange, but oh-so-pleased. She felt comfortable around him and even though he'd been here a week, she'd already trusted him in several life or death situations. Someone, she knew that each time, he'd do the right thing.

"I know this whole setup has been weird from the get-go, Nate, but I'm really glad you're here. I can't believe how well it's gone. I thought it was crazy to place that bid, but I'm so glad I did."

He was staring at her now. She felt the burn of his eyes against her face as she watched the road, moving into the slow lane as she passed a slow-moving silver van. His hand rested against her right arm, squeezing gently.

"Me, too. For the first time in a long while, I felt pride in my work.

And it meant something. It mattered to someone, even the smallest gesture meant a lot of comfort."

She wanted to lose herself in his green eyes and the passion there. Not just for her (she saw that clearly when he looked at her), but for something, a cause, a conviction, or just reaching out to someone. She'd never met anyone like Nate before.

She let go of the wheel with her right hand, steering with her left, and gripped his hand, stroking her thumb across his smooth knuckles. He entwined his fingers in hers, leaning his face against her hair, lips against her ear. Sending shivers down her spine.

"God, I'm attracted to you, Kadence," he whispered, nuzzling his face against her hair.

It was all she could do to keep her car on the road, wanting to grab him with both hands and feel his arms around her. Holding her like she hadn't been held in such a long time.

She shuddered, gripping the wheel with her left hand as he smoothed a hand against her hair.

"I think I'd better watch the road, don't you?" she said with a grin.

"Sorry," he said with a sheepish grin and let go of her right hand, his other hand sliding away from her neck.

She pulled in a long, deep breath, wanting only to feel his hands against her skin, but they were at least an hour from Hackberry.

"So am I," she said, grinning at him as she took hold of the wheel with both hands again.

He laughed and settled back into his seat, but she saw the pain in his eyes. Something was holding him back. But what? She desperately wanted to know.

Nate pulled his cell phone out of its clip and flipped it open.

"Damn, missed two calls."

"Were they important?"

He paged through something on the little screen and his face darkened.

"Nothing that can't wait," he said finally and pushed the phone back into its clip.

Looking annoyed, he stared out the passenger-side window and said nothing the rest of the way to Hackberry. All the way back to the house, she wondered who he was annoyed with: a person or a situation.

# THIRTEEN

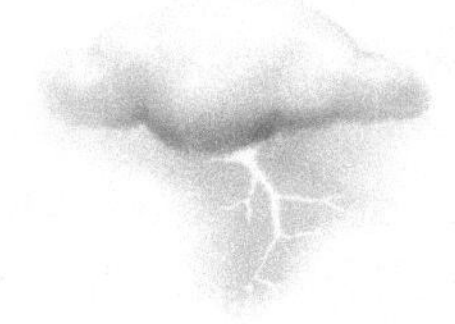

After a hot shower, Nate changed into a Redskins sweatshirt and his last pair of clean jeans. He'd need to do laundry tonight. Elsie hugged Kadence and they chattered away about what was happening in the city. The old lady seemed comfortable here with Kadence who seemed very fond of her. Even her two cats looked content, looking a little fatter and fluffier since they'd been gone.

Nate stood on the porch, smelling fried potatoes and ham sizzling in the kitchen, punctuated by laughter. He glanced through the window, cell phone in hand, and watched them cook and talk. He felt a deep sense of comfort in this place that he hadn't realized he could feel. The lazy calm and simplicity, the smell of the sweet grass and tinge of salt air. The Spanish Moss hanging from the massive Live Oaks, creak of the wraparound porch as his Merrell's crossed it, waiting for Corrina to answer the damned phone.

She never failed to answer it in the middle of dinner with him or when he was speaking to her. She even slept with that thing by her ear.

He felt cold, a chill that he just couldn't shake shivering through him as he waited for her to pick up. The smell of fried potatoes was starting a sour turn in his stomach, his side hurting. Too much exertion over the past few days.

*Come on, Corrina. Pick up!* He was just about to close the phone when her clear voice said hello.

"Corrina? It's Nate."

"Oh…Nate…I wasn't expecting you to call tonight."

He frowned. What did that mean? "You sound distracted. Were you asleep?"

"Oh…no—not asleep." She gasped.

"What's wrong?"

"I'm fine. Darling. What's up?" She giggled.

"Are you drunk?"

"No. No, I'm sorry, what do you need? My wuv."

She sounded strange, patronizing. Almost drunk, even though her speech wasn't slurred. She'd probably had a glass or two of wine. Enough to bring out that hint of cruelty she hid well. Corrina didn't handle alcohol well. She was a mean drunk, so he tried to avoid drinking with her beyond a glass of wine with dinner.

"You called me," he replied, doing his best to hold in his annoyance. "Left two messages, telling me to call you right away."

She was quiet a moment, the connection sounding fuzzy.

"Corrina, if this is a bad time, just tell me and I'll call you later."

"No, no. It's fine. I just wanted to see how you were doing, that's all. And to ask you something."

He paced past the open window, stopping in front of the steps leading into the yard. He rolled his eyes. It was like talking to a three-year-old. And she hadn't called to see how he was doing. She never did. It was always pretext to something else.

"Ask me what, Corrina?"

"Well…would you mind if I used your theatre tickets?"

"Of course not," he replied. "You know I never use those things."

A present from his mother. She bought them every year for him, calling from France to tell him about the season's offerings and urging him to go. And every year they lay untouched on his dresser, unless Meredith was able to drag Ren to one of the trendier plays. He'd have agreed to go if his mother agreed to visit, but she rarely got to the States anymore. Always work or her husband's busy schedule that kept her from visiting. He'd been over there twice and stayed at their villa in Mireval, but she was always too busy for much more than a quick visit.

Corrina giggled softly and he thought he heard a whisper in the background.

"Who's there with you, Corrina?" he asked.

"No one. It's just some boring TV show," she said in a clipped voice.

Another muffled sound. A voice. He was almost certain.

"Ssssh," Corrina hissed in the background.

"Is someone else there?" he asked, growing suspicious.

"Of course not," she said, her voice sounding almost hypnotized.

"You sound funny, Corrina."

"I'm wonderful, Nate. So, are you bored yet? Ready to end this silly little auction thing and come home? Daddy wants to have dinner with you when you return. He's interested in hearing all your little flood stories."

Nate gritted his teeth. *Why did she have to treat everything like it was trivial? Did she not hear how callus she sounded? How cold and unfeeling it was to refer to the Gulf Coast devastation as some little flood story?*

"Little flood stories?" He clenched his hand into a fist, trying to hold back his anger and resist the urge to bite her head off. "Do you have any idea how many people have died down here? Mothers searching for toddlers swept away. Husbands watching over the bodies of their dead spouses. Whole families wiped out. There are so many dead they don't have places to even house the bodies for burial."

"Nate, stop," she cried, her voice sounding teary. "You're scaring me."

He fell silent, not caring how the truth affected her. She always turned it into something about her. His little flood stories scared her. He wanted to wretch.

"Ren will get the tickets for you," he said finally. "As you can see, I'm a thousand miles away right now."

*Oh, really, Nate, dear? And how are you, my love? How was your trip? How are you feeling after your accident? I miss you so much. But enough about you. Let's talk about me now.*

"Okay," she said. "Call me tomorrow and I'll tell you all about the play!" Her voice perked up again with that clueless optimism she'd carefully cultivated. The tone that said, *as long as my surroundings are rosy and I get what I want, the rest of the world's okay, too.*

"Enjoy the play," he said and reached toward the End button to hang up. As if he gave a damn about some play.

"Wuv you, Nate," she said.

He winced. He couldn't say that to her. He wouldn't. "Bye, Corrina," he replied and hung up the phone.

He snapped the phone back into its clip and stepped down into the yard, following the wheel ruts to the end of the driveway. The surrealness of that phone call overwhelmed him. He'd heard another voice in the background, one she'd tried to hide. But why? It didn't make sense.

He sighed. Ren had witty, articulate Meredith with a degree in Math and a position at a research firm. Meredith cared about the people around her and she loved Ren with all her heart. Everyone knew it. Everyone saw it. But Ren was his own man, able to date and work as he chose. He'd chosen Meredith; he hadn't been setup with her like some 19th century arranged marriage.

Disgusted, Nate kicked at the gravel. If he'd just stand up to his father and ignore the noose of expectations that tightened around his throat, then maybe he could be his own man, too?

And disappoint Senator Logan and the Honorable Judge Coleridge? Yeah, right. He shoved his hands into his front pockets, but the sharp pain that cut through his left side made him wince.

Even now, standing in the September Louisiana sun, he still felt cold despite the burn of the summer heat against his face. Beads of sweat clung to his freshly shaved upper lip and he wiped it away with the back of his hand. He rubbed his side, the vague pain reminiscent of his recently ruptured spleen.

*Maybe he was just tired?*

He hadn't slept last night or the night before that. And his right forearm still ached from the dog bite. He pushed up the sleeve of his sweatshirt, looking at the punctures. A little red and puffy, but healing. *Maybe he'd just call it an early evening and crash?*

He went inside and Kadence held up a full wine glass at him, but he politely declined, touching his stomach. She looked a little disappointed, but she took a quick sip from her glass and returned to the skillet sputtering with oil and browning potatoes. He wandered into the warm kitchen and settled himself at the kitchen table, watching Kadence cook.

She wore a white tank top and those cut-off shorts, her light red hair pulled into a ponytail. Slim waist, small firm breasts, and all legs, freckles sprinkled across her nose and cheeks, on her shoulders. She laughed with Elsie who wore a yellow t-shirt and baggy green shorts. She sipped a glass of wine with Kadence, telling her about the first time she saw a movie in New Orleans.

"Nate, you don't know what you're missing here," said Kadence, tapping her wine glass.

"My brain's saying yes, but my belly's saying no," he said, offering her a smile. He shivered as a chill rolled through him.

Kadence studied him a moment as she turned the potatoes in the cast iron skillet with a metal spatula. Elsie turned the slices of ham, browning one side now. Kadence reached over to a stainless-steel pan and stirred what looked like over-cooked green vegetables. He frowned, catching her attention.

"I'll bet you don't even know what these are," said Kadence, laughter in her eyes.

He shrugged. She was right. He hadn't a clue.

"Child, haven't you seen collards before?" Elsie asked with a chuckle.

"Can't say I have," said Nate.

Kadence held up the faded greens with a spoon, a piece of bacon draped over it. "These are good southern greens: collards, mustard, and turnip greens. Pour a little vinegar on 'em and serve 'em with a little red beans and rice for a Cajun twist."

"Now, that's heaven, this," said Elsie as she reached over to a boiling rice and tomato mixture and inhaled the spicy scents.

His stomach twisted at the thought and he felt badly. This time yesterday, he'd have devoured all of it willingly and asked for seconds. But tonight, he just wanted to sleep.

Kadence wiped her hands on a towel and handed the spatula to

Elsie who turned more of the browning potatoes. She moved over to the table and bent toward him.

"Nate, you're not looking so good. Are you all right?"

"Feeling a little under the weather tonight. I think I'll try the leftovers tomorrow, if that's okay with you. I'm going to go lay down for a while."

He saw the concern in her eyes as she reached out to his forehead, laying a cool hand against his brow. Her lips parted, eyes widening.

"Nate…I think you've got fever." She took him by the sleeve and eased him up from the chair. "Come on, let's get you to bed. I'll find the thermometer and see if I need to call a doctor."

He waved her off as he rose from the chair, letting her lead him toward the stairs. "That's not necessary, Kadence. I'll be fine after a good night's sleep."

"Sure you will," she said, leading him up the stairs. "Why are men always such babies about being sick?"

"I just don't need you fussing over me when you've got better things to do," he said as they reached the top of the stairs.

She turned around, grabbing him by the shoulders. She ran her fingers through his hair, her brown eyes soft with concern. *God, he wanted to kiss her.*

"Nate Logan, when are you going to understand that you're just as important as anyone else in this world? You're not a burden. In fact, I paid good money for you and you've been worth every penny."

He laughed, wincing immediately as pain tugged at his left side.

"What is it?" she asked as his hand moved toward his left side then stopped. "Your side hurt?"

"A little."

"Come on," she said, gripping his hand and pulling him toward his bedroom. "We're getting you to bed."

He'd thought about that a lot this week, but this hadn't been how he'd pictured it. He sat down heavily on the edge of the bed and kicked off his Merrell's while she turned down his quilt.

"I'll be back in a few minutes with a thermometer," she said and hurried out of the room.

He stripped off the sweatshirt, his skin turning to gooseflesh as the cold shivered through him. He snaked off his jeans and laid his clothes in the chair beside the bed. Down to his boxers, Nate slid underneath the warm quilt, his teeth chattering. The soft down pillow cradled his head as he sank against it, his temples starting to throb.

The stairs creaked with Kadence's hurried footsteps. She sat down on the edge of the bed beside him, one of those ear thermometers in her hand. Gently, she turned his head and tugged his earlobe down, sliding the thermometer in his ear. In a second or two, it clicked and she slid it out.

"Nate! It's 102.3. You're really sick." She laid the thermometer on the nightstand beside the clock.

He groaned. Just what he needed. Another spasm rippled through his left side and his breath caught as he lurched a little, his hand moving to his side.

"Let me see," she said, pulling back the covers. Her fingers brushed down his goose bumped flesh, finding the scar from his splenectomy. "What's this?"

"Old surgery scar," he replied.

She frowned. "Doesn't look so old to me."

*A couple of weeks was old enough*, he thought as her finger traced over the scar.

"I'll be fine tomorrow," he replied. "Just need to sleep it off, that's all."

She nodded, brushing a tangle of blond curls out of his eyes. "Rest easy, Nate. I'll make you some soup."

"Don't go to any—"

Kadence pressed her fingers to his mouth, silencing him. "Don't you dare say it's trouble to heat up soup or I'll slug you. Got it?"

He laughed, nodding as she pulled her fingers away from his mouth.

"I'll bring you some Tylenol for that fever," she said, stroking her fingers down the side of his face. "Thirsty?"

"How about a Coke?"

"Pepsi?" she asked with a shrug.

"I'll suffer through."

She crossed her arms, a smirk on her face. "You'll drink one of my Pepsi's with reverence, Mister."

He chuckled. "Because it's yours, I will."

She patted his arm. "Be right back. But seriously, Nate, you're no trouble. You're a pleasure and don't let anyone tell you differently."

He reached out and caressed her cheek with a shaking hand. All he wanted was to hear those words again from those full, kissable lips. She closed her eyes a moment at his touch then gently, she pressed his hand back against the quilt.

"Get some sleep," she said and rose from the bed, hurrying down the stairs. He heard her light steps creaking down the stairs and felt his eyelids closing.

---

It seemed late, the room looking dim-lit and almost surreal as he awoke, his head pounding out a rhythm of fever through his veins. His face was a mask of sweat, his breathing hard and fast against whatever infection was hammering his body. The doctors had warned him about being more susceptible to infections without his spleen, but he hadn't expected to get sideswiped this soon by something.

Kadence sat beside him on the edge of the bed, her hand stroking his hair as she pressed a cold washcloth against his forehead. But she was fading into the room, the pounding in his head overwhelming him. It was all swirling together into a wildness that his brain couldn't manage. The steady thunder in his head became the rhythmic buzz of a boat motor, and he was trawling through Ninth Ward, through eight feet of dark water. Images of the car crash mixed with thick, black flood waters smelling like gas and oil as they burbled around him and he struggled against them.

"Water's rising," he whispered. "Get out—gotta get out!"

Metal gouged metal, shooting sparks, guard rail collapsing. Burn of air bag, breath exploding from his chest.

He gasped, jolting with the impact.

"Easy, Nate—you're fine. You're fine."

Her voice was muffled by the pounding in his ears and his ragged breaths.

"He's mighty sick," said a raspy voice somewhere beyond his bed.

"I know," said Kadence. "His temp's rising, too. Almost a hundred and four. If it goes past that, I'm calling Jim."

"Jim? Who's that?" asked the woman.

*Was that Elsie? He wasn't sure.*

"A good friend of mine," said Kadence. "Works at the fire station."

"Jim, the debris' sinking. Throw me the rope. The rope!"

He thrashed against the water rising around him, metal twisting against him, blocking the door. And the car was sinking.

"Nate, it's not real," she said, hands pressing against his shoulders as he tried to sit up. "It's the fever. You're safe."

"Car's sinking…Ren, throw me the rope!"

He had to sit up or drown. But the metal was pinning him in the car. He felt the cold flood waters against his face and bolted, the metal giving way at last. He was on his feet, swaying, the thundering noise aching through his brain. He was so cold.

"Nate!" Kadence shouted, grabbing hold of his arm.

The debris pinned his arm and he struggled against it, his arm finally slipping free as he lurched forward. Something hit the floor beside him, his gaze watery as he clutched his aching head and plunged ahead.

The plank. He had to reach the plank and climb up into the boat or he'd drown.

"Marty, where's the plank?" he demanded, staggering forward, the tilted image of a board swaying ahead of him. He lunged for it. Missed.

"Nate!"

Kadence's scream throbbed through his ears as the first bite of wood slammed into his side, the next smacking his chin. Another hit his shin as he tumbled down the debris pile head first. Into black flood waters.

HE AWOKE TO BURNING PAIN THROUGHOUT HIS BODY, THE ROOM'S LIGHT still fever-dim, quilts bunched around his aching limbs. Kadence was stretched across him, holding him down with both arms. The crook of his right arm burned and he tried to reach over and rub away the burn, but he couldn't move his arms.

"He's coming around, Kay," said the familiar voice. Jim.

"Did we save Shawna?" Nate asked, his voice sounding so weak that it startled him.

A hand patted his shoulder. "Yeah, Nate, we got to her in time. Good work."

Another voice he didn't recognize was on the other side of the room.

"It's sepsis," said the calm voice. "Probably from the dog bite. And being without his spleen didn't help either."

"He's lucky that's all he lost in that accident," said Jim.

"Ren?" Nate called.

Kadence whispered that he was fine and stroked his fiery forehead.

"How'd you find that picture, Jim?" Kadence asked.

"My buddy in D.C. sent it. He knows the first responder who was on the scene that night. Nate's damned lucky to be alive if you ask me. If that hadn't been an SUV, he wouldn't be here right now."

Kadence's strong hand was caressing his face again.

"So, y'all gonna admit him, Clark?" Jim asked.

"I'll call Dr. Ferguson, get him to send out some more antibiotics. I'm going to drip a couple of bags into him tonight. That should get him to feelin' better, maybe knock that fever down a notch or two. Knock out the delirium."

A face hung above his and in a few moments, it swam into focus. Jim.

"Nate," he said with a chuckle, "promise me you're not going to dive down any more staircases tonight."

"What's that mean?" Nate asked, frowning.

Jim patted his shoulder. "It's okay if you don't remember. I'm sure Kay here'll tell you about it in the morning." Jim's face slipped into a haze again. "Clark, he didn't break anything, did he?"

"Bruised a few ribs, but he's fine otherwise."

Nate squinted at the figure in blue and white standing behind Kadence. Balding, thin moustache, short with a slight belly. He wanted to sit up, but Kadence still held him down. He struggled until finally Jim's hands joined Kadence's against his shoulders.

"Easy there, Nate," said Jim as Nate collapsed against the pillow, drenched in sweat. "Just lie still, buddy."

"Where am I?" Nate asked, glancing around.

"Still in Hackberry," said Kadence, her hand against his forehead again, smoothing the blond hair out of his eyes. "You're in your room, Nate, and you're safe. We're not in New Orleans anymore."

"Or your SUV," said Jim in a soothing voice.

"So, they removed his spleen?" Kadence asked. "After the accident."

"Looks like it," said the man called Clark. "Pretty recent, too."

"The news story was dated August 25th," said Jim.

Kadence glared at him, those kind brown eyes burning with anger. "He arrived here in Lake Charles on September 2nd. He was probably fresh out of the hospital when he boarded that flight. No wonder he's looked so tired."

Jim slouched on the other side of the bed. "So, you gonna return him as damaged goods, Kay?" he asked with a snort.

"No," Kadence snapped. "But I'm not very happy about the lack of disclosure."

"Guess you didn't read the fine print," Jim said, grinning at her.

Kadence rose from the bed and returned in a moment or two with a glass of water. She bent over Nate, pressing the glass to his lips.

"Here, drink this," she said, her voice soft and comforting.

He took a sip of the cool water that soothed his dry throat.

"Okay, I'm gonna head on home," said Clark. "Jim, when the second bag's empty, you can remove the IV."

"Will do," said Jim, mocking a salute. "I still remember my EMT training."

Clark patted Nate's arm. "You get better now, Mr. Logan. We'll check on you in the morning. See how you're doing."

"Thanks," said Nate, his voice raspy.

The room grew darker, the voices fading as the pounding in his head reverberated louder. He felt the dark flood waters licking at his heels, the horrible summer heat clinging to him as he closed his eyes.

# FOURTEEN

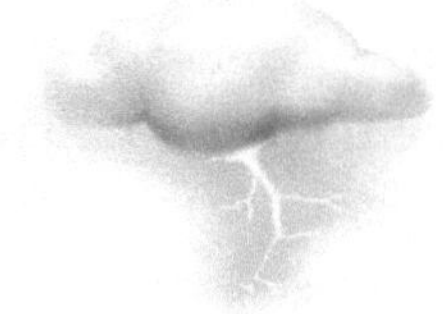

Kadence leaned against the headboard, watching Nate sleep a little easier as the antibiotics dripped into his veins. She still felt shaky, remembering his wild-eyed strength as he'd slipped past her and Elsie, his delirium a raging fire. And his horrible plunge down the stairs. She cringed. It was a miracle he hadn't broken his neck. And now, he was septic, requiring heavy doses of antibiotics.

She'd convinced Elsie to go on to bed when Jim and the paramedic arrived. She hadn't meant for any harm to come to Nate. The whole auction thing had been a lark, yet from the moment he'd stepped off the plane, everything had been deadly serious. Including her attraction to him.

"I know that look, Kay," said Jim, pointing at her as he sat at the foot of Nate's bed. "None of this is your fault, so don't you even go there."

She shrugged, sitting up to adjust Nate's covers. His breathing was a little easier. Maybe the antibiotics were already helping?

"I'm just furious that he didn't tell us he'd just gotten out of the hospital."

The image of his SUV, a mass of twisted metal around that light pole, made her shiver. And the trauma poor Nate must have gone through. But worse, that picture carried her back to the night that Tom died. The eerie similarities haunted her, made her hands shake and her heart hurt. Tom's had been a one-car accident just like Nate's, yet Tom died at the scene and Nate had walked away.

Jim nodded, his gaze falling to the patchwork quilt. "I feel bad, too, I guess. Here he was missing a spleen, probably weak and shaky as hell and we drag him into that septic soup."

"Well, he should have said something."

"Would it have made any difference?"

"What? Of course, it would have!" She crossed her arms and stood up from Nate's bedside to pace. "If I'd known about the accident, I'd have delayed his trip down for starters. Then we'd have been past the rescue efforts. Just thinking about the days he sat there with that festering dog bite without even some antibiotic ointment makes me crazy."

"It's all moot, Kay. Looks like we caught it in time and he'll be just fine."

Kadence picked up the accident picture that Jim had printed off her computer and stared at it a moment, her heart squeezing. "But why didn't he tell us about this?" she demanded, shaking it at Jim.

Jim raised his hands in the air. "Probably just stubborn male pride. He wanted to be treated like an equal, not an invalid. Probably didn't want you thinking he was a wimp or too good to get dirty."

She sighed. All of those reasons made good sense and probably explained a lot, but it made her angry to see his lack of concern for his own health. No wonder his friends had been so concerned about him, especially being in those flood waters. They knew his spleen was gone and that he was very susceptible to infections now.

"Maybe he didn't think it was any of our business?" Jim offered.

"What was the cause of the accident?" she asked. "Do you know?"

Jim nodded. "Sleep deprivation."

A chill touched her skin, remembering Nate not sleeping for two days out in the field. Had he been in that shape the night he'd hit that light pole? Apparently, he had been.

"Think he's one of them workaholic types?" Jim asked.

She gave him her best *duh* looks.

"Guess even I could have answered yes to that one." He rose from the bed and dropped down in a wicker chair on the other side of the bed, propping his feet on the wicker ottoman. Jim looked tired tonight, no doubt still recovering from the New Orleans rescue efforts.

"Nate doesn't strike me as a guy who gives up on anything. Even when he should."

*Just himself,* Kadence thought with a sigh. She kept glancing over at Nate, afraid he'd crawl out of bed and fall again, but for the moment, he seemed to be sleeping.

"He was determined to fall down those stairs, whether I wanted him to or not."

Jim chuckled. "Nah, Nate's all right."

Nate moaned, shifting in the bed and mumbling something about flood waters. Kadence moved to his side again, a hand against his face, caressing, soothing.

"You're fine, Nate. You're safe."

"My buddy in D.C. said Nate didn't remember the accident at the scene. Had no idea what had happened to him. That's not always a good thing. It might hit him hard later."

She nodded, knowing that's exactly what had happened. He'd had nightmares that first night. Memories of the accident; she was almost certain.

"It did," she replied, glancing over at Jim. "That first night in camp."

Jim's eyes widened as he sat up straighter. "You serious?"

"He was shouting in his sleep," she replied, a hand against Nate's bare shoulder. "I had to wake him up and when I did, he was wild-eyed. Must have blindsided him a little. Something he hadn't expected so soon." Or ever. Piling those memories onto the horrors he'd seen that day in New Orleans must have been hard.

Jim ran a hand across his face, tan and unshaven. Of course, Jim *always* looked like he needed a shave. "My hat's off to him. We've put him through the ringer and he's still standing. More or less." He grinned at her. "You're looking awful cozy there, Kay."

She pulled her hand back from Nate, standing up to refill his water glass. "I was just checking his fever, smart guy."

"Sure ya were," he said with a snicker. "What are you so afraid of, Kay?"

*Of falling in and losing a second time.*

She couldn't go through that kind of heartache again. Or the guilt. If she'd been better skilled or had just paid more attention. If she'd just done the right thing that night, Tom might still be alive. Instead, she'd let him bleed out on the highway.

*Why didn't Jim understand how hard this has been on her?* Especially with the anniversary of that night fast approaching. *Didn't he realize that she'd bungled the scene.* And it cost Tom his life. Maybe he didn't? She'd been the first one on the scene.

"More pain," she answered finally, still clutching the water glass in her hand. "Or having to go through that kind of loss again."

Jim rose to his feet and walked over to her. He took the glass out of her hand and set it on the nightstand. Then he put his arms around her, hugging her close.

"I know. There are so many nights when I've wished it'd been me to respond first that night. To have found him first and spared you that extra agony."

She felt the tears stinging her eyes and she wrapped her arms around him, trying to hold back the pain so he couldn't see it.

"But you know what?" he said, gazing into her eyes. His own eyes were watery now as he shared his pain. "If I had, you wouldn't have had that moment to say goodbye."

She clenched her eyes closed as the tears filled her eyes.

He brushed his thumbs across her eyelids, wiping away the hint of tears that threatened to fall. "See, no matter what happened that night, Kadence, you were with Tom when he died. You held his hand when he passed from this earth."

A tear slid down each cheek and she thrust her hands up to wipe the rest away before they fell.

"It was only a moment, but you got to say goodbye to him. That's somethin' precious you gotta remember. You gotta cherish. No matter what happened next."

She nodded. Jim was right. She wouldn't trade those last seconds of Tom's life for anything (except to have him back in her life).

Regardless of her own failures that night, she'd been with him when he died.

"I never thought about that until now. Thank you."

He smoothed the hair out of her eyes then hugged her again. "He'd want me lookin' out for you, so I've gotta say this to you, Kay." He nodded toward Nate who shifted with a groan in the bed. "I know you feel somethin' for Nate there. Don't know if it's anything or everything, but whatever it is, you gotta find out."

She nodded, stepping back from him as he let her go. She wanted to find out, wanted to delve beneath Nate's calm, unassuming facade to find the man beneath it. The man who put himself last to everyone else. The man who only wanted to help others. She wanted to know what he wanted, what he yearned for, what he needed out of this life. But some questions needed answers first—like who was Corrina.

She'd heard Nate's conversation on the porch this afternoon. She'd heard it all through the open window. He'd almost yelled at her on the phone, something about *little flood stories*. She'd heard him tell her he loved her, but he hadn't been convincing. Kadence wasn't sure if Corrina was a real girlfriend or someone he had to deal with in some capacity. He looked so disgusted when he'd hung up the phone.

"Jim," she said, studying his face a moment. "What if he's already got someone?"

Jim pointed at Nate's left hand that gripped the edge of the quilt. "See a ring there?"

She shook her head.

He smiled. "Where there's a ring, there's trouble. Where there isn't, there's always a chance."

Kadence threw her arms around him, hugging him hard. "Thanks," she whispered.

Jim patted her on the shoulder then shooed her over toward the bed. "You stay with him while I grab a beer," he said. "Then we'll check that IV and disconnect him so he can sleep." He reached the door, but turned around, his face looking tense. "You want me to stay tonight? In case, you need some help?"

She cringed. "Would you mind? I'll make you the best breakfast you ever had."

He held out his arms, cocking his head to one side. "How can I refuse an offer like that? Be right back."

His boots pounded down the stairs as she sat down beside Nate and laid her hand against his forehead. Still burning up. He let out a groan, shifting his body with a sudden jolt.

"Look out! Look out!" He thrust a hand up over his face, gritting his teeth against some unseen impact.

"It's okay," she said in a soothing voice, saying it over and over. She leaned down and kissed him on the cheek then continued to stroke the hair out of his eyes.

In a few minutes, Jim returned with a bottle of Miller Light in each hand. He pressed one into her hand.

"Thought you could use one, too."

She thanked him and twisted off the cap. The beer was cold and wet. That's all she cared about. Jim flopped down in the wicker chair, his feet rasping against the canes. She took another sip then set the beer on the nightstand, picking up the wet washcloth she'd laid there.

Nate shifted his body with a mumble and a sharp inhale. She folded the cloth in half and pressed it to his overheated forehead, holding it against his brow. Nate relaxed a little.

Finally, he lay still and she picked up her beer.

"Kadence?" Nate called in a raspy voice, his eyes opening.

"I'm here," she replied, gazing down at him with a patient smile.

"You go on to bed," he said in a feverish voice. "It's late and you're exhausted."

"So are you," she said, stroking the side of his face. "The company's good, though, so I'll just stick around."

His mouth lifted in a faint smile. "Thanks, but I know you're tired—"

She laid two fingers against his dry lips and gently shushed him. "Just rest. Thirsty?"

When he nodded, she set down her beer. With the glass in one hand, she slid an arm under his bare shoulders, lifting his head enough for him to drink the water.

"Better?" she asked.

He nodded, closing his eyes a moment.

She patted him on the shoulder, feeling his smooth skin against her fingers and she wanted to comfort him.

"So, why didn't you tell me about your car accident?"

He shrugged.

"Or the fact that you'd just gotten out of the hospital? Minus your spleen."

"Didn't seem relevant," he replied.

She felt her anger stir. "Didn't seem relevant? What do you mean by that?"

"Thought I'd just be doing some financial advising," he said with a sigh. "Not trying to rescue flood victims. Besides, it just never came up. Until I was actually out in a boat, I didn't think about it."

"You could have died, you know?" she said, crossing her arms.

He was frowning, the dark circles under his eyes making him look sleepier than usual. "What do you mean?"

"The accident. You fell asleep at the wheel, didn't you?"

His jaw tightened. Finally, he nodded, bowing his head. "Too many late nights after work, I guess."

"Were you partying?"

"No. Wining and dining clients, Kadence," he said, his breath becoming a little more ragged, his eyes looking weaker. "It's part of the job—that I hate, but it's something I have to do."

*Okay, so he hadn't been out partying hard, getting drunk, risking his life and other people's, too. He'd been working.*

"How many hours a week do you work, Nate?"

He groaned, laying a hand against his side as his face scrunched in pain. He drew in a quick breath.

"Eighty, eighty-five...why?"

She felt her stomach drop into her feet. "My God, Nate—that's over two full time jobs! Are you crazy? I don't know exactly what you do there, but I know you're working too hard."

"Jesus, Nate," said Jim, rising from the wicker chair to sit on the edge of the bed. "No wonder you wrapped yourself around a light pole. You work eighty-five hours and then take clients out for the evenin'? When do you sleep?"

"Apparently, at the wheel," Nate replied with a thin smile that disappeared as quickly as it arrived.

Jim laughed and took a swig of his Miller Light. Then he wagged a finger at Nate. "That's only funny because you're alive to tell the tale. You know that, don't you?"

"Yeah," Nate said with a nod.

"Kay's awful concerned about you."

He stared up at her as he reached over and took her hand in his. His hand shook with fever as she stroked his hand.

"I know I've only known you a week or so, but there's something familiar about you," she said. "Something comfortable. So, I'd like to keep you around awhile, okay?"

"Not sure what I did to deserve you," he said, his whole face brightening from the grey shadows haunting his face. "But I'm good with that."

Jim rose from the bed and set his beer on the dresser. He moved over to the IV, checking the level of the antibiotic dripping into Nate's arm. He tapped the line with thumb and forefinger.

"It's a little slow, but you're over halfway through this second bag of antibiotics."

"What do I have?" Nate asked.

"System-wide infection, but we're gettin' it under control. Clark's gonna check on you tomorrow and I'm stayin' the night, to make sure you don't do anymore stair divin'."

Nate squinted at Jim with tired eyes, the dark circles hollowing out his face a bit. "Who's Clark?"

"Paramedic," said Jim, retrieving his beer from the dresser. "Works for Lake Charles. He was on call tonight, so I tapped him when Kadence called me."

"Thank him for…coming out so late," said Nate, his eyelids closing.

Kadence smiled. Poor man was fighting hard to stay awake. But he was quickly losing the battle.

"Sleep, Nate," she said, pressing the cold washcloth to his forehead.

It took only a few minutes for Nate to fade into deep sleep. Kadence picked up his empty water glass and moved to refill it. As she reached the doorway, a cell phone chimed. Nate's, she realized. She set down the glass and hurried over to dresser—and Nate's phone. The name, Ren appeared on the display, so she opened the flip phone.

"Hello?"

"You're not Nate," said a wary voice. "Where's Nate?"

"Is this Ren?" Kadence asked.

"Yes. Is this—Kadence?"

She smiled. Ren had a smooth voice, sounding laid back but personable. "Yes, Kadence Harlowe. Listen—Ren, I answered the phone because Nate's taken ill."

"What?" Ren fell silent and, in a moment, she heard him whispering to someone in the background. "Kadence, what's happened? Does he need anything? A doctor, an ambulance—"

She was a little surprised by Ren's concern, but also very impressed. She knew right away that Nate meant a lot to Ren.

"He's resting comfortably right now, but he's got a pretty high fever."

"Meredith, I'm asking," he said to someone in the background. "What's the diagnosis, please?"

"Sepsis, but—"

"Dear God! Sepsis?"

"He's going to be fine," Kadence said as forcefully as she could, trying to get Ren to hear her.

The phone crackled and Kadence heard another voice on the line.

"Kadence, this is Meredith Hudson, Ren's fiancée. What can you tell us about Nate's condition?"

She sounded equally concerned, but a little calmer than Ren.

Kadence felt her voice crack. "He's—uh, got a system-wide infection and we're pumping antibiotics into him right now. The paramedic is coming back in the morning to determine whether Nate should be moved to a hospital."

"This is all my fault," Ren said in a pained voice.

"I feel responsible, too," said Kadence, pressing her forehead against the phone's screen. "He got bit by a dog he rescued. The paramedic thinks that's how he got the infection."

"He's missing a spleen, did he tell you that?" Ren asked.

"We only found out tonight about the accident and his splenectomy. If I'd known, I wouldn't have taken him into the devastation like that."

Meredith sighed. "He'd have never told you if it meant keeping him on the sidelines. He pushes himself way too hard."

"I've seen that," said Kadence. "Watched him risk his own life to carry a little girl out of flood waters."

"What? Nate did that?" Ren's voice was a mixture of surprise and reverence.

"Yes, just one of many things he's done, Ren. He's a real gem."

"He's the best friend I've ever had," said Ren. Kadence heard the smile in his voice.

"Don't you worry. We're taking very good care of Nate down here. When I saw your name on Nate's cell phone, I thought I should let you know his condition."

"Well, thank you, Kadence," said Ren, "Meredith and I really appreciate you telling us. God knows we'd have never heard it from Nate."

*How much did they know about the cause of Nate's car accident?*

"Ren, could I ask you a personal question?"

"Sure, ask away," said Ren.

"Nate's car accident. What do you think caused it?"

A heavy sigh hissed through the phone.

"Look, I know what the first responder said," said Kadence. "Said it was sleep deprivation, but—"

"But what? He was asleep at the wheel when he left for home. He'd been up all night before that, handling clients."

Ren's anger was unmistakable.

"I'm asking because I'm worried about him. He's been having flashbacks of the accident."

"They said he wouldn't remember," said Meredith to Ren.

"I know, but no one knew for sure," Ren replied. "Kadence, listen, Nate's had a rough time of it lately," said Ren. "And with the accident memories surfacing…"

"You're thinking he should return to Arlington?" Kadence said, the words almost sticking in her throat.

"Maybe that would be best?" said Ren. "Get him back into the hospital and get his health on track."

Kadence chuckled. "Of course, you and I both know he'd never agree to that."

"Ren, hold on, honey," said Meredith. "It sounds to me like Kadence has everything under control and is taking good care of him. Probably just what he needs."

"Kadence, Nate almost died that night. He hadn't slept in nearly two days, pushing himself to handle several people's jobs at once. He works too hard."

"That was my speculation," said Kadence.

"So, where's Nate now? Can I talk to him?" Ren asked.

"At my place in Hackberry, but he's asleep right now. We've got an IV at his bedside, pumping antibiotics into him. As soon as his fever breaks and we get some food into him, I'll get him on the phone to you."

She'd have to sit on him to keep him in bed, but that might not be such a bad exercise, Kadence thought with a grin.

"Sounds like Kadence has everything under control," said Meredith. "Is there anything we can do from here?"

"Not right now," said Kadence. She had to restrain herself not to blurt out Corrina's name and ask questions, but she held it back. "I just wanted to make sure someone knew about his condition. The paramedic is confident that we got the infection in time. Is there anyone you'd like me to call for him?" Corrina perhaps? Kadence wanted to know who she was to Nate.

"No, no," said Ren, "You're doing plenty. We'll contact Nate's Dad and anyone else who needs to know. Kadence, I really appreciate everything you're doing for him."

"We think the world of him," said Meredith. "Sounds like he's a little special to you, too, Kadence?"

"Yes. I mean, I'm uh, taking very good care of him and you don't need to worry. I'm sure he'll call you in a couple of days."

"Nice talking to you, Kadence," said Ren.

"Bye, Kadence," Meredith replied.

"Nate's got some wonderful friends. Bye now."

She closed the phone, clearing the connection.

"The in-laws?" Jim asked, smirking at her as he stood by Nate's IV.

"No," she snapped. "Two of Nate's best friends. One's his business partner. They seemed very nice and very worried about him."

Jim adjusted the bag of antibiotics then moved toward Kadence. "He'll be fine. He's got about ten more minutes left on that dose."

Kadence picked up the empty water glass and hurried into the bathroom to fill it. She returned and set it on the nightstand before sitting down on the other side of the bed to watch him sleep.

# FIFTEEN

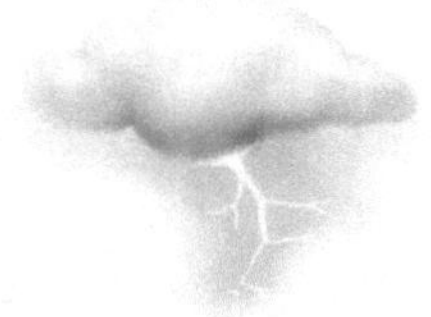

It was evening the following day when Nate awoke, still battling a high fever. He felt exhausted and only stayed awake long enough to drink some liquids at Kadence's insistence. All through that night and the next two, he heard voices, footsteps, and lots of creaking on the stairs. Interspersed with dreams and images he'd wanted to forget.

He lifted his head from the pillow, seeing Kadence curled up beside him on the bed, a pink afghan draped across her. Her breaths were steady and deep as he sat up. She looked angelic lying there, red hair in waves across her face, cheeks dusted with freckles. She wore a lavender tank top and those eye-popping Levi's cut-offs, the white pockets showing beneath the frayed hems.

He leaned over her, the pounding in his head much softer now, and brushed a lock of hair out of her eyes. He let his fingers linger against her pale face, soft cheeks, long lashes. She looked tired.

She was so beautiful, lying there in the balmy silence, her quiet breaths the only sound in the room. He pressed his lips against her cheek, smelling hints of lavender and sandalwood as he kissed her. All this time, she'd stayed with him in this room, watching over his fevered sleep, easing his restlessness.

He was moved by her tender care, intoxicated by her unflinching support. Intoxicated by her. As soon as he could get out of this bed, he'd take her out for a nice dinner. No business. All personal. To thank her properly. Who was he kidding? He was really falling for her.

He thought back to the strange phone call he'd had with Corrina, the whispers in the background. In less than three months, they were to be married and the thought sickened him. The only thing he and Corrina had in common were the social circles their parents traveled. This engagement was a farce. And he was no Jay Gatsby. Not even a good Nick. Corrina loved the lifestyle not the man. And until he'd come to Louisiana, he hadn't even recognized the charade. A social game wealthy parents played with the media and their children. And considering the lavish wedding presents, no one ever really suffered. Much.

But he was done with party games. His life wasn't a social play put on for the benefit of others. It belonged to him and he was taking it back. And that started with breaking off his engagement with Corrina. He'd do it in person. As soon as he got back to Arlington.

He planted another soft kiss against Kadence's cheek, brushing his lips across her full lips, exploring the curve of her chin and her long, graceful neck.

Her eyes rolled open and she stared at him a moment as he leaned over her. Finally, she smiled at him.

"Looks like you're feeling better," she said.

"I am," he said, "thanks to you." He brushed his fingertips through that thick red hair and traced them down the side of her face to cup her chin.

She reached up to him and laid the back of her hand against his forehead. Nate sighed.

"Fever's broken," she said, propping her elbows behind her.

"That's what you think," he said, leaning toward her lips.

Her lips parted as he pressed his mouth to hers in deep, covering kisses. Her hands stroked across his bare chest as he laid back against the pillows, his body pressed against hers.

"God, you feel good," she said between kisses, her hands moving across his shoulders and up to his hair, gathering handfuls of curls in her fists.

He wanted to roll her under the quilts and take his time with those cut-offs, but the illness betrayed him, sapping away his strength. A wave of weakness hit him and he groaned as the room tilted.

And those wonderful hands stopped moving across his body, holding onto his shoulders now and pressing him back under the quilts. Alone.

"As much as I'd love to take advantage of your weakened state, I'd better let you rest," she said. She kissed him on the forehead and rose from the bed.

"Just my luck," Nate said with a groan.

She leaned over him, her hair tickling the side of his face. "For now," she said and kissed his lips, nibbling his lower lip before she sat up.

He held onto her hand, squeezing. "Thanks," he said.

She stepped away from the bed, letting her fingers slide through his. "My pleasure, Nate. Be right back with some soup for you."

THE NEXT DAY, NATE SHAKILY DRESSED IN JEANS AND A RED POLO SHIRT. He smiled. Kadence had washed all his clothes while he'd been ill.

Slipping into his Merrell's, Nate stepped out of the bedroom and creaked down the stairs to the kitchen. The room smelled like cinnamon. Elsie sat reading the *Lake Charles American Press* in a yellow robe, a steaming cup of coffee setting in front of her.

"Well, Nate Logan," she called, all smiles, as he stepped into the kitchen. She set down the newspaper and pushed out a chair for him. "Boy, you look like death on toast. Get yourself into one of these chairs for you fall down."

"Think I'll do that," he said and sat heavily on one of the straight-backed chairs.

She patted his arm.

"Your stomach up to some coffee?"

"Think so," he said and grabbed one of the ceramic mugs, turned upside down beside the old-style, stainless-steel percolator that sat on a hot pad. The percolator was heavy in his fist as he filled his cup. His hand shook a little, but he didn't spill the coffee. He picked up the cup with both hands and brought it to his mouth, sipping gingerly. It was rich and warm, strong like he liked it.

Elsie watched him a moment or two.

"You the first Yankee I ever saw could handle good Southern coffee straight up," she said finally.

He laughed. "It's very good." He glanced around, not seeing Kadence anywhere. "Hey, where's Kadence?"

"She at the university. Teachin' classes today. She'll be home for dinner." She pointed toward the phone on the wall. "She left you a note."

A grin spilled across his face as he rose to retrieve the message. Tucked behind the phone, it was written on blue paper. He picked up the folded piece of paper and opened it.

"Nate, I'll be at the university until four or so. Call me if you need anything. Otherwise, I'll see you tonight around six. Hope you're feeling better. K"

Smiling, he refolded the note and slid it into his jeans pocket. Then he returned to the table to drink coffee with Elsie. Percy, her tubby tabby, sauntered into the room, the tortoiseshell cat, Diva, following behind him. Percy wound his way between Nate's legs and then Elsie's, on his way to the food bowl against the wall. Nate reached down and patted both cats as they passed by.

"How are you doing so far, Elsie?" Nate asked. "I know this must seem so far from home."

She nodded and leaned back in the chair, looking frail this morning. She was a petite woman with thin, hunched shoulders and papery, wrinkled skin.

"It's been a change, this," she said and gazed over at Percy gorging himself on dry food. Diva poked her nose around him to eat, too. "I think they adjustin' better'n me."

Nate laughed.

She stared into her cup a moment, that unwavering smile still on her face. He admired Elsie for that smile. No matter what, she'd held her head high and smiled, like she was saying to the world, *you'll never get me down.*

"It's hard. Not havin' a place of your own no more. Waitin' for them screwball FEMA people and the insurance settlements. Every day, I wait to see what gon' happen next. Like a three-ring circus, this."

Nate took another sip of his coffee. "What are your plans? Gonna stay on with Kadence? She really enjoys your company, you know."

Elsie's smile broadened. "She's become like a daughter to me. And we get on nice. Maybe someday I'll go back home? Ninth Ward was all I knowed. The only place I knowed since I left my momma's home in Baton Rouge." At last, that intrepid smile faded a little, pain flickering her dark eyes. "But so many died there. It's hard to think about goin' back in the face of that. Someday, I'll be ready though." She glanced around Kadence's spacious kitchen. "But I feel at home here. Kadence got a nice place that she's sweet enough to share."

Strangely enough, he felt at home here, too. The laid-back lifestyle appealed to him and he admired the straightforwardness of the people. They told things like they were, no candy-coating. No politics, he thought with a sigh. People did things their own way here and it worked for them.

"Me, too," said Nate.

That smile broadened as Elsie reached out and patted him on the hand.

"She's done a lot of worryin' over you these few days. When you pitched down them stairs, she thought you'd a killed yourself. Them tears were fast and furious until we got you back in bed."

Nate bowed his head. "This was hard on her, I know."

"Only 'cause she cares about you, silly boy," said Elsie. "Wish you Yankee boys had more moxie. She needin' someone like you in her life, Nate, but you gotta show her you care, too. Otherwise, she's just gon' keep guessin'."

He laughed. Elsie was right. Maybe he did need more moxie, to tell his Dad and everyone else trying to orchestrate his life where to blow their notes? He wanted to know her better and the only way he could find out how they'd be together was to end it with Corrina. He dreaded his father's reaction more than Corrina's. Oh, she'd rage. She'd scream and break things. With all the melodrama she could summon.

It was all about appearances after all. She could do her worst, because it wasn't his problem anymore.

Now, Dad's disappointment and the guilt trip he'd lay down, with only first-class accommodations, would be hard to take. He'd deal with that on his return to Virginia. But he'd made up his mind. He wouldn't marry a woman who treated him like this year's fashion accessory. No matter what political gain it handed the Senator.

Suddenly, Nate felt the weight lift from his shoulders. He was free. Finally, he was free to own his own life. He grinned, leaning back in his chair.

"Well, ain't you the cat who got the canary," said Elsie. "What's that look about?"

"Moxie," he said with a wink at her and rose from the chair. He had some phone calls to make.

---

KADENCE ARRIVED HOME AROUND SIX O'CLOCK AND NATE MET HER AT THE door with a glass of chardonnay and a daisy from the field beyond the house. It smelled like dried grass, but the petals were crisp and bright, like Kadence. She wore navy pants and a cream-colored camisole beneath a linen jacket. Smelling like lavender and sandalwood.

"What's this?" she asked, grinning as she set her briefcase inside the door. She had that playful look in her eyes, wanting him to come closer.

"How was your day?" he asked, pressing the wine glass in her hand and kissing her gently on the lips before he handed her the daisy.

"Getting better by the moment," she replied, leaning into him for another kiss. "I could get used to this." She tucked the stem of the daisy behind her ear and took a sip of the cold wine.

She sniffed the air, her eyes widening. "What's that wonderful smell coming from the kitchen?"

The fettuccine! He ran back to the kitchen to find the sauce nearly bubbling over the pan. Elsie passed him a wooden spoon and he stirred down the cream and garlic. The noodles were still bubbling away, ready in about three minutes.

Elsie hunched over a cutting board, slicing tomatoes for salads. She had three white bowls already filled with lettuce.

"Y'all even set the table," said Kadence, moving toward the square table in the corner.

He nodded. A yellow tablecloth, three navy placemats and white plates. He'd just lit the red tapers before she pulled up. Nothing fancy, but she seemed to appreciate his effort.

Kadence turned toward Elsie who carried over the first salad to the table and set it on one of the plates.

"He hasn't been doing too much, has he, Elsie?"

She laughed and picked up the other two bowls from the counter. "He's tried to, but I kept him distracted."

Kadence put her hands on her hips, frowning at him, but the smile beneath bled through.

"How are you really feeling, Nate?" she asked. "And don't tell me what I want to hear."

He poured more cream and garlic into the pan and stirred it with the wooden spoon. The fresh garlic made his mouth water.

"I'm more than a little shaky," he said, "and tired, but ready to get out of bed."

He moved his glass of chardonnay that set too close to the box of fettuccine noodles he'd found in her pantry. Lucky for him she liked real cream in her coffee, otherwise he'd have ordered a pizza delivered. Fettuccine made a much better impression—unless he burned the sauce. He'd just keep the pizza delivery around as plan B.

"Any fever today?" she asked, moving toward him.

"No," he said, but her hand was already against his forehead. And he smelled that warm lavender sandalwood again.

"Feels cool," she said as he slid his arms around her waist.

"That's what you think," he said against her ear in a soft voice.

"It's boiling," she whispered.

Nate frowned. "What?"

"Your alfredo sauce."

He cursed and let her go, diving for the wooden spoon to stir down the rising cream sauce. Kadence giggled behind him. As he stirred, he felt her hand rubbing his shoulders. Then she stepped away, sitting down at the table, glass of wine in her hand.

"How was class today?" Elsie asked.

Nate's timer for the noodles beeped, so he flicked off the burner and carried the noodles to the sink where his colander was perched in the sink. He dumped the steaming noodles in to drain and returned to his sauce.

"Not bad," said Kadence. "Passed out study guides for Friday's exam and returned some long overdue homework assignments. Then had office hours, so it was a long day."

Nate added the noodles to the sauce and stirred in plenty of parmesan cheese before carrying the large pan of alfredo to the table. He spooned out generous portions of fettuccine onto all three plates and returned the pan to the stove.

The oven timer buzzed and he grabbed a towel off the sink, sliding out the hot bread. He dumped it into a basket and set it on the table.

"This looks delicious, Nate," said Kadence, watching him as he sat down beside her, wine glass in hand.

"It's the only thing I know how to cook," he said with a shrug and took a sip of his wine.

---

AFTER DINNER, NATE CLEANED UP HIS MESS AND LOADED THE DISHWASHER. The sun was just setting across the field as he refilled his wine glass. That's when his cell phone rang. He slid it out of his belt as he walked into the sitting room where Elsie and Kadence had sat down.

"Hello?"

"Hey, Nate, it's Jim."

Nate stepped back into the kitchen, his voice low. "Thanks for calling me back. Are they able to finish the plaque by Friday?"

"Yep, all set. We'll have the ceremony on Saturday afternoon. She's comin' in to grade some papers that day—be alone. We'll give her a smaller version of the one that'll hang in the firehouse."

"Excellent! I don't want it to upset her, but maybe it'll help her get through the day."

"Tom meant a lot to all of us, Nate, so you settin' up an education fund for firefighters in Tom's name is the bomb. She'll love it, Nate, I know she will. It'll mean a lot to her."

He sat down at the table, cleared of the supper dishes now, table-cloth in the washer.

"I hope so. She's going to have a rough day that day, so having something positive to mark it, for the community to remember, might help."

Jim was quiet for a moment.

"You there, Jim?"

"Yeah. Look, Nate…I've thought about this a lot today and there's one condition I'm not gonna be able to meet."

"What's that?" Nate asked, frowning. He took a sip of his wine, the glass almost empty.

"I can't keep the donor's name anonymous."

He felt a knot twist in his stomach. "Why not?"

"Because, Nate—she deserves to know it was you. It's not right otherwise."

"But it's not important who donated the funds. What's important is to remember the loss. To remember her Tom." He fiddled with a stray spoon, unused and left behind on the table.

Jim didn't respond.

"But it's not about me, Jim," he said, his voice taking on an edge he'd tried to hold back. "This is about her loss. Her grief."

"It will be," Jim insisted. "But she has to know it was you. I'm sorry. It's just gotta be that way."

He ran a hand over his eyes. "All right. But don't make a big deal about it, okay?"

"I won't. We'll present the plaque to her on Saturday mornin' when she comes by the station."

"Thanks, Jim. I owe you."

Jim's laughter echoed through the phone. "Of course, you do. You're buyin' the beer on Saturday night."

"I'm on it then," said Nate with a laugh. "Talk to you later."

He closed the phone and slid it back into its clip before tossing the spoon in the sink.

"Nate?" Kadence called from the sitting room.

"Be right there," he replied and grabbed the corked bottle of chardonnay out of the refrigerator. He carried it and his glass into the sitting room. "Anyone need more wine?" he asked.

Elsie nodded, sitting down on the couch. Nate set down his glass on the coffee table and refilled Elsie's glass, handing it to her.

"Thanks, honey," she said.

He turned to Kadence who was standing by the front door. His breath caught, eyes wide at the sight of those white pockets hanging out of her faded cut-offs and against those long legs. And that white tank top hugging her breasts in soft cotton curves. God, he wanted to get into those cut-offs.

"You okay?" she asked with a chuckle.

"I'm much better than that," he said, holding out the wine bottle. "Need a refill?"

She nodded and he approached her, tipping the bottle to her extended wine glass. When it was full, he pulled the bottle away and filled his own glass as she took a long, slow sip of wine. She motioned with a nod toward the door.

"Porch swing?" she asked.

All he could do was nod and follow her outside. He set the bottle and his glass on the weathered round table beside the swing. Kadence sat down on the swing, sipping her wine as the swing creaked in the growing twilight. Cicadas rattled away in the treetops, the air alive with night voices. The air smelled sweet with cut grass and a hint of salt from the Gulf.

He sat down heavily beside her, the day starting to catch up with him. Damn. Not now. He had things to do.

She glanced over at him then set her wine glass down. "You okay?" she asked. "Suddenly, you're not looking so good." She swiveled around to him, hands against his forearms.

"I'm fine. The tiredness just sort of hit me, that's all."

Kadence let go of a soft sigh and settled back against the swing, watching him.

"That was really sweet of you to fix supper tonight."

"Glad to do it," he replied, his hand sliding onto hers, stroking the supple curve of her forearm, the rounding of her upper arm muscles, the line of her shoulder blade as it disappeared beneath that thin tank top.

She closed her eyes a moment, drawing in a long, slow breath of pleasure.

"That's nice," she said as he kneaded her shoulder.

She settled into the crook of his arm, her head nestled underneath his chin as his arms enfolded her, wrapping around her middle to draw her closer. Her right leg pressed against his left, her foot running up and down his calf in long, slow strokes that were driving him wild.

Her right arm draped up and around his head, drawing his mouth toward hers. He sipped those full lips, nibbling her bottom lip, taste of chardonnay lingering. She moaned, arching her back as her lips pressed hard against his. His tongue brushed hers as he kissed her deeper. Her right leg crossed over his until she was in his lap and his left hand was sliding over her breasts, over her stomach, that cotton fabric in his way. He ran his hand down her jean-clad hip and down her silky right leg. And up again. Back to that tank top.

Her hand was against his left leg, on his thigh. Driving him wild as he slid his fingers underneath the hem of her tank top, traveling across her stomach and at last, underneath that bra. He cupped her left breast, fingertips tracing.

"Oh, God, Nate," she gasped, arching her back as she pressed harder against him.

His cell phone rang, but he ignored it, laying Kadence back against the gently rocking swing. His ribs ached with the movement, but he'd worry about that tomorrow.

"Aren't you—going to get that?" she asked after the fourth ring.

He shook his head as he leaned down to cover her mouth with his. A moment later, the phone inside rang and she giggled. He laid his head against her shoulder, laughing.

"Damned phones," he muttered, helping her up to sit beside him in the swing.

"Kadence?" Elsie's voice rang out and the front door opened. "Phone's for you."

Nate propped his elbow on the swing's armrest, a sour look on his face. Kadence chuckled, poking him in the shoulder as she rose from the swing.

"Be right back."

She was gone for several minutes. Nate grabbed his wine glass and emptied it, feeling the warmth in the pit of his stomach, already missing Kadence beside him on the swing.

When she finally returned, she looked…well, out of the mood, a little pensive and distracted.

"Everything okay?" he asked as she sat down beside him and grabbed her wine glass.

She cradled it in both hands a moment, staring out across the darkening fields. The security light hadn't come on yet.

"Yeah," she said, at last looking at him with a lighter expression, a smile appearing at last. "It was Marty. He wanted me to know about the memorial at the station house on Saturday afternoon."

"For Tom?" he asked, stroking the hair out of her face.

She nodded, a hint of distance in her eyes now. "He'll be gone a year on Saturday."

"I can't imagine how hard that's been for you," he said in a soothing tone.

But she seemed to pull back from him now, her shoulders squared, her gaze past him now. Finally, she stared into her wine glass again, both hands cradling it. "I'm just not sure if I'm ready to move on yet."

He kept stroking her hair. "It's okay if you're not, you know. Only you can decide when, Kadence. Don't let anyone push you. Including me."

Holding in a sigh, he patted her on the arm and rose from the swing, but she gripped his arm, gently tugging him back.

"Please," she said, not meeting his gaze. "Don't go."

He sat back down beside her and she laid her head against his shoulder, eyes teary. As gently as he could, he slid his arm around her shoulder and held her close to his chest. With his feet, he set the swing into solemn motion, a lazy swing as night darkened the fields.

Kadence fought against the tears that ran down her cheeks, sweeping them away with her fingers. "I'm sorry," she said, her voice cracking.

"It's okay to miss him, Kadence," he whispered and kissed her on top of the head. "No shame in tears."

As she cried silent tears in the darkness, Nate kept up the swing's steady rocking, but fear hovered in his stomach now. Was it just grief sending her into his arms? Or something more? Regardless, he knew his relationship with Corrina was over. But he couldn't help but feel a staggering sense of disappointment. He'd wanted more than thirty days.

Only two weeks now, he realized, knowing week two was winding to a close. And he had no idea what she was thinking. Maybe that's all she'd wanted? A little comfort to get her through the first anniversary?

Nate stared out across the fields as the security light clicked on, casting a crisp burst of yellow light across the dark yard. The faint buzz was quickly lost among the cicadas scritching. Shadows of moths fluttered across the yard as they collected around the yellow wash of light.

He laid his hand against her shoulder, stroking her arm as she sniffled. For now, he had to be patient. She was still grieving for her Tom. Until she'd worked through that pain, she wouldn't see him as anything other than some guy she bought off the internet. And the clock on that rental was ticking fast.

# SIXTEEN

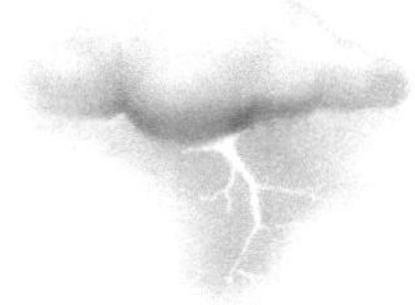

On Saturday, September seventeenth, Kadence left the house early. Nate had still been asleep, so she'd crept past his door and down the stairs in her bare feet, not wanting to wake him. These past few days, he'd been nothing short of wonderful and she'd taken that for granted, unable to let herself enjoy his company and his caring ministrations.

She smiled, running a hand through her hair at the memory of him serving her breakfast in bed yesterday. He'd set a tray of scrambled eggs and cheese and a steaming cup of coffee across her lap. And daisies.

Her first impulse had been to dump the tray and get him under her covers, but she'd let the feeling pass, knowing today was almost here. And the guilt had weighed on her again, holding her back from everything. She'd thanked him for the breakfast, offering nothing but her warmest smile. He'd excused himself quickly, leaving her to eat in unwanted silence.

Today, with the sun warm against the world, the events of a year ago ached through her brain as she drove north toward Lake Charles.

"Oh, Tom, it's so complicated now," she said above Evanescence's *My Immortal* lamenting through the car.

God, she didn't want to hear this song today, of all days. She flicked past several country music stations until she found a classic rock station and *Sister Golden Hair's* easy strains distracted her as signs for Highway 10 appeared.

Of all days to grade an exam. Giving a lecture would have been a welcome distraction rather than sitting there in silence with her own thoughts. But unfortunately, today was Saturday. Without even a class to focus on, she'd have to distract herself with exam results. As if this day weren't hard enough, the fire station was giving a memorial for Tom.

Maybe she'd have supper with the guys afterward? Maybe Po-boys and beer near Big Lake? Or Tom's favorite restaurant, she thought with a sigh. But the thought of sitting there eating without him turned her stomach.

She missed his turns of phrase and that warm Cajun way he had about him, a man who spoke French better than English. She wasn't a native of Louisiana. Not even close, having grown up in Maine. She'd taught at McNeese State for a decade now and considered Louisiana home with its bayous and comfortable ways.

She never dreamed she'd be here one day without Tom, but here she was, still breathing and living a year later. And now, there was Nate tugging at her heart in a way she couldn't fathom. In a way, she grew more attached to him as the days passed.

Her breath caught. But in two weeks, he would leave her, too. Her eyes stung at the thought.

She turned onto Highway 10 heading east and in a few minutes, she exited onto the Loop, heading for Ryan Street and Kaufman Hall.

***

ALL THROUGH THE DAY, SHE GRADED EXAMS AND HOMEWORK, HER MIND heavy with memories, of things she and Tom used to do. The weekends at Big Lake with all their friends. He'd pick her up after work, those dark eyes full of mischief as they'd head down 27 to Big Lake.

Calcasieu's waters looked steely and luminous against the fiery sunset as firefighters and their spouses and dates showed up, carrying fresh caught shrimp and spotted trout, coolers of beer, and spicy Cajun carry-ins. Jim and his girl du jour, Marty and Annie, Jake and Sally... all of them crowding around the fire pit, stoking it with wood until it roared like a pyre into the night.

Four months ago, Marty broke up with Annie. Jim was still playing the field. Sally dumped Jake just before Thanksgiving last year. And Tom...Tom was gone.

But for a brief moment of time, they'd all been together, laughing, celebrating, living. None of them knowing just how short their time was in this moment. And how quickly and irreversibly those moments slipped through their fingers. She remembered last Labor Day weekend, the sizzle of shrimp and cayenne grilling in the humid darkness, smell of woodsmoke and Miller beer, roar of fire and laughter as Zydeco played in the background. Tom's arm around her shoulder, holding her close, his Old Spice cologne faint against the smell of burning wood and garlic. His lips crushing against hers, wanting more and more of her with every kiss.

As she sat there watching the dreamy summer night cast all of them in surreal perfection, she knew this was the brightest this moment would ever shine. She knew it would never be better than this and she'd felt its fragileness, like a sand dollar plucked out of Gulf waters. Too much pressure and it would crumble into fragments.

In the end, all she could do was hold it in the palm of her hand and immerse herself in its rounded perfection, knowing if she tried to carry it home and keep it somehow, it would turn to dust. So, she threw herself into that night, knowing she may never come this way again. That was September 5th, 2004. Twelve days later, Tom died in a car accident.

Tom had always lived his life in the present, carefree and easy. To see her struggling through the days with a lifelessness and lack of joy...it would have hurt him deeply. No, it would have killed him.

After the end of her office hours, with one or two students stopping by to discuss the exam, Kadence walked out of Kaufman Hall and across the campus to her car parked on Lawton. Parking was much easier on Saturdays. She climbed in and started the car, Tom's memory raw against her nerves. She took a deep breath and drove south toward Big Lake Road and Fire Station Number Eight.

JIM MET HER AS SHE PULLED UP TO THE STATION AND LED HER INTO THE small white building, past the pumper truck and into the small office/classroom with its white walls, eclectic mix of old tables and chairs, and concrete floor. Where Tom once taught fire safety to parents. Where she'd taken CPR courses and learned how to start the trucks. The air smelled a little musty, traces of Lysol tanging the air.

Her jacket and pants hung with the other firefighters' gear that lined the wall beyond the pumper truck, Harlowe on the sleeve. The long office's faded ivory walls were mostly covered with framed photos, including one of Tom standing in full firefighter gear, fighting a barn blaze outside Lake Charles. The spattered concrete floors needed a coat of paint like they always did.

At the far end were two folding tables and a small kitchenette, old Harvest Gold stove and refrigerator, where the guys ate. She'd spent a lot of time in this quaint little station, remembering the time she'd kissed Tom right out of his boots at that refrigerator door. The memory made her smile.

"You doin' okay?" Jim asked, a hand against her back.

She nodded as several firefighters in their dark dress uniforms filed into the room to stand at the table. A cloth covered something large that hung on the wall opposite the refrigerator and she squinted at it.

Jim stuck his head out into the garage.

"Come on, guys, Kay's here. We're ready."

Four other firefighters shuffled past her, some squeezing her arm, some whispering condolences, like they had a year ago on her first trip back without Tom.

Marty stepped into the office and gave her a warm smile as he put his arms around her.

"How you doin', girl?"

"Okay," she replied.

Marty glanced behind her and then around the room. "Hey, where's Nate?" he asked, frowning.

"I came alone," she said.

Marty's face scrunched as he cast a glance at Jim who stood beside her. "But I thought Nate was—"

"Later," Jim growled through gritted teeth.

Marty hurried toward the table, leaving Kadence to wonder what that had been about. She leaned toward Jim, starting to ask when all of the firefighters stood at attention, including Marty, as the Fire Chief entered the office.

Jim said a few words and then introduced Chief Brooks, a stocky man in his late forties. He talked about Tom's nine years of service to the department and his impeccable service record. He talked about fires Tom had fought, comrades he'd supported, and how he'd even tried to save a teenager's life the night he was killed.

Kadence let the tears well in her eyes and fall onto her cheeks, her stomach twisting with old, sour guilt. Why hadn't she done more to save him? Why?

Jim slid his arm around her shoulders, holding her close as the tears welled in his eyes.

"And now, it gives me great pleasure to introduce the Tom Bujeau Memorial Education Award, to be awarded each spring to an exceptional firefighter to further his or her education."

Chief Brooks, a tall square-shouldered man with greying hair and bushy moustache approached the wall and removed the gold cloth hanging there. Revealing a large black and gold plaque with Tom Bujeau Memorial Education Award engraved and centered at the top. In the right-hand corner was a color picture of Tom. In the left-hand corner was an American flag. Below the award name were empty name plates, ready to be engraved with the names of recipients.

The room filled with applause and whistles, the excitement evident. Kadence wiped away her tears and leaned toward Jim. Tom had always talked about going to college and finishing his degree. There hadn't been enough time and now, that moment had passed.

"Jim, this is wonderful," said Kadence. She squeezed his arm. "Who donated the—"

Chief Brooks approached her, smiling as he extended a small plaque toward her, held in his white-gloved hands. All the firefighters stood at attention again.

She turned to face him.

"Kadence, I'd like to present you with this plaque to honor Tom Bujeau's memory and mark the anniversary of his death. Our deepest sympathies to you on this difficult day, but it's our hope that this award will help ease the pain."

He extended the plaque to her and she took it in shaking hands, running a finger across Tom's name, knowing in her gut that it didn't have to be this way. Tom could have still been alive if she'd done her job right.

The tears rushed down her face again as Chief Brooks shook her hand and called for a moment of silence. In that moment, the clock on the wall ticked steadily. Someone coughed. A boot shuffled across concrete. And her heart pounded against her chest, her stomach twisting into knots.

"Thank you," said Chief Brooks. "The education endowment is bein' setup by Nate Logan of Logan Financial out of Arlington, Virginia. A big thanks to Mr. Logan for his generous contribution."

Everyone clapped as Kadence felt the heat rise at her temples. Nate had done this. Without asking her. Without even telling her about it.

She felt the anger quiver through her. Her grief was none of his business. He hadn't even known Tom and here he was making this day about him instead of Tom. He had no right.

Kadence stormed out of the office, running past the shiny white pumper truck as she yanked open her car door.

"Kadence, wait!" Jim shouted.

She slammed the door and started the engine. Slamming her foot against the gas, she squealed away from the curb, heading south to pick up Highway 27. And to tell Nate Logan where to put his endowment.

# SEVENTEEN

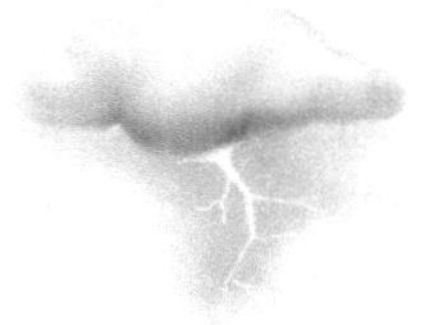

Nate heard Kadence's car pull up and he froze, sitting on the couch with Elsie, watching the news on Channel 7. How had she taken the award? He hoped well.

He'd cringed through the news and the story about his rescuing little Shawna Martin, being interviewed in Mobile with her aunt at her side. As if that wasn't bad enough, Elsie had cut out Arbaugh's stories from the paper, describing Nate's heroism in Lower Ninth Ward and his unique status as a rented executive for charity. He hadn't expected to ever see these articles and he wished they hadn't appeared today of all days. Kadence had enough on her mind without seeing all these things lying on her couches.

He started gathering up the stories when the front door banged open. Kadence stood in the threshold, her furious gaze pinning him.

"Nate Logan, you had no right to interfere in this!" she shouted and threw her purse onto the library table by the door.

Nate cringed. She'd found out it had been his endowment. He wanted to kick Jim for letting her know the source.

He rose from the couch, setting down the stack of newspaper. He held out his hands as he moved tentatively toward her. He'd never seen her that enraged before.

"I just wanted to do something for you," he said, still moving toward her.

"You never knew him!" she shouted. "So, you just waltz in here with your money and try to even buy his memory from me!"

She threw the plaque at him, the wood slamming into his shoulder as he caught it with a wince. Damn, she had a good fastball.

"I'm sorry."

"You had no right! Everything's not for sale, you know!" She poked her chest with her thumb, her eyes burning with rage. "Including me!"

"Kadence, I—"

"God, I hate you! Just stay away from me."

She turned and ran outside, slamming the door shut behind her. She ran down the porch stairs and across the driveway, gravel crunching under her feet.

He'd only wanted to honor the memory of the man she'd loved. Nothing more. Why had Jim insisted that he reveal himself as the donor? He set the plaque down on the library table, his face burning with embarrassment as he rubbed his shoulder. He shoved his hands into his jeans pockets as he walked away from the door, averting his gaze from Elsie.

"It's a hard day for her," said Elsie, somewhere behind him as he wandered into the kitchen for a beer.

"I hadn't meant to make it worse," he replied, pulling a bottle of Miller Light out of the fridge and twisting off the cap. He tossed the cap into the trash and took a long drink.

When he turned around, Elsie stood in the doorway, looking a little unnerved.

"I knowed ya didn't. People react funny to grief is all. You never know what that's gon' be neither."

He nodded, feeling like a bastard. He took another sip, the anger finally poking him in the gut. Grief or not, that hadn't been fair. He hadn't deserved that.

Nate set down his beer and moved past Elsie, but she grabbed his arm.

"Where you goin'?"

"To talk to her. I can't let this go."

"More moxie than I thought," she said with a grin and let him pass. "Good luck."

He pulled open the front door and rushed down the stairs, glancing around the yard for a flash of red hair, an echo of her voice, but only silence gripped the humid air, smelling of dry grass.

He followed the driveway, past the tick and settle of her Accord as it cooled down, a trace of motor oil in the air. When he reached the end of the drive, he stopped. Across the street was an open field, a huge oak tree standing in its center. No out-buildings anywhere, just that big oak tree standing tall with branches stretched high into the September blue sky.

He walked through the dry grass that whipped and whispered against his Levi's as he moved toward the oak's massive trunk. Wide enough for Kadence to stand unnoticed behind.

As he approached, he heard the muffled sound of crying. When he reached the tree and stepped around it, he found her laying against it, face pressed against her sleeve, shoulders heaving.

He dropped down on his haunches, still an arm's distance from her.

"Kadence?" he said in a timid voice.

"Go away," she snarled, not raising her head from her arm.

"No," he snapped. "I'm not going away. I care very much about you and I'm not going away, so go ahead and scream at me."

"Dammit, Nate! Leave me alone!"

He clutched her arms, pulling her up to face him. "Like you have been, Kadence? It's been a year. What happens when it's two then three? Do you still want everyone to leave you alone?"

She raised her hand to slap at him, but he held her arm extended so she couldn't. He watched as her anger unwound into sorrow and she wilted in his grasp, her voice raw with sobs. He pulled her into his arms, holding her tight and safe against him as he stroked her wonderful red hair.

"It's okay," he said in a hushed voice.

"No, it's not okay!" she shouted. "It'll never be okay!"

"Why?" he asked, his chest aching with her grief.

"Because I killed him!" Her sobbing intensified, her whole body shaking. "Don't you understand? It was my fault!"

"No, it wasn't your fault."

"It was!" she screamed. "I saw the femoral puncture, but I—I couldn't stop the—the bleeding! I couldn't get the tourniquet on. I didn't call the ambulance soon enough! It was all my fault!"

"No," Nate shouted. "No, it wasn't! Kadence, Jim saw the autopsy report. Tom's femoral artery was torn open. He was bleeding out and there was nothing you could have done to stop it. Nothing!"

She held onto him, her fingernails digging into his flesh, but he kept his arms around her, trying to get through to her.

"Kadence, the artery wasn't repairable! It was too far gone. Not even a surgeon on the scene could have saved Tom."

At last, he felt his words sink in as her grip on him eased. She met his gaze with puffy, swollen eyes.

"Unrepairable?" she said, her voice hoarse and barely above a whisper.

He nodded emphatically at her. "Completely. Jim said it was a miracle he was still alive when you got there." His gaze softened as he ran his thumbs across her face to wipe away her tears. "All this time, you've been blaming yourself. You need to give yourself a break. There was nothing anyone could do, Kadence. Nothing."

She nodded, looking a little shell-shocked, the acceptance creeping into her face. Nate pulled her into his arms again, cradling her and this time, she let him.

"I'm so sorry, Nate," she said, her voice cracking. "I'm so sorry for what I said."

"It's okay," he said, stroking her hair. "Just wish I'd known what a great right arm you have. Next time, I'll duck."

She laughed. "Did I hurt you?"

Nearly severed his clavicle from his deltoid, but he'd never admit it. "Nah, I'm fine."

"Good," she said and pressed her lips hard against his, knocking him off balance and into the grass.

IN TEN MINUTES, JIM'S RED TRUCK AMBLED UP THE DRIVEWAY, TWILIGHT IN the air. Nate sat beside Kadence on the swing, his arm around her. Jim looked concerned as he walked up the porch steps and moved toward the swing.

"Kay? You all right?" he asked, his eyes dark with worry.

He cast an uncertain look at Nate, no doubt seeing her puffy, red-rimmed eyes and shaky demeanor and he nodded.

"Sorry I ran out on you, Jim," she said, staring back at him, no emotion in her face.

"You okay with the award and all?" he asked, laying a hand on her shoulder.

She nodded.

"She's been blaming herself for Tom's death," said Nate.

Jim frowned and he dropped down on his haunches beside her, shaking his head. "Kadence, no—how could you even think that! There was nothin' you could have done. Nothin' anybody could have done." He lifted her chin. "Don't you understand? Tom bled out. In two minutes, he was gone. I know you were first on the scene, but you couldn't have saved him, hon—he was too far gone."

Nate rubbed her shoulders. "See, you've heard that from me and an actual, credible source. It wasn't your fault, Kadence."

She let out a chuckle and finally nodded.

Jim stood up and hugged her. "God, I feel terrible, Kay. I had no idea you been walkin' around blamin' yourself all this time."

Another car pulled into the drive. A blue, beat-up old Chevy Grand Prix. Marty piled out and rushed toward the house, a case of Sam Adams in his arms. He set it on the porch, sounding winded as he leaned against the railing.

"Thought maybe you could use some liquid comfort tonight, Kay," said Marty.

She smiled as she rose from the swing, Nate and Jim on either side.

"Yes, thanks, Marty." She motioned to the door when Nate opened it. "Come on in."

Nate threw in a frozen pizza and they all sat around the kitchen table, reminiscing about Tom. Even Elsie sat with them, drinking a beer and eating pizza.

"And you threw it at him?" Jim replied, nearly spitting out his beer as Kadence set the memorial plaque on the kitchen counter.

Marty let out a belly laugh and Jim joined him. Nate rubbed his shoulder where the plaque had hit him.

"I'm telling you, she's got a mean fastball."

Jim laughed harder, pounding the table with his hand.

"I'm really sorry, Nate," she said, rubbing his shoulder as she stood behind him.

"It's okay," he replied with a smirk. "Guess my dream of playing major league ball is over now."

It was late when Marty and Jim finally left, Elsie having gone to bed nearly two hours before.

"If you need me, you call," said Jim, kissing Kadence on the cheek as he stepped onto the porch. Marty was already on the driveway.

"I will. Thanks guys. You're real gems."

Marty waved and ambled toward his Grand Prix. Jim hopped into his truck. Both motors revved in the darkness and chugged down the lane, disappearing into the night.

Kadence hugged herself as she moved toward the kitchen to turn out the lights. Percy wound past her legs and headed toward the hallway and Elsie's bedroom. Nate followed Kadence up the stairs, walking behind her with tired steps. She stopped in front of his door, turning to him.

"Thank you for what you did today. I know you didn't have to—"

He covered her mouth with his, hands caressing her face as he kissed her long and hard.

"I did it for you," he said, still holding her face in his hands. "Only for you." He smoothed the hair out of her eyes. "Good night, Kadence," he said and flipped on the light in his room.

"Good night, Nate," she said from the hall.

He closed the door and heard her footsteps pad past the bathroom to her room. Sighing, he leaned against the door, feeling like he should have said more. Should have done more. She still looked lost, watching him close the door—like she'd wanted to say something. Whatever it was, she'd left it unsaid.

He sat down on the bed and kicked off his Merrell's. After pulling off his jeans, he folded them and laid them on the dresser along with his red polo shirt. Down to his boxers, he crawled into bed, still thinking about how lost she'd looked. He reached up and flicked off the light and rolled over, closing his eyes.

But not even an hour later, he awoke to sobs. He sat up, turning on the light, and listened. Muffled sobs down the hall from Kadence's room. He opened his door and paused, listening for quiet, but her sobs still carried.

Nate padded into the hallway, past the bathroom, and to her bedroom door, halfway ajar. In the darkness, he saw her silhouette under the quilt, shoulders shaking, body turned away from the door.

"Kadence?" he called, stepping into the room.

"Did I wake you?" she said in a soft, tear-strained voice.

"I wasn't asleep yet," he replied and sat down on the bed, reaching out to cup her face.

She threw her arms around him, her sobs renewing, and he held her close. She wore only a yellow t-shirt, the thin fabric warm against his bare chest.

"I know it's hard," he said against her ear, "and it's okay to let out your grief."

Her face was against his chest, her skin against his, but all he wanted tonight was to comfort her. He pushed back her covers and slid beneath them, still holding her against him. She trembled, her teeth chattering, her face still hot with tears.

"Everything's going to be okay," he said in a soothing voice as he stroked the hair out of her eyes.

It took her over an hour, but she finally fell into an exhausted sleep against him. Still holding her, he turned on his side, spooning her against him, and closed his eyes.

# EIGHTEEN

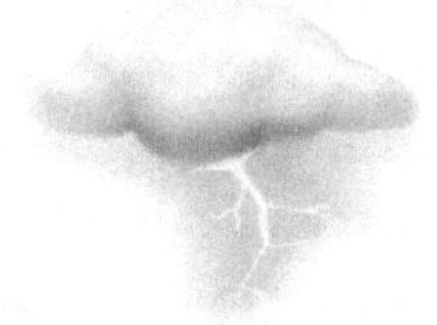

Kadence awoke in Nate's arms, his breath warm against her neck, face pressed against her shoulder. She'd slept better last night than she had in months. She rose on her elbows and watched him sleep. No nightmares had touched him (or her) last night and she was grateful for that. She had no idea how long he'd have them about the accident, but she hoped they were behind him now.

At that moment, with the early morning light washing pale gold across him, his warm presence pressing against her body, she knew she loved him. She'd known him only two weeks, but he was unlike any man she'd ever known, with a rare need to help everyone, sometimes to the detriment of himself. She reached up to a blond tangle of curls against his forehead and with her index finger, she brushed it back.

Selfless bordering on reckless, that was her Nate Logan.

He'd held her all night, too, comforting her with no expectations, no strings. She wanted to know what lay behind his eyes, but she felt terrified, knowing what lay behind her own. She'd fallen hard for him and she was in deep now. With his return to Virginia only two weeks away, she was scared now. Scared he would walk away and leave her. But he had to feel the same way about her. Didn't he?

She smiled at him. Lying here, his right arm pinned beneath her body and had probably lost feeling hours ago, he had to feel more than friendship for her.

He had to. She'd felt the spark.

Leaning down, her hair brushing his cheek, she ran her lips across his in whisper-soft kisses, across his chin, down his neck, until his eyes rolled open.

"Hi," she said, smiling at him.

"Hi," he said in a sleepy voice, returning her smile.

He rolled over onto his back and pulled her onto his chest.

"How're you feeling this morning?" he asked, a hand against her face, thumb rubbing gentle circles against her cheek.

"Better," she said, leaning down to kiss him again. Longer. Deeper. "Thanks to you."

"It was just a ploy to get into your bed," he said with a grin. But she knew better. He'd done nothing but hold her the entire night.

"So that's what that was," she said, smiling.

He leaned up and kissed her, a seriousness touching his eyes. "You understand that Tom's death wasn't your fault, don't you?"

She nodded. "You and Jim explained enough times to finally get through."

"Good," he said and kissed her again.

All she wanted to do was lay in bed with Nate the rest of the day.

The echo of his cell phone chirped into the hall and he sighed. "The next bridge I go over, I swear I'm gonna heave that thing into the bayou."

It was early. She hoped it wasn't bad news.

With another sigh, he let her go and slid out of bed. "I'd better find out who it is."

So much for lying in bed with Nate all day, she thought with a groan. She rose from the bed, intending to take a shower and start the day. Maybe pack him and Elsie in the car for a trip down to Holly Beach for the day?

By ten a.m., they were southbound for Holly Beach. Nate seemed a little distracted, sitting in the back seat and staring out at the bayous and lakes as they headed for the coast. Even Elsie noticed his tuned-out demeanor.

Kadence watched him in the rearview mirror. She'd put on her green string bikini with him in mind, wearing it beneath her favorite cut offs and short white tank top. But he hadn't seemed to notice yet.

"Nate, everything okay back there?" Kadence asked finally.

He glanced at her, almost a sadness in his eyes. "Yep, fine."

"Then why don't I believe that?"

He sighed, rubbing a hand through his hair.

"The phone call?" she asked, studying his expression in the rearview mirror.

"Yeah. Just had a lousy conversation with my dad."

"Wanna talk about it?" she asked and offered him a smile.

His eyes darkened. "It was one of those *it's your duty, son* conversations. Him talking and me listening—some conversation. But all of it was just orders."

She felt a stab of nerves in her stomach.

"Do you have to do something you don't want to do?"

He nodded, looking forlorn. "According to him, I do. He's unhappy when I defy him, as he puts it." He propped an elbow against the door and rested his chin in his hand. "I suggested he get some Prozac because he's going to see a lot of defiance in the near future."

Kadence laughed which brightened his face, but there was a certain degree of misery hiding in those fluid green eyes. She knew that whatever situation he was fighting his father over wasn't resolved yet. She could only imagine what his father thought was Nate's duty. And with his overly helpful personality, she imagined that he got taken advantage of a lot. And that probably didn't rule out his father.

"I'll call Ren tonight and get his take on the situation."

He rubbed his eyes with thumb and forefinger, looking tired. Not the *I didn't get enough sleep* kind of tired. It was the life-weary kind of exhaustion that came from trying to please everyone. He was a good man, someone who rarely thought of himself. Whatever was expected of him by his family was weighing heavily on him.

In twenty minutes, they were rounding the southern edge of Calcasieu Lake or Big Lake as they called it. Nate seemed absorbed by the scenery, his expression filling with serenity. Elsie seemed content, too, but Kadence worried that she might feel frightened of the Gulf—after nearly drowning in her own home. But Elsie insisted that she was fine with the beach and that she'd enjoy the trip. Nate had jumped at the idea, too, telling her how much he loved the ocean.

After Highway 27 curved past West Cove and Mud Lake, the Gulf of Mexico rose in front of them, stretching long and steely. The glitter of sunlight on water was intoxicating as she rolled down the window, smelling the clean salt smell. Not the fetid briny stink that still clung to New Orleans. No, this was fresh, clean salt air.

Nate rolled down his window, too, inhaling a warm breath of air.

"That's wonderful," he said, closing his eyes.

Kadence parked the car along the road that stretched parallel to the beach and everyone piled out. She ran toward the beach, kicking off her flip flops when she felt the soft sand at her feet. The wind was brisk and warm today, fluttering across her face and billowing in her hair. She put on sunglasses and looked west at the endless line of telephone poles curving around to frame the long stretch of sandy beach.

Nate was beside her in the sand, short sleeve shirt open and flapping in the wind, and tight-fitting blue swim trunks. But his eyes were focused on her short, sheer tank top and she grinned.

"Nice suit," he said with a smirk.

She pulled the tank top over her head and his eyes widened a little, but when she snaked off her cut-offs, his eyes were popping, his mouth practically hanging open.

"You're sweet," she said, kissing him on the cheek.

"I have another word for it," he said, taking hold of her shoulders.

She laughed, ducking under his arm and ran into the surf. Nate chased after her.

Elsie laid a blanket on the sand, wearing a white t-shirt and blue shorts. She took off her flip-flops and grinned as she ran her toes through the sand, looking pensive as she looked out at the water.

Nate was beside Kadence in the water now, his arms sliding around her waist as he took a good, hard look at her bikini.

"There are no words," he said, shaking his head. "Just intense reverence. Kadence, you blow me away."

He leaned down and kissed her with the most passionate kiss she'd ever felt. It slammed down her arms and into her knees. It staggered her. She stepped back in the warm water, nearly falling, but he grabbed her hands.

"I'm going to need a lifeguard if you do that again," she said, out of breath.

He laughed and stepped back into a wave that broke just above his knees.

"It's kind of rough, isn't it?" he asked, struggling against the next wave that hit him at the kneecaps.

Kadence nodded, a hand over her eyes as she gazed out at the white caps chopping up the water.

"Lots of waves out there today. Wonder if there's a tropical storm near the Gulf."

She'd watch the Weather Channel when they got back to make sure. New Orleans was still too fresh in her mind to ignore the weather. Besides, September was prime hurricane landscape. Surely, everything had settled down after Katrina. In this corner of Louisiana, they hadn't had such a brutal storm in forty or more years, not since Audrey killed 390 people in the surrounding parishes. Before Katrina, that's all anyone had talked about.

She and Nate played in the water for hours while Elsie read a book, stretched out on her blanket. When the sun edged over the Gulf, drifting west toward Texas, hunger made them decide to go home. They climbed into the car to pick up fresh shrimp from a stand in Holly Beach. Iced in a cooler, the shrimp sat in the back seat with Nate as Kadence drove north toward Hackberry.

In thirty minutes, they were back at the house. Nate carried in the cooler while Kadence lit the gas grill on the porch. Elsie took the towels and blankets to the washing machine and went to her room to change.

Kadence hurried into the kitchen and whipped up a spicy marinade as Nate cleaned the shrimp, tossing them into a large ceramic bowl.

Kadence tossed olive oil, chopped onions, garlic, basil, chili sauce, and Dijon mustard into a bowl and whisked it together. Nate opened the refrigerator, pulling out a half-full bottle of chardonnay. He uncorked the bottle and splashed wine into her marinade.

"Hey," she said and dipped her finger into the mixture.

She held it up to Nate's mouth and he pressed it to his tongue. "A little black pepper and it'll be perfect."

She grabbed the peppermill off the counter and ground a healthy dose of pepper into the marinade before she poured it over the shrimp. Nate grabbed a spoon and gently stirred the shrimp into the mixture. When he'd coated all the shrimp, he carried the bowl out to the grill.

"Back in a minute," he said with a wink. "Pour me some wine."

She slid three wine glasses out of the cabinet when the phone rang. She picked it up, balancing the cordless on her shoulder as she rinsed the marinade bowl.

"Hello?"

"Kadence, it's Teddy Arbaugh."

"Ted! Good to hear from you." She turned off the water, set down the bowl, and gripped the phone in her right hand. "Listen, the stories you wrote for the paper were incredible. I especially liked the one about little Shawna Martin and Nate. My rented executive."

"Glad you liked them. And you'll be happy to know that Shawna's doin' fine with her aunt. The woman seemed very protective of her niece, so Shawna's in good hands."

He'd found out some information about Nate. She felt it as he hesitated, making a little more small talk than she was used to from him. Her stomach ached and she almost regretted asking him to search now.

"Arbaugh, I know you didn't call me to talk about tonight's sunset."

A heavy sigh hissed through the phone and she gripped it hard.

"No, and I wish I had." He paused again. "He's engaged, Kadence."

It was a sharp blow to her chest that staggered her. She knocked the bowl into the sink as she gripped the edge of the counter to keep from taking a step backward.

"What?"

"Engaged. Big society engagement, in all the East Coast social registers. Nate Logan, son of Senator Lee Logan, to wed Corrina Coleridge, daughter of the honorable Judge Evan Coleridge. A November wedding is planned."

She sank back against the cabinets, sliding to the floor. A November wedding? My God, it was a month after he went home.

"No," she said finally. "That can't be."

"I triple checked my sources, Kadence. I'm sorry. It was the last thing I expected. He seems like a standup guy, someone who wouldn't lead a woman on."

She bit her lip to keep the tears from springing to her eyes. So, she was just a thirty-day fling after all.

"Wish I had better news, kiddo," he said.

"Me, too," she said, trying to keep the shake out of her voice.

"But not everything in the papers is black and white," said Arbaugh. "Don't forget that."

"Thanks for checking for me, Ted. I appreciate it."

The silence between them mounted, growing more awkward by the moment.

"You take care, Kadence."

"Goodbye, Arbaugh," she said in a hoarse voice and hung up the phone.

Kadence sat there a few moments, finally summoning the strength to get to her feet and pick up the bottle of wine on the counter. She poured herself a big glass and drank it down fast, trying to numb the pain rising through her like flood waters.

# NINETEEN

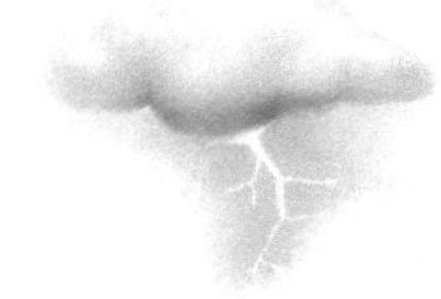

When Nate returned from putting the shrimp on the grill, he saw a marked change in Kadence's demeanor. Cold. Avoiding him. He poured himself a glass of wine, watching her hurry out of the kitchen. Laundry, she'd said, not even looking at him.

Confused, he leaned against the kitchen counter, wine glass in hand. Had he done something to upset her? Or was she still grieving over Tom? He didn't want to pry, but her behavior made no sense.

He grabbed tongs and a plate from the kitchen and returned to the grill. With fragrant smoke rising around him, he turned the shrimp.

What had just happened during those five minutes he'd been gone? He went through their conversation forward and back, trying to figure out what he'd said (or hadn't said). As he closed the grill lid, turning down the heat a bit, he decided to give her space. Instead, he paced the porch, wine glass in hand and thought back to the morning's phone conversation with his dad.

"You're not backing out of this wedding," Senator Logan had barked at him. "I worked hard to arrange that meeting with the Judge's daughter. Besides, she's charming and beautiful and would boost your career."

Nate hadn't even held back his anger at his dad's response.

"Did you not hear one word I said?" he'd snapped at his father, bringing about a surprised pause. He'd never spoken to the old man like that before and it had taken him off guard. "I don't love her. I never did. I just tried to so I could please you, but I can't go through with this."

"Nate, Nate, this isn't about love," his father had said in his best Senator's voice, turning on the rhetoric. "This is about something greater. It's about a partnership between two families. The forging of a new alliance—"

Nate shoved a hand in his pocket, remembering how he'd cut off his dad in mid-pontification. Dad never talked to him. It was always at him, like the man was appearing before some congressional committee.

"This isn't a war, Dad," he'd snapped. "It isn't some old-world alliance. This is my life. Not yours. Not the Judge's. Mine."

"I'm not discussing this any further, Nate." His tone had been tight-lipped, the anger controlled for now. "You're defying me and I don't like it. Not one bit."

"Then you'd better get some Prozac, Dad," he said, the edge apparent in his voice, "because you're going to need it."

"Dammit, Nate! It's your duty to the family to make this marriage work and you *will* go through with it. Someday, when you run for president, you'll thank me."

Nate had burst out laughing at the insanity of his comment. He would never go into politics. Never.

"That's your dream, Dad, not mine. And my duty to this family doesn't extend to who I marry. That's my decision."

The line fell into razor sharp silence.

"It does if you want to remain in the will."

Stunned, Nate could only sit there with the phone pressed to his ear. He'd never heard threats from his father before.

"You do what you have to do, Dad," said Nate with a sigh. "And so will I."

"Think about that long and hard, Nate," said his Dad. "I don't know who you've met down there or what you think you've found, but a hot piece of tail isn't worth it, I can assure you. They never are."

"You have no idea what you're talking about, Dad."

"Have your fling, Nate. Then come home. I'll expect a call from you in a few days, assuring me that this marriage is still on."

"It's not a fling," he'd shouted, but the line went dead.

He'd hung up, expecting Nate to do as he said, like he expected an employee to follow his dictates. Nate had always been the good son. Obedient to his father's wishes and dreams, even when they'd conflicted with his own. As an only child, caught between two strong-willed parents, he'd always played the peacemaker, the negotiator. This time, he would assert his own will. Even if it cut him out of the Logan will. There were plenty of cousins around to soak up the estate.

The sizzle of the shrimp returned to his foreground and he rushed back to the grill, turning them again. Almost done. One more time he turned them and when they were ready, he plucked them off the grill with the tongs, filling the plate with shrimp.

When he carried them inside, he found only Elsie sitting at the dinner table. She'd made two salads and set them out along with a box of croutons and a bottle of balsamic vinaigrette.

He set the hot shrimp on the table and sat down beside Elsie, glancing around.

"Where's Kadence?" he asked.

Elsie shook her head as she reached for the dressing. She unscrewed the cap and sloshed out a little vinaigrette into the lettuce and tomatoes.

"She wasn't feelin' well. Said she was goin' to bed."

He jumped up from the table, but Elsie grabbed his arm.

"Let her alone for now, child," she said, her gaze unblinking. "This ain't no time for moxie."

"But I want to help—"

She shook her head. "You cain't help if'n you're the cause, now can you?"

It wasn't an accusation. More an observation, but he felt sick inside, knowing he'd hurt her somehow. But how? He'd wracked his brain for the answer, but he'd come up with nothing.

"She's upset because of me?" he said finally, dropping down into his chair.

Elsie nodded. "Don't know why. But I know love when I see it. And she loves you, Nate. Mebbe she sees the calendar and how soon you'll be gone?"

Today was September eighteenth. By October third, he'd be on a plane home. Long enough to tie up his affairs in Arlington and figure out his next move. But he was coming back. Maybe that's what she needed to hear from him? Some assurance of where she stood. He needed to say the words to her, he realized.

"Then maybe I need to show her the date I'm coming back."

Elsie's head snapped up from her salad and she grinned.

"You're comin' back?"

He nodded emphatically as he cast a look at the stairs, wanting to run upstairs and tell her.

"How could I not?" he replied. "Her buying me off the internet was the best thing that ever happened to me."

Elsie patted his arm, returning her gaze to her salad.

"Then you'll just have to tell her that."

He speared two shrimp with his fork and laid them on his plate. In the morning, he'd tell her everything.

---

But on Monday morning, when Nate woke up, he knocked on Kadence's bedroom door. No answer. After two more knocks, he pushed open the door to find the bed made.

"Kadence?" he called, clomping down the stairs.

Percy wound around his feet, making him step over the pudgy tabby.

"Kadence?"

Elsie called him and he hurried down the short hallway to her bedroom.

"Elsie, you seen Kadence?" he asked, stopping outside the half-open door.

She was sitting on the bed, Diva in her lap.

"She done gone out, Nate. It's her class day. Got an exam to give back to those kids. Said she'd probably stay in Lake Charles this evenin', too. Take care of some things."

He felt the burn in his chest. She was still avoiding him.

"Why?" he asked.

"There's a school meetin' this afternoon and one at the firehouse, too. 'Bout the tropical depression headin' for Florida. They say it's gonna strengthen. Storm could cross into the Gulf."

"Tropical depression, huh?"

Elsie nodded. "May be comin' this way, Nate? She'll have a lot of work to do as a—what do you call dem? First Responders?"

"That's it," he said, distracted. "First Responders."

He'd never been through a tropical storm before. But they were probably far enough inland to avoid the brunt of it. Probably get lots of wind and rain.

She reached out and squeezed his arm. "Don't you worry none. She'll be home tomorrow mornin'. And you'll get your chance to talk to her."

"Thanks, Elsie," he said, patting her arm.

"And tonight, I'm gonna cook for you. Best Cajun cookin' you ever had, this."

"Looking forward to it, Elsie."

---

ELSIE COOKED UP A SPICY BATCH OF CHICKEN GUMBO AND PO-BOYS FROM last night's leftover shrimp. She'd wanted to make him a muffuletta sandwich, but without salami, she said it just wasn't the same. After supper, he cleaned up the kitchen for her while she watched the evening news.

He had just turned on the dishwasher when he heard the weather report blare in the next room.

"It's comin' this way, Nate," Elsie shouted with a gasp, a hand to her mouth.

He stood transfixed, watching the map of the southern United

States and the storm swirling toward the tip of Florida. Tropical Storm Rita.

"It's uncertain whether this storm will strengthen into a hurricane," said the meteorologist. "Aerial reconnaissance reports that without a well-defined eyewall, sustained winds will most likely top out around seventy miles per hour. However, once Rita reaches the warm waters of the Gulf, it could strengthen. Mandatory evacuations have already been ordered for the Florida Keys in advance of Rita's arrival. We'll keep you up-to-date as we know more."

Nate walked outside to the porch swing and rocked in the humid night, his thoughts still on Kadence. What happened to turn her mood so drastically yesterday? So much that she didn't even want to see him? He had to get this settled between them.

He slid his cell phone out of its clip, seeing three missed calls. He looked at the numbers, surprised when all three were from Meredith Hudson. Had something happened to Ren? His stomach did a somersault as he dialed her number.

"Hello?" she said on the third ring.

"Meredith, it's Nate, returning your call. Is everything okay there?"

"Nate!" she cried, her voice brimming with excitement. "I'm so glad you called. I've been dying to talk to you all day."

"About what?" he asked.

"I've got some…uh, news for you. About Corrina." She sounded pleased about something, eager to break some news about her. He stiffened.

"Corrina?"

"Uh huh, darling Corrina."

"Meredith, who's on the phone?" Ren in the background.

"Are you at our place?" Nate asked.

"Yes," she said, almost a purr in her voice. "Ren is cooking dinner for me tonight." She lowered her voice. "He thinks his fettuccine is better than yours, but it's not. Save me, Nate."

Nate laughed. Ren had taken several gourmet cooking classes after he'd first met Meredith. She'd been a sous chef in training at the Arlington Bistro, working her way through college. He'd sent a dish back and she'd come out to the table for clarification. Ren was lost right then and there. He thought of himself as a chef in training, but Ren had a long way to go yet.

"It's one dish," said Nate, holding up his index finger. "The only thing I know how to make and he can't stand it because it's better than his."

Meredith giggled. "Oh, nothing, Ren," she said into the background.

"Just don't let him overcook the noodles or burn the cream," said Nate in a low voice. "Usually, he does both."

"I'll watch him," she said, laughing.

"What was that?" Ren replied. "That Nate?"

"Yes, sweetie," said Meredith, her voice muffled. "He said he wished he could be here for your fettuccine tonight."

"Because he knows mine's better," Ren shouted.

Nate chuckled.

"You said you had some news about Corrina?" Nate replied, hoping she'd eloped with her driver to Buenos Ares.

"Last night, I was at the Four Seasons. At a cocktail party given by Corrina's mother—more bridal stuff. Y'know, rented suite and all that."

Nate could almost see her rolling her eyes.

"Bradley Wilcox escorted her to the little soiree and stayed at her side all evening. They were whispering and giggling like a couple of teenagers."

He sighed. "She's always with that guy."

"Well, I stepped into the back bedroom to call Ren to come pick me up. That's when I heard these…sounds from the walk-in closet."

Nate stiffened. "Sounds?"

She giggled. "Like two pigs going at it."

He couldn't say anything, a cold feeling in the pit of his stomach.

"Nate, she's cheating on you."

Her words slapped him in the face. "What?" he said, finally.

"I opened the closet door and found Bradley on top of her, her dress hiked up to her shoulders, his pants at his ankles. Going at it like dogs in heat."

He sank back in the swing, his feet planted against the wooden porch.

"Shit," he said finally. "I'm such a fool."

The line crackled as Ren picked up on the other line.

"Buddy, I wish I could say I was sorry, but I've hated that woman from the first day I met her. Maybe now you'll come to your senses and dump her before you regret it?"

"I told my father yesterday that I wasn't going to marry her."

Ren cheered in the background.

"Seriously?" he said. "How'd your old man take it?"

"Threatened to write me out of the will if I didn't marry her."

Meredith gasped. "You're not serious."

"Told him to do what he had to do. But this little bit of news may make our breakup easier. Though, I doubt Dad'll believe she's cheating on me. He just wants the Coleridge name for his in-laws."

"That's awful, Nate," said Meredith, her voice sympathetic.

"Just wish I could prove it to him, show him somehow."

She giggled again. "You can."

Nate frowned. "How?"

"I have two words for you, Nate," she said, laughing. "Camera phone."

Nate broke out in a belly laugh, sending the swing into a mad arc across the porch.

"You didn't, Meredith? You didn't actually get shots of them, did you?"

"I caught Bradley's best side. But it's best not to look at them after eating."

Nate held his stomach, he was laughing so hard.

"Meredith, I don't know how to thank you," he said finally, leaning his head against the back of the swing as it slowed down. "You just saved my life."

"Anything for Ren's best friend. Besides, I just want to see you happy, Nate. You deserve it."

"Thanks, Meredith. I think I've got a shot at it now."

"With Kadence, you mean," she said in a knowing voice.

"Yeah," he replied. "With Kadence. Or at least I hope I have."

"Well, I'll keep these photos safe for you," said Meredith. "Talk to you later, Nate."

"Bye you guys and thanks. You made my day." He closed his phone and slid it back into its clip, wanting to shout his relief to the half-moon overhead.

Corrina was cheating on him. It was the best news he'd ever heard.

# TWENTY

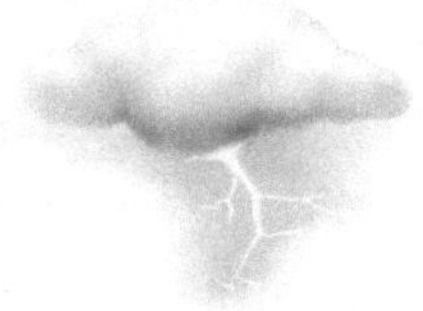

On Tuesday morning, Kadence woke up in Jim's spare bedroom in south Lake Charles. She took a quick shower and dressed in jeans and a chambray shirt. Then she wandered out to Jim's kitchen.

It was an old house, the floor sloping slightly in the dark green kitchen. His table was an old sixties model with beige vinyl chairs and flecked Formica top. The wood cabinets had been painted a dark green, the walls a pale green, cracked linoleum in another shade of beige. The air smelled like old bacon grease as she set down in one of the squeaky chairs beside Jim. He sat reading the paper, gold and red flannel shirt over his jeans, the sleeves cut off and his LCFD baseball cap propped on his head. He hadn't shaved yet, his tanned face a little dark with stubble.

"Hey, Kay, how'd you sleep?"

The twin bed was manageable, the foam pillow hurting her neck a little, but it was better than facing Nate. He knew all along he was getting married, yet he'd deliberately led her on, making her think they had something more. But in the end, it was just thirty days. For charity. She felt crushed.

"Good, thanks," she lied.

Jim gave her a *yeah, right* look and poured her a cup of coffee from the old percolator on the table.

"So, you gonna tell me what happened or do I have to keep guessin'?"

He slid the coffee cup toward her and the half jug of milk. It wasn't cream, but she'd make do. She poured a generous draught of milk into the cup and swirled it around before sipping it.

"I just wanted to stay in town last night after the storm meeting at the station."

He took a sip of his coffee. "Sorry, Kay—I'm not buyin' that."

"Suit yourself," she said and took another sip. Needed more milk. She poured in a little more milk, the color softening to a pale caramel as she swirled the cup in her hands.

"If I need to punch him for you, just tell me."

"No need for that," she replied. "He won't be here long enough to bother."

Jim frowned, setting down his cup. "Is this about him leavin' soon?"

She shook her head. Before Arbaugh's call, it had been. But she'd called up Arbaugh's sources online. She'd seen the engagement announcements herself. Saw his smiling face with that sneery-faced platinum blonde beside him, massive diamond perched on her greedy little fingers. The photo disgusted her. Nate disgusted her. How could he marry a creature like that?

From every article she'd dug up on Corrina Coleridge, the words selfish and over-privileged screamed back at her. Besides that, she seemed clueless about the world around her, her thoughts no deeper than which designer purse was trendier this season. It dripped from every clueless interview she'd given. If that woman was Nate's ideal, then she'd never known him at all.

"He's getting married," Kadence finally blurted out, biting her lip.

Jim spilled his coffee, his mouth falling open as he grinned at her.

"Did he propose?" he cried.

"What? No, he's engaged, Jim. To some bimbo socialite back in Arlington. I found out yesterday."

Jim's face darkened, the anger gritting his teeth. "Did he tell you?"

She shook her head, her gaze falling to her coffee cup again. "No, Arbaugh found the story for me."

Jim slammed his hand against the table. "That snake!"

He snapped out of his chair, moving toward the back door. When he grabbed his truck keys, Kadence jumped up and grabbed him around the waist.

"Where are you going?"

"To beat some manners into him," said Jim through gritted teeth, pulling away from her.

"Jim, no!"

She rushed out into the car port, the gravel hard against her bare feet. With his boots on, he was in his truck before she could stop him. She jerked open the truck door as the motor rumbled to life.

"Jim, don't!"

"He's not gonna jerk you 'round like this! I'm gonna bust his nose for him."

He was in full-tilt Cajun rage now and Kadence couldn't stop him from pulling out of the driveway.

She ran back inside and grabbed her duffle bag, sliding her feet into her flip flops. By the time she'd gotten out to her car, Jim was long gone. She jerked open her car door, throwing her duffle inside, and started the motor.

---

She hoped that the forty-five-minute drive to Hackberry would cool his temper. She wanted to kick herself for opening her mouth. Jim was way overprotective of her, considering it his duty after Tom died. She was furious with Nate. Never wanted to see him again, but she didn't want him to get beaten up either. And she couldn't even call and warn him. She'd left her cell phone on her dresser.

Kadence drove as fast as she could down Highway 27, knowing he'd still get there before her. At last, she turned into her lane, swerving around the corner and up the gravel driveway. Her stomach sank. Where Jim's truck was already parked.

She shut off the motor and shoved open her car door. In time to hear a sharp crack echo across the lawn. Her stomach twisted into a knot. From the backyard.

"Get up, you bastard!" Jim's hot voice roared in the silence.

"I'm not—going to fight you, Jim!" Nate answered.

Crack! A muffled groan.

"I said get up and take what's comin' to ya!"

"Jim, please, listen to me—"

Crack! A thud against the ground.

Kadence ran around the side of the house to find Jim towering over Nate who lay in the grass, his face bloodied. Jim's fist was bloody, too, knuckles scraped raw. Against Nate's face, she realized, wincing.

Jim grabbed him by the shirt, his fist slamming Nate's face again. His lip split, blood spilling down his shirt.

"Not gonna—fight you, Jim," Nate muttered through a swollen lip.

"Jim, stop!" Kadence shouted, but he was already cocking his fist.

Crack! Nate slammed against the ground again and this time, he didn't get up. Her heart wrenched as she ran toward him, falling down beside him.

Jim cradled his right fist against his shirt, the anger dissipating.

"Bastard admitted he was engaged," Jim said with a snarl. "Sorry, Kay, but I had to school 'em."

Jim huffed as he walked over to the garden hose and flicked it on. He dragged the hose across the grass and stuck his thumb over the nozzle, pointing it at Nate's face.

Nate jolted, looking disoriented, his eyes swollen to slits.

"Get up, Logan," Jim snapped. "I'm not done schoolin' you yet."

Kadence gritted her teeth, rushing at Jim, her palms slamming against his chest. He dropped the running hose into the grass.

"Oh, yes you are," she shouted. "School's out."

Nate struggled to stand up and when he'd drawn himself to his feet, Jim lunged at him, landing a hard blow to his gut and his chin. Laying him out again on the lawn.

"There," said Jim, brushing his hands together. "School's out now."

Kadence moaned, staring down at Nate unconscious in the wet grass, a cut above his eye bleeding profusely.

Jim stepped over Nate, moving with shaky steps to turn off the hose.

She knelt beside Nate, tears in her eyes, her heart breaking as she smoothed a bloody curl off his forehead.

"I never meant for this to happen," she said with a moan.

"Seeya tomorrow, Kay," said Jim, walking away.

"Oh, no you don't, Jim Hawkins," she shouted, standing up. Her hands snapped to her hips. "Don't you dare walk away and leave him unconscious on my lawn!"

"Call a paramedic," Jim snapped, but she ran at him, jerking him around.

She pointed toward Nate who lay still beside the hose. "Now, you help me get him inside or so help me, you'll wish you were never born."

He stood there staring at her a moment, then finally, he shoved back his cap with scabbed up knuckles, still looking angry, and moved toward Nate.

---

NATE AWOKE ON HIS BED, BLOOD DRYING AGAINST HIS THROBBING FACE. His temples pounded with pain and he remembered Jim standing over him, fire in the man's eyes. From the light streaming into the room, it was morning. But was it still the same day? Had he missed last evening entirely?

"Are you engaged, Logan?" Jim had demanded.

Nate remembered the sigh hissing from his lips as he'd nodded. "Yeah, I guess I am," he'd replied.

That was a mistake.

Jim's fist had smashed into his mouth before the rest of his intended sentence had even reached his tongue.

Everything else from that point was fuzzy. But the one thing he knew for certain was in Louisiana, they took care of their own. Jim had liked him once, but whatever Kadence told him had turned the guy into a madman.

But he was starting to piece things together now (not his face, yet, but that was next on his list). The only thing Jim had asked was if he was engaged. Kadence must have found out about his engagement to Corrina.

He felt miserable now. Granted, he should have told her about it, but she could have confronted him before getting her buddy Jim to break him up like this.

Guess this was the Louisiana way of telling him he'd outstayed his welcome. There was no use trying to explain anything to Kadence now. Judging from the beating he'd taken, she'd made her feelings perfectly clear.

The room spun a little as he struggled to his feet, finding his Merrell's beside the bed. He held onto the nightstand as he worked his feet into the shoes.

Everything tilted, going black a moment and he slumped back against the bed, gripping the headboard until it had passed. Holding his head, he moved toward the closet and slid out his suitcase. It took him three tries, but he managed to lift it onto the bed.

He opened the luggage and emptied the dresser drawers he'd filled, tossing everything into his case. He grabbed the old pair of Nikes and threw them inside along with the clothes he'd hung in the closet. Just needed his toiletry bag and he'd be finished.

Staggering into the hallway, he grabbed the railing, using it to get to the bathroom. His face was a hideous mass of cuts and bruises staring back at him from the medicine cabinet. He turned away, the dizziness forcing him to sit on the edge of the bathtub. He waited out the spin, leaning his forehead against the wall.

Finally, the spinning passed, his ribs aching as he rose from the bathtub. His toiletry kit lay on the back of the toilet, so he tucked it under his arm and returned with slow steps to the bedroom. He tossed the case into his luggage and zipped it up. He dragged it out of the room and to the top of the stairs. It bumped against every step until finally, exhausted, he reached the bottom step. He sank down on it, leaning against the wall to stop the swirling in his brain.

"You oughta get yourself right back up those stairs afore you fall."

It was Elsie's worried voice as she knelt beside him.

"I'm fine," he muttered, not even trying to sound convincing.

She frowned at him, her dark, wrinkled hand reaching toward his face.

"He done tore you up good, yesterday," she said with a hiss. "You were out the whole day." She frowned at the suitcase beside him. "Why you got your suitcase, Nate?"

He pointed to his face. "I'd say the message was pretty clear, wouldn't you? I'm gonna call a cab to the airport."

Her eyes turned watery. "Honey, you ain't gonna get you no cab out here now."

"Why not?" he asked, laying a hand to his throbbing lower lip.

She pressed her hand against his forehead. "Rita's comin' this way. She done strengthened to a Category three and gettin' stronger. They orderin' mandatory evacuations south of Highway 10. Everybody's busy battenin' down the hatches."

"Where's Kadence?" he asked, not particularly wanting to see her, but he wanted to make sure Elsie had a place to go if the authorities made them evacuate.

"She and Jim went out for plywood to nail over the windows." Elsie gripped his arm. "Rita's gonna come, Nate. They say she's gonna be worse than Audrey."

"Audrey?" he asked.

Elsie nodded. "Hurricane Audrey. She killed nearly four hundred when she passed through these parishes about fifty year ago. They afraid the N'Orleans levees gonna break again and reflood everythin'."

He squeezed her hand. "We've gotta get out of here then, before it hits."

Elsie smiled at him, her expression haunting as she shook her head no.

"Not gonna run no more, Nate. I'm too old. I'm gonna stay here with my cats and ride it out. If I survived Katrina, I can survive Rita."

He shook his head. "Elsie, you can't! It's too dangerous. If they're calling for mandatory evacuations—"

"Don't you fret none," she said. "I've lived too long to let another storm take me. We'll be fine."

He felt his heart twist. That meant Kadence was staying, too.

"Kadence won't evacuate?"

She nodded. "Said she was stayin' right here. But, Nate, you go on out of here. Before you cain't."

No, he wasn't leaving. He couldn't. No matter what had happened between him and Kadence, he wanted to make sure Elsie was safe. And Kadence. He still loved her, not that it would do him any good.

"Elsie, listen to me," he said, taking her face in his shaky hands. "We've gotta get you upstairs. Move everything you care about upstairs. Then we'll need food and water up there, too."

Elsie grinned at him, nodding. "I knew you wouldn't leave her like this. I knew you had moxie."

He let her go and started back up the stairs, dragging his suitcase up one stair at a time. He shoved the suitcase inside, adrenaline kicking in, and struggled down the stairs again. He grabbed every bottle of water from the refrigerator and carried it upstairs to the bathroom, setting them in the bathtub.

Four more trips he made, carrying food and water upstairs. His stomach ached in time with his face, but he tried to shut out the pain, concentrating on the food. Then flashlights and batteries. Finally, can openers and anything else he found useful.

By the time he'd finished, the house was darkening as plywood sheets were nailed across windows. It was just past four o'clock when he flicked on his bedroom lights and laid down, still feeling shaky. He was nearly asleep when his cell phone rang. He slid it out of its clip, saying hello.

"Nate? What's happening down there?"

Ren, he realized.

"Preparing for a hurricane."

"Where exactly are you?" he asked.

"Near a town called Hackberry. On Highway 27. Why?"

Ren's breath hissed out. "That's in the evacuation zone. When you planning to leave for safer ground, Nate?"

He hesitated. "I'm…uh, not. Going to ride it out in Hackberry."

"Are you crazy? In case you don't know it, you've got a Category 5 hurricane bearing down on you right now. And that little town you're in? It's directly in the path of this monster. Nate, please—it's not worth your life. You've got to get out."

"I'm staying here."

Ren fell silent for a moment. "That's insanity! This monster's got sustained winds of 165 miles per hour. Do you hear me? 165 miles per hour! They're predicting storm surges up to twenty feet, Nate." His voice went deadly quiet. "Please. You've gotta get out of there."

"Can't, Ren," he replied. "Sorry."

"Did something happen?"

He wanted to spill the whole terrible story to Ren, but it wouldn't help. He'd lost Kadence.

"Looks like I'm coming home earlier than expected. Probably see you before the thirtieth."

"Okay, buddy, but please—take care of yourself and be careful. Don't drown on me, okay?"

"If anything happens…you'll take care of things for me, won't you?"

"Don't talk like that, Nate."

"Just say you will, Ren."

Ren was quiet for several long moments. "You know I will," he said finally.

"Talk to you soon," said Nate, closing the phone.

---

By ten o'clock that night, Hurricane Rita's maximum winds were steady at 175 miles per hour. Nate stayed in his room and slept. He didn't want to face Kadence much less Jim who was downstairs in the kitchen. Nate heard his loud voice and the clink of silverware.

Finally, around midnight, someone knocked on his door. He was awake, but ignored it. Two more times, someone knocked, but the third time, the door opened.

"Nate? You awake?"

Kadence, he realized. He didn't rouse from the bed, instead lying on his side.

"What is it?" he asked, summoning as much professional distance as he could.

"Just wanted to check on you, see how you were," she said.

"Why?" he snapped, not turning over to face her.

"Because I feel terrible about what happened, all right? And I wanted to make sure you were okay."

He didn't respond. What was left to say? She hadn't even given him a chance to explain, to tell her how much he loved her and that he was breaking off the engagement.

"Don't worry. As soon as the storm passes, I'll be out of your way for good. And I'll refund you the difference on your donation."

She closed the door and he heard her footsteps creaking on the stairs. Outside, a low rumble of thunder pierced the calm, warning of the approaching storm. At that moment, he didn't care if he survived it or not.

That's when his cell phone chimed in the darkness. He cried out as he struggled to pull the phone off the nightstand. Jim had done a number on his ribs. His father's cell number glared back at him as he flipped open the phone.

"What?" Nate snapped. He was in no mood for more orders. Not from anyone.

"Nate, what's this I'm hearing about you riding out a category five hurricane down there?"

"What about it?"

"So, it's true?" his Dad replied. "You've got an MBA from Harvard, but not enough sense to heed a mandatory evacuation."

"Guess not, Dad. Sounds like it's all for the best, isn't it?"

"Nate, what's the matter with you?" Dad sighed his *my kid's driving me crazy* sigh. "This is about that girl, isn't it?"

"Not so much, Dad. More about finding out that Corrina's cheating on me. Has been since for months. With Bradley Wilcox."

"Oh, nonsense, Nate," his father sputtered. "Where'd you hear something like that?"

"A very credible source. There's photographic evidence to support it."

His dad sighed again and fell silent. Finally, he heard paper shifting.

"Look, Nate, sometimes couples see other people. It happens. Even you're seeing—"

"Don't you dare accuse me of cheating on Corrina. Because I haven't."

He'd wanted to several times, but he hadn't. He'd wanted to do the right thing and break up the engagement before he'd started seeing Kadence. But that wasn't a concern now.

"Okay, son—settle down. I didn't mean to imply impropriety on your part. I just wish you could see what this political alliance could do for you. For us."

"I'm not interested," Nate said. "Look, it's late and I'm tired."

"Maybe you'll be interested if it involves Logan Financial?"

Nate rolled his eyes. "Going to fire me if I don't marry Corrina?" He couldn't care less. He could get a job anywhere.

"No," said his dad. "Just Ren."

Nate felt his hands go cold as he held the phone to his ear.

"You wouldn't," he said in a quiet voice.

"That's just the start of it," his father replied, his tone razor sharp. "I have friends in a lot of places. Chancellors, college presidents—the promise of a donation could make a lot of trouble for your little professor."

"You leave her out of this!" Nate shouted, the rage trembling through him.

"I'll expect you back to work on the third. If you're not, Ren won't be there when you return. And that woman may be in for hard times. Very hard times. Try to be careful, son. Goodnight."

Gritting his teeth against the scream of rage he wanted to let loose, Nate threw the phone against the floor. The casing shattered, buttons and antenna skittering across the wood.

He couldn't let Ren be fired. Or some fabricated scandal by his dad ruin Kadence's career. Now, he had no choice but to return and marry a woman he not only didn't love, but despised.

# TWENTY-ONE

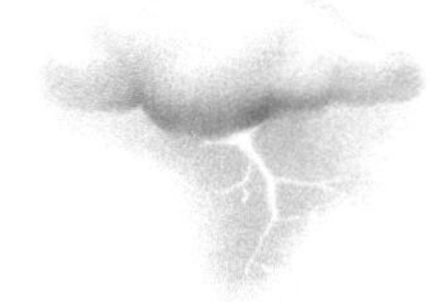

Kadence walked down the stairs and into the kitchen where Elsie sat sipping a Pepsi.

"Wouldn't talk to you still?" Elsie replied.

She shook her head, dropping down in a chair across from Elsie. She picked up her can of Pepsi and took a hard drink that hurt all the way down.

"He told me he'd be out of my hair as soon as the storm passes."

She set down the Pepsi and pressed her hand to her forehead, fighting back the tears. The memory of him lying all broken up in the grass made her sick to her stomach. She'd never meant for that to happen. Why couldn't she have stopped Jim? Why hadn't she just kept her big mouth shut?

She wanted to run upstairs and wrap her arms around him, tell him how sorry she was. She'd seen the blood, the swollen eyes and lip. She knew he was hurt, but he'd refused anyone to look him over. Kadence winced. He wouldn't even look at her. That hurt most of all.

"What made Jim beat him up like that?" Elsie asked. "It was a rotten thing to do."

Tears threaded down Kadence's face and she bowed her head, the top of the Pepsi can brushing against her forehead.

"It was horrible and it was all my fault."

"He'd been wantin' to talk to you, but you was still in Lake Charles. Seemed awful perky about somethin' that night. Like he'd gotten some good news."

She could only imagine. Probably got an early flight out of Lake Charles. He couldn't wait to get out of here now, but honestly, she couldn't blame him.

"He's engaged to be married, Elsie."

"What?" Elsie cried, nearly spilling her Pepsi. She quickly righted the can that almost fell onto its side. "Married?"

"It's been in all the Arlington newspapers. I saw them myself."

Elsie shook her head, her dark eyes looking hard. "I don't know what's goin' on in that head of his and I don't know nuthin' about no engagement. All I know is that he sat in this kitchen and told me he was comin' back here. After he done went home for a while."

"What? Are you sure, Elsie? He said he was coming back?"

She nodded. "He made a point of tellin' me. Said he had to go home and take care of a few things before he could come back. But he said he was comin' back."

At first, Elsie's news made her grin, but she knew everything had changed now. Why hadn't she kept her big mouth shut? Why hadn't she just waited to talk to him about the situation? Now, it was hopeless.

Rain peppered the windows, a clap of thunder in the distance. Hers and Elsie's gazes snapped to the window, boarded up now.

"Weatherman said we'd see scattered storms first," said Elsie.

Kadence rose from her chair and went to the refrigerator. She pulled out a Coke from the six pack she'd bought for Nate yesterday and carried it up the stairs. She lingered outside his door for several minutes, finally gathering the courage to knock. Once. No response. Twice. Nothing.

On the third knock, she opened the door.

"Nate?"

"What?" he asked still with his back to the door.

She walked over to the bed and set the Coke can on the nightstand beside him.

"Brought you a Coke," she said in a quiet voice.

He turned his body toward her on the bed and she couldn't help but gasp when she saw his face.

"Oh, God, Nate—I'm so, so sorry about yesterday."

Nate just shrugged. His eyes were nearly swollen shut, his bottom lip twice its normal size. Deep black bruises ringed both eyes. The cut above his eye probably needed stitches.

That's when she saw the cell phone parts scattered across the floor. She picked up the cold can of Coke and pressed it into his hand.

"Drink this. And I'll be right back."

She didn't hear the tab pop until she'd stepped into the bathroom for Band-Aids, a washcloth, and some Neosporin. She returned to his bedroom, seeing his packed suitcase by the door, and her heart bounced into her throat as she climbed onto the bed. Sitting cross-legged, she tilted his face toward her and gently dabbed away the dried blood.

He winced, pulling back, but she held his head firmly, gently washing away the blood from his face. Once she'd removed the dried blood, she could see the cuts that needed to be dressed.

The one above his left eye was bad, so she applied ointment and butterfly closures. She put a small bandage over another cut on his chin. Then she lifted the can of Coke out of his hands and gently touched it to his left eye. He winced, pulling back, but she held the can there a moment then two. She took hold of his hand and laid it against the Coke can.

"Hold that there. I'll be back with an ice pack."

"Not necessary," he said, not looking at her.

"Yes, it is," she said, smoothing hair out of his eyes.

She rose from the bed and hurried down the creaking stairs to the kitchen. She fumbled through the freezer for a bag of peas then carried it upstairs to him. With easy movements, she took the Coke out of his hand again and laid the bag of peas there. Then she maneuvered his hand to his eye to hold the bag in place.

"There. Is that better?"

He shrugged.

"Thank you for carrying all the supplies upstairs. Especially when you didn't feel like it."

"No problem," he replied.

She cringed, missing the closeness they'd had, remembering the night he'd held her in his arms all night. She wanted that Nate back. Not this sullen and distant man who'd been pushed too far.

"Get some sleep," she said, rising from the bed to pause in the doorway.

---

SCATTERED THUNDERSTORMS ROLLED ACROSS SOUTHWESTERN LOUISIANA much of the day on Thursday. By Friday, the outer rain bands were sweeping the Louisiana shores, spawning squalls and thunderstorms. And tornadoes. Rita was predicted to make landfall by four a.m. Saturday morning. The hurricane winds had weakened some, down to one hundred and forty-something, but the forecasters were still predicting a Category three landfall. And Hackberry was right in her path.

Kadence didn't want to evacuate. She had nowhere to go and neither did Elsie. Or Nate. With a storm surge of ten plus feet expected, the three of them would ride out the storm on the house's second floor. And pray she held together.

"Oh, mercy!" Elsie cried, rushing into the kitchen where Kadence and a very quiet, very bruised Nate sat drinking coffee.

"What's the matter?" Kadence asked.

"One of the N'Orleans levees done broke again. Done re-flooded Ninth Ward."

Nate finally reacted to this news, his battered face scrunching into a sad expression.

"That's your neighborhood, isn't it?" he replied.

She nodded, tears in her eyes.

"I'm so sorry, Elsie," said Nate. He rose stiffly from his chair to put his arms around her.

"It's so sad to see her go under again."

He kissed Elsie on top of her head and let her go. Kadence envied Elsie at that moment, wanting to feel Nate's arms around her again.

"It only hours away now," said Elsie. "Guess I better get the cats locked upstairs now."

She left to attend to the cats and Nate sat back down, wincing. Kadence watched him, feeling so awful.

A squall of wind screamed across the house, the drive of rain dull against the plywood covering the windows. Nate's gaze flicked to the plywood and she wondered what he was thinking.

"Ever been through a hurricane before?" she asked.

He shook his head. "Not even a tropical storm."

"The storm surge is the worst part. That and the tornadoes. They're saying a fifteen-foot storm surge could send sea water flooding over the coast and inland. Hackberry's going to flood."

He pointed at the sitting room. "How tall's that ceiling?"

Distance to the top of the stairs is what he wanted to know.

"Eight feet."

His jaw tightened. "Storm surge will reach the second floor."

She nodded, knowing he was right. Maybe staying had been a foolish idea after all? But Elsie had been adamant about not leaving. She couldn't leave her alone here.

"Is there an attic?" he asked.

"Yes. The stairway is across from the bathroom."

"We'd better put the food and water up there. And a saw to cut through the roof."

She nodded, rising from her chair. "I'll get the saw and meet you upstairs.

---

For nearly an hour, she and Nate hauled bottled water and canned food upstairs to the attic. It was a small room with one window and a pointed roof. She had an old dresser up there and some boxes. Nate set the food on top of the dresser along with the saw and can opener. She noticed that he'd grabbed a bag of cat food for the cats, too. And the upstairs litter pan that set in the bathroom.

His silence was driving her crazy.

"Nate," she said, her voice exasperated. "We've got to talk about this, otherwise I'll go mad from guilt."

His gaze met hers, but that flicker of hope she'd always seen there was strangely absent.

"You've already said you're sorry about this," he said, pointing at his face. "Apology was accepted."

She took two steps toward him, but stopped herself from taking his hands in hers.

"I want everything to be all right between us." She shook her head, turning away finally when his expression didn't change. "I want to go back to that day at the beach."

"Me, too," he said, the sadness in his voice. "Trouble is, I don't know how to get back there."

Another squall screeched around the eaves and the house shook, rain pounding the roof. Rita's outer rain bands were probably battering the coast now. And poor Holly Beach, she realized. She hoped everyone got out in time.

She turned back to him, laying a hand against his bruised face, gently stroking. "I never meant for this to happen."

"It's okay," he said, not looking at her.

"No," she said, her fingertips tracing his jaw line. "It's not okay."

With a slow rise of her left hand, she touched his side and he flinched away from her touch. She slid her arm around him, drawing closer to him until she was embracing him.

"I don't know how to tell you," she whispered, "how much you mean to me."

He squeezed his eyes closed, his left hand weakly pressing against her back. "You just did," he said, his arms at last sliding around her.

---

THE THREE OF THEM SLEPT UPSTAIRS THAT NIGHT. ELSIE LOCKED THE CATS in the attic and slept in Kadence's room, Nate alone in his room as the winds howled across the house. It was a shriek of such pitch and velocity it made his skin crawl. And the rains pounded the house with such force, the droplets sounded like nails pounded through wood. With each gust of wind, growing stronger and more violent as midnight slipped toward two a.m., Rita drew closer.

Around two-thirty a.m., she slammed into the Louisiana shore, gobbling up homes and businesses, inundating the shores with fifteen feet of sea water that rushed inland to swallow up the world.

Sometime after three a.m., Nate heard water rushing into the house. He bolted up from the bed, ignoring the pain, and sank into his Merrell's before rushing to the railing. The smell of salt and silt filled the house, the shine of black water surging across the floor.

The house gave a moan, the lights sputtering, and finally the power bled away. Leaving them in darkness and rising water.

Nate felt his way back to his room and found the flashlight on the dresser. He flicked it on, returning to the railing. As hurricane force winds pounded the house, the thin ray of flashlight caught the water flowing across the wood floors.

Outside, the crash of wood and projectiles echoed above the crackle of thunder and rush of wind. And the steady flow of water into the house. He shined the light downstairs. Couches were floating now, chairs and tables overturning. Lamps toppled, water bubbling. It was already up to the third step.

He rushed into Kadence's room.

"It's flooding downstairs," he announced his voice calm despite the danger. "We'd better get to the attic."

Elsie was already on her feet, moving toward him, Kadence a little slow.

Nate followed Elsie into the hallway as she gripped her own flashlight, pointing it toward the attic stairs. He waited at the bottom while she opened the door and slid inside, careful to keep Percy and Diva from escaping.

When Kadence didn't follow Elsie out into the hall, he hurried back to her room. Finding her dragging out a box from under the bed.

"Come on," he shouted, above the roar of rain and wind pounding the roof. "It's rising fast!"

She hurried to the door, box in her arms, and stopped to grab a flashlight then she followed him to the stairs.

"Hurry," he urged, shining the light along the attic stairs so she wouldn't fall.

When he heard the door creak open, he moved toward the railing to peer down at the flood waters. Shining the light on the stairs sent his heart up into his throat. Halfway up. If that surge was higher than twenty feet, they'd have to climb onto the roof.

He swallowed hard. If he could cut through the roof fast enough for them to escape.

# TWENTY-TWO

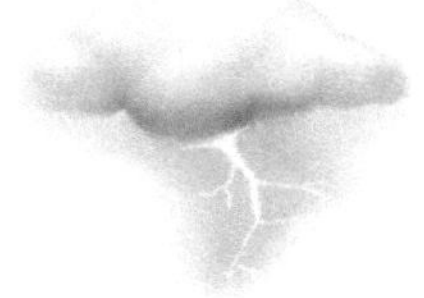

Kadence called to him as he turned away from the first-floor stairs. The flow of water was disturbing as he climbed the attic stairs and carefully opened the door, sticking his foot in the opening in case Percy or Diva decided to dash out.

"It's halfway up the stairs," he announced in a grim tone, stepping inside and closing the door.

"Storm surge is coming in," said Kadence, looking worried. "We're twenty minutes from the coast, so it's going to be bad."

Elsie huddled against the wall, Diva in her arms.

Nate knew if the surge rose the full twenty feet (or higher), sea water would reach the attic door. Or fill the attic.

They huddled on the floor in darkness, only a thin stream of light visible from Nate's flashlight as the wind ripped at the house. Shingles popped off the groaning roof, the sound like gunshots.

Outside, wood splintered, metal crashed, slamming into the house. The noise was horrendous. Like a freight train bearing down on them. And the squeal of wind shaking the house. It felt like a tornado, earthquake, and flood waters were hitting the house at the same time. But the house was mostly brick. Nate hoped the brick would hold it together as the dirty side of the storm—as Elsie had called it—passed over them.

A massive tree smashed through the roof, cracking the attic open like an egg shell. The warring, angry sky was pitch black, rain whipping past in horizontal sheets.

Kadence grabbed Elsie, shielding her from the debris falling through the gaping hole and off the uprooted oak tree. Parts of the roof tore away in the shrieking winds as Nate shuffled Kadence and Elsie into a protected corner of the attic, out of the wind and rain.

Below, more wood cracked, the sounds of shattering and smashing deafening. Parts of the house were giving way. If the downstairs walls collapsed, the whole house might crumble into the storm surge and they'd drown in the currents. Wind screamed over the house, the squall nearly constant now. Could this old place take much more?

The outside wall of the house swayed with every wind gust as the three of them huddled behind the dresser. Percy and Diva crouched underneath it.

Another tree trunk hammered into the hole in the roof and slammed through the attic door, splintering it.

Elsie covered her head, clutching Kadence around the middle. Percy and Diva scrambled into the corner behind them, cowering behind an empty box.

Nate crouched beside Kadence and Elsie, trying to cover them with his body as the entire house shifted with a groan. Something below gave way and his heart hammered into his throat. Something big.

"What was that?" Elsie shouted.

"I'll go check!" Nate yelled.

He staggered up, flashlight gripped like a life preserver, and crept toward the ruined attic door.

"Nate, be careful!" Kadence shouted above the roar of wind.

He stepped over the broken hunks of tree limbs, slipping on the rain running all over the unfinished floor boards and down the stairs. He caught himself by grabbing hold of the door frame then made his way down the stairs.

The second floor was mostly dry (except for the thin stream of rain water) when he stepped onto it and edged his way toward the top of the stairs. To his horror, they were gone. The entire staircase had crumbled in the current.

A gaping hole of swirling black water lay below.

He shined his flashlight toward the kitchen. But it was a pile of rubble now, the walls stripped to their frames and wobbling in the winds. Tangles of aluminum roofing, insulation, and the remnants of kitchen cabinets wrapped around the remaining walls buffeting in the wind and swirling waters. Couches and tables slammed into the walls from the force of the current. Glass broke.

The first floor was nearly submerged, the rushing water less than four feet from the second floor. And still the water was rising.

He backed away toward the attic stairs, climbing over debris and through water until he reached the safety of the attic. Water still poured in from the torrential rains, running down the stairs in a wider swath now.

"How bad is it?" Kadence shouted as he crouched beside her.

"Kitchen's gone! So are the stairs!"

"The kitchen?" she gasped. "Maybe the brick will hold?"

He nodded. "Hope this thing weakens soon or the house won't be here anymore."

***

For hours, Rita pounded the deteriorating house and the three of them crouched in the corner and waited. It was all they could do.

Finally, Nate rose from the floor, flashlight in hand. "I'm going to check the water levels."

"I'm coming, too," said Kadence, pulling herself to her feet.

She turned on her flashlight and stepped over the broken tree trunk onto the stairs. Nate followed behind her, shining his flashlight ahead of her until she reached the second floor. She took tentative steps forward, the rain making the floor slick as she moved toward the stair railing.

When he shined his flashlight below, he felt the cold chill hit him. It was all underwater. Right up to bottom of the railing.

"Oh, God," Kadence said with a gasp.

She grabbed hold of the railing to steady herself. And it gave way.

Nate watched in horror as she fell through and into the churning flood waters.

"Kadence!" he screamed.

He tossed the flashlight onto the attic stairs and threw himself into the rising water.

The salt water burned his eyes, furniture and God knew what pummeling him as the current drew him downward into the blackness. He sucked in a breath just before his face went under. Ahead, he saw the thin trail of light. Only a foot or so in front of him.

He kicked his legs, pushing off what might have been a submerged sofa, and stretched his arms toward the flailing light.

Missed.

With lungs burning, he kicked harder, bouncing off something solid that sent a wave of pain through his side. But the light had shifted to his right.

He clawed and fought the churning water until his feet hit something—part of the staircase maybe—and pushed him above the water line.

Gasping for air, he pulled in several breaths until he could hold his breath again. Then he dived under the salty surface, fighting the thick water to swim toward the pale, yellow light.

He was thrown into her nearly limp body, the flashlight still gripped in her hands. Wrapping both arms around her, he held on tight and kicked up, hitting the ceiling.

A wave of panic hit him as he fought the current, swimming toward what he hoped was the stairway—and that fading corridor of air.

He hit the wall hard, nearly knocking himself out, the water pressing him against it. His lungs burned as he fought to reach the edge of the second floor.

Finally, he broke surface and lifted Kadence's face above water. He clawed at the wall, trying to push himself that last foot toward the landing. Where he could lift Kadence out of the water.

He was nearly washed underneath it, but he caught the edge with his left hand.

Water and debris pounded him as he held on despite the pain, and lifted Kadence up with his right. With one hand, he lifted her the last four inches to the landing, pitching her forward.

She gagged, expelling sea water then coughed hard as she clawed at the wood to pull herself onto the landing.

That's when something slammed into his legs, tearing his one-handed hold off the landing.

"Nate!" Kadence screamed, trying to grab his hand, but she was just a moment too late.

# TWENTY-THREE

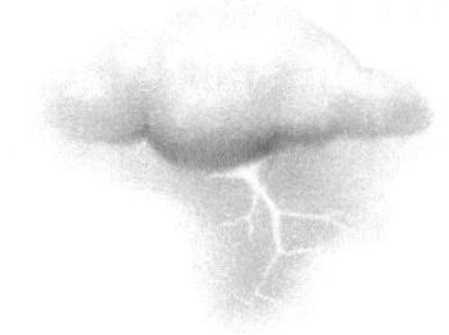

Nate fell backward into the swirling water, the debris tangling around his legs, dragging him deeper until he felt the wood floor against his knees.

He struggled to put his feet on the floor and then pushed off, shooting up through the water as the current dragged him forward. If he got sucked into that short hallway, where Elsie's bedroom had been, he'd drown.

He rose until his head cracked against the ceiling.

Fighting the fiery pain exploding through his head and the sudden tilt of the world, his hand raked across the light fixture. Still attached to the ceiling.

Grabbing hold, the current buffeting him, he swiveled his body, kicking out until he felt his foot strike the wall. It was the light fixture over the stairs, he realized.

He had a fifty-fifty chance of swimming the right direction.

But the sound of Kadence's voice pierced the roar of water. His lungs burned for air as he listened again. The sound was to his right.

He lunged right, kicking and flailing until he felt his arm hit wood.

The landing!

He grabbed hold of the wood and pushed his body upward. And found air.

"Nate!" Kadence lunged across the slick floor toward him. Grabbing his wrists.

Nate dug his foot into the wall enough to leverage himself out of the water and onto the landing.

He gasped and wheezed, collapsing on the floor, the sea water burning his throat as he sucked in gulps of air.

Kadence collapsed beside him, her hands still clutching his wrists.

"You saved my life," she shouted, her voice a hoarse rasp.

His chest hurt too much to respond. All he could do was nod. And the water was still rising.

"Attic," was all he could sputter as the coughing tore through his chest.

She helped him up and they both staggered toward the stairs. Kadence went up first as Nate grabbed his flashlight. He looked back, shining the light on the landing. The water was three inches from the edge. He turned away and stumbled up the stairs.

When he reached Elsie, he dropped to his knees and leaned against the wall, still huffing for breath.

"Nate, you okay?" Elsie asked, looking horrified when she saw his soaked clothes. "What happened?"

He slid down the wall, closing his eyes and feeling the mud caked in his hair, on his face.

"Railing broke on her," he said.

Elsie's eyes widened, her hand flying to mouth. "Dear God!" she cried, turning to Kadence. "You're lucky you both wasn't killed!"

Kadence huddled against the wall, her red hair soaked and mixed with mud and marsh grass. "We nearly were," she replied, her eyes closed. "When I fell through, he jumped in and pulled me out."

Nate squeezed his eyes closed, wishing the current had taken him. Given time, he might have eventually patched things with her. But unless he married Corrina, he risked ruining his best friend's career. And Kadence's. Nate knew his father well enough to know the man didn't make idle threats. That had been a promise. One Nate wasn't going to test. He owed Ren a lot. He wouldn't ruin Ren and Meredith's life for...for what? For thirty days. For a woman who bought him off the internet?

He sighed, the ache in his chest terrible now. How crazy was that?

———

With every hour, Rita trudged north, moving farther and farther away until around afternoon, the sky lightened. And the rain stopped. At its highest, the storm surge had reached the attic's third step. But it was starting to recede now.

In the stark, hot silence, the same that he remembered from New Orleans, they sat in evening darkness and ate from the cans they'd carried into the attic. Nate ate spaghetti, Elsie and Kadence munching on ravioli. When Kadence finished, she carried pillows up from the soggy second floor and they stretched out and slept. Or tried to, in Nate's case. He lay awake most of the night, trying to find a way out of marrying Corrina.

On Sunday morning, he awoke to the sound of buzzing. A boat motor, he realized.

"Kay! Kay, you all right in there?"

Nate recognized the voice immediately. Jim.

Kadence raised her head from her pillow. "It's Jim!" she cried, getting to her feet.

Elsie sat up, Percy and Diva entwining around her.

"He gonna rescue us?" Elsie asked.

Kadence grinned. "Hope so."

"Kadence! It's Marty! Answer us!"

He watched her run down the attic stairs.

"Up here, Jim! You're gonna need a ladder."

"Got one in the boat," Jim shouted.

Nate stretched and got to his feet. Stiff and aching, he limped down the stairs, Elsie peering out.

He reached the landing just as a silver ladder slapped against it. Elsie was behind him now, a box in her arms, a towel draped over the top. Percy and Diva mewed pitifully beneath the towel.

"Watch your step, Elsie," Nate said, hands on her shoulders as he steered her toward the ladder.

Marty popped up at the top and reached his arms toward Kadence.

"You're a sight for sore eyes," Marty said, grinning at her as she hugged him.

"So are you, Marty. What are you, two doing here?"

"We volunteered. Wanted to make sure you was okay."

"Thanks, guys," she replied through teary eyes. She turned to Elsie. "You first, Elsie."

Elsie handed the cats to Kadence as Marty stepped down a few rungs, making room for Elsie to descend.

"I'm gettin' to be an old hand at this," said Elsie with a chuckle as she hobbled down the ladder.

Nate stared out at the six feet of water still filling the devastated house. It was only partially standing now, torn from its foundation, but still upright. It would have to be bulldozed and rebuilt. Then his gaze met Jim's unblinking stare. He nodded with a slight tilt of his head at Nate. Nate returned a quick nod, his gaze returning to Elsie.

"How you doin', Nate?" Marty asked, squinting at him.

"Still alive," Nate replied. "How'd Lake Charles handle the hurricane?"

"Had a lot of damage, six-foot storm surge in places, but we came through all right. Holly Beach is—is just gone. Only stilts where houses used to be. There's hardly anythin' left standin' in Cameron either."

Nate shuddered, remembering all the houses along that beach.

"But so far, nobody's died," Marty said, his voice sounding tinny as he reached the boat below. "And that's some good news."

Marty pounded up the ladder again and Kadence held out Elsie's cats to him. He carried the box like it was a baby and gently set it in Elsie's lap.

Nate looked up. Kadence was staring at him, but she didn't say anything. Those big brown eyes looked sad, no doubt the realization of her house's condition setting in now.

"You next, Kadence," Marty called from below.

She cast one last look at Nate then turned and climbed down the ladder. She moved with slow, sure movements, hand over hand until she reached the boat. Jim threw his arms around her, holding her in a long embrace.

"I was worried sick, Kay. Wish you'd listened to me instead of ridin' this one out. You're lucky nobody died."

Marty stared up at Nate a moment.

"You plannin' to come down, Nate?" he asked with a chuckle.

He turned and started down the ladder. As he swung his leg into the boat, he saw a water moccasin slither through the water.

"Whoa," Marty cried, jerking back from the side of the boat. "I hate those things."

Nate sat down in the nearest seat as Marty picked up a paddle. Jim grabbed another paddle and they canoed away in the dark, standing water toward open water. What used to be fields and streets. He'd never seen anything like it in his whole life. The heat balled up like wool, like it was trying to soak up all the water. He felt the sweat already masking his face. He ran his hand across his bruised face, wincing at the dull pain.

It was the first thing he'd felt since yesterday.

Jim started the motor with a whine and the boat glided through the flood waters.

"How you doin', Nate?" Elsie asked, her voice low as Marty and Jim chattered with Kadence.

"Not sure. Kind of numb, I think."

She patted him on the leg. "It'll get better. Took me days to get any feelin' back in me. What you need now is some rest."

He watched Kadence's animated face recounting something to Marty and Jim and that dull ache moved into his chest. He'd lost a lot in this storm and it was just starting to hit him. It was the end of September—what day, he wasn't quite sure. But it was the end of something.

Elsie glanced over at Kadence then him. "She says you're engaged. That true?" Her voice was quiet so that only he could hear her.

He squeezed eyes closed and nodded.

"Were you gonna tell her?"

He sighed, bowing his head. "No. I didn't think I'd have to."

When he looked up, Elsie's dark eyes were hard, angry.

"I thought I could go back home and call it off before she had to know about it."

Her eyes turned watery, a frown pulling down her features. "You was gonna break up with your girl back home?"

He nodded, casting a long look at Kadence. "But I can't now."

"Why not?" she asked, her tone sad.

Because he'd have to ruin his best friend's life to save his own. And Kadence's. That was something he couldn't do. Besides, he'd already ruined things with Kadence. There was no point in changing anything now, except his return flight home.

"Because things are…are complicated now. I have an obligation to fulfill. If I don't, two people I care a great deal about will suffer greatly. And that's not fair."

Elsie's hand was on his arm in a motherly gesture. "Do you love her? The girl back home?"

He stared at Elsie a moment or two then shook his head. "No," he said finally, looking away. "And I never will."

The thought of spending the rest of his life with Corrina made him ill, the sound of her baby talk phrases making his skin crawl. But to protect Ren and Kadence, he'd go through with it. He watched Kadence laughing with Jim and Marty, feeling very alone. It wasn't like he was giving up anything.

---

It took three days for the flood waters to recede and authorities to allow anyone back into Hackberry and down Highway 27. Power poles had toppled like toothpicks from the wind and surge. Trailers smashed like pancakes. Water still clung to the roadsides and stood in fields, many of the puddles housing fiddler crabs now. Fire ants swarmed over debris piles and aluminum roofing lay crumpled like tissue paper along the roadsides. Cloudy-eyed fish lay everywhere, staring up at the sky, the smell putrid.

For several days, Nate worked alongside locals in Hackberry to clear debris and anything else he could do. He also helped the Lake Charles firefighters with the clean up on Kadence's house, helping her salvage anything worth saving and loading it into the back of Jim's truck.

On September twenty-ninth, they left the ruined house for Lake Charles where Kadence had rented a small house for her and Elsie. In Jim's neighborhood.

After Nate had helped unload everything at the small place, he loaded his suitcase into Marty's old Grand Prix. Kadence was inside unpacking. It was time to go.

"Appreciate you giving me a ride to the airport, Marty."

"Glad to do it, Nate," said Marty, clapping him on the shoulder as Nate opened the passenger-side door. "Sorry to see you go."

"Nate, wait!"

He turned to see Elsie hobbling toward him, wearing a blue house dress and flip flops. He pulled her into a tight hug.

"Gonna miss you, Elsie," he said, trying to keep his voice from cracking. "You take good care of yourself." He took her hand and pressed his business card into her palm. "If you ever need anything, please—call me, and I'll be right there. I promise."

"Aw, Nate, I'm gonna miss you somethin' terrible." She kissed him on the cheek, running her arthritic hand through his hair. "You still gettin' married?" she asked in a whisper.

"Pet Percy for me, huh?" he said and climbed into the Grand Prix.

With a lump in his throat, he waved at Elsie as Marty pulled away from the curb, heading for I-10 and Baton Rouge.

---

THAT EVENING, NATE FOUND HIMSELF IN A HOTEL NEAR THE BATON ROUGE airport. His flight to D.C. left first thing tomorrow morning. He'd just called Ren to let him know he was alive and on a morning flight out of Baton Rouge. He laid face down on the bed, the ache spreading through his body, mixing with dread. He thought about buying a ticket west, of just closing his eyes and pointing to a map. Anywhere but Arlington and the looming wedding. November fifth. It felt like the end of the world.

---

THE NEXT DAY, HE ARRIVED IN D.C. AROUND THREE O'CLOCK AND FOUND Meredith and Ren waiting for him as he walked toward baggage claim.

"Nate!" Ren shouted, running toward him, Meredith a step behind him.

Ren stopped short, his mouth falling open. "My God—what happened to you?"

Meredith enfolded him in her arms. "I'm so glad to see you," she said in a soothing voice. He hugged her, glad to see some friendly faces. Ren hugged him, too, but his face was tight with worry.

"I was going crazy hearing all the devastation in Cameron Parish."

"He called your cell phone hundreds of times," Meredith added.

Nate didn't tell them he'd broken it into a million pieces.

Ren slid an arm around his shoulder as they walked toward baggage claim.

"You okay?" he asked finally. "I've never known you to be this quiet."

Nate shrugged. "I'm okay. Just need some adjustment time."

He saw Meredith mouth, "he's not okay" at Ren who nodded.

They were right. He wasn't okay. And he couldn't tell Ren about his father's threat against him either. No, like or not, he had a wedding to attend. And an unfaithful bride to love, honor and cherish—if he didn't choke on the *I Do's*.

They waited about fifteen minutes at baggage claim and Ren filled the silence with work talk, a big account he'd landed, and a reminder that Nate was still without a car.

"That's great, Ren," said Nate, pulling his battered suitcase off the conveyor. "I knew you'd handle everything just fine without me."

"So did I, but it wasn't nearly as much fun, my friend," he said with a smirk.

He pulled the bag toward the exit, Ren on one side, Meredith on the other.

"Hey, Nate, there's this great new restaurant we want to take you to," said Meredith, smiling, her short dark hair wavier than he'd remembered.

"You get a perm?" he asked, squinting.

She grinned, twisting a lock of hair around her finger.

"Looks great, Meredith," he replied.

"See," she said, poking Ren in the stomach. "Nate noticed. He knows how to treat a woman."

Ren just rolled his eyes.

"Anyway," said Meredith, taking hold of his arm. "It's called Creole House and it's authentic Cajun food. It's delicious!"

He felt his jaw tighten, his body stiffening at the thought. He had no desire to remember Louisiana right now. None at all.

"I'd rather not, Meredith, but thanks. I'm sure it's very good."

Meredith gave Ren another look, but Nate didn't care. He didn't even want to think about Cajun anything right now. Her dark eyes turned sad and she hugged him as they walked toward the parking garage.

---

THE RIDE HOME WAS QUICK. MAYBE BECAUSE HE WAS EXHAUSTED OR because Meredith and Ren had kept the silence at bay. When he finally got into the apartment, he wheeled his suitcase into his bedroom. He kicked off his shoes and plopped down on his bed, the room looking so strange after being gone a month. Right now, it all felt like a bad dream as he stretched out.

Everything had a clean smell to it. Like soap and lemons, unlike the smell of mildew and rotting fish that he'd smelled for days in Louisiana after Rita.

Ren stood in the doorway, leaning with his arms crossed, studying him.

"Didn't they feed you down there? Meredith thinks you look really thin."

"They fed me," he said with a sigh.

"I really like Kadence," Ren replied. "We talked a long time the night you got sick."

He sat up, eyes wide. "You talked to her?"

"Yeah, she was really concerned about you." He grinned. "So, what's the word on you, two? Any couple's news in the making."

Nate's face darkened. "No, that's long dead."

"Oh, come on, Nate," he said, prodding. "She was practically in tears as she explained how you'd gotten sepsis, how bad she felt. Especially when she found out about your car accident."

He laid back down, putting a hand over his eyes. "Can we talk about something else?"

"Sure." Ren was quiet for a moment or two. "You're really serious? But you were gone on her when I talked to you last."

"It's over, Ren," he snapped. "Drop it."

"But I thought you were breaking off the engagement?" he said, staring at Nate in surprise.

"The engagement's back on, Kadence is out of the picture, so let it go—dammit!"

He turned over on his bed, away from Ren's shocked stare.

"Oh, my God...say it isn't so." Ren rushed around the bed and grabbed him by the shoulders. "You're not still going to marry Corrina, are you? Nate, you can't! She's trash!"

Nate couldn't look him in the eye. "I'm going to take a nap now," he said and turned away, closing his eyes.

"I can't believe you're still going to marry that bitch after what Meredith saw. Nate, she doesn't deserve you."

There was nothing he could say. He had no choice but to marry Corrina now. It was out of his hands.

# TWENTY-FOUR

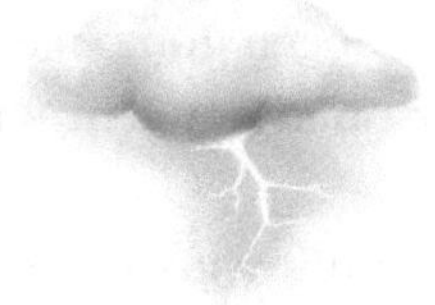

Kadence stood on the porch of her little blue rental house, feeling lost as the sun set. The afternoon heat still clung to the air, refusing to let up. The white camp shirt she wore over baggy green shorts helped keep her cool. In the back yard, Jim and some of the guys from Station Eight were cooking the burgers she'd bought on a portable grill. Feeding them was the least she could do since they'd helped her move her stuff.

Laughter rose above the clink of beer bottles and drone of classic rock from the radio, but all of it sounded tinny, hollow. She took a long drink of her Miller Light, wondering where Marty and Nate had gone.

She'd thought a lot about Nate's engagement these past few days as she'd salvaged the remains of her possessions from the house. But she realized tonight, standing here watching the blaze of gold and pink along the now calm sky line, that none of those things mattered except him. Watching him disappear into the raging flood waters made her face the possibility of losing him head on. And she never wanted to feel that way again. No, Nate was the only thing she'd wanted out of that house.

When he got back, she needed to tell him how she felt and even if it didn't change anything, she would at least know that she'd tried. That she hadn't just let him go without a fight. She'd risk the embarrassment and anything else. She knew that now.

Elsie stepped onto the porch, hobbling a little as she pulled up a white plastic chair to sit beside her. Her flip flops slapped against the cement as she shifted her feet.

"It's really getting late," said Kadence, staring down the street for Marty's blue Grand Prix. "Where are they? Burgers are almost ready."

"Where's who?" Elsie asked, folding her hands in her lap.

"Marty and Nate. They've been gone over two hours."

Elsie reached up and gripped her arm with a strength that startled Kadence.

"Child, didn't you hear him say goodbye?" she asked unblinking.

"Goodbye? No, did he already go back to the hotel?" She set down the beer, turning toward the house. "I've got to call him then, see what time he's coming over tomorrow."

Elsie didn't let up her grip and Kadence frowned, staring at her.

"Kadence, he done gone to Baton Rouge. Got a flight home tomorrow mornin'."

Her heart smashed against her rib cage, the breath spilling out of her lungs.

"What? Home?"

Elsie nodded. "I'm sorry, honey. I tried to talk him into stayin' one more day, but he wouldn't change his mind. Not one lick."

Kadence slid down to the porch step, hugging the railing. She felt chilled to the bone despite the humid Lake Charles night. She'd never see him again. The realization bit deep into her stomach that twisted into knots. She couldn't halt the flood of tears pouring down her face, so she covered her eyes, trying to hide the pain. Elsie was standing beside her now, a hand stroking her hair.

"I know it hurts, honey."

"Kay?" Jim called from the front door. "Kay, what's the matter?"

He hurried past Elsie to sit on the steps beside her.

"What's the matter?" he asked, his gaze falling on Elsie.

"Nate left for Baton Rouge tonight."

He laid a hand on Kadence's arms, drawing her hands away from her face. "Hey, now—don't cry over that piece of work. He's not worth it."

She shook her head. "I know," she said with a sob. "But I love that piece of work."

He pulled her against him, rocking her as she cried on his shoulder. She'd lost Nate to that sneery faced blonde and she didn't understand why. It just made no sense to her, but knowing he was gone made her heart hurt. She wished she'd never seen that Auctionanza ad. But more than that, she wished she'd confronted him about the engagement. If she had, maybe he'd still be here.

# TWENTY-FIVE

Over the next month, Nate endured yet another bridal shower, two cocktail parties, and a rehearsal dinner. Corrina had planned a Four Seasons wedding extravaganza, complete with seven-course, sit-down dinner and high tea the next afternoon before they jetted off to some small Pacific island near Papua New Guinea.

At each party and event, Nate hung on the periphery, watching Corrina put on her scripted performances for the press and anyone else watching. And always, just off to the side, watching her every movement was Bradley. They disappeared once for about fifteen minutes and he wondered if she was having sex with the guy while he stood down here pretending to be her fiancé.

He'd been home five days before she'd even bothered to return his call. Not that he'd even wanted to talk to her, but with Dad twisting his arm to the breaking point, he had to at least play the couple farce.

Ren wandered over to him at the party, Meredith on his arm. He smelled the faint, sweet scent of Meredith's perfume and watched how she looked at Ren. She loved Ren; it was there in her eyes. But when he looked into Corrina's pale eyes, all he saw was that self-centered expression of hers, always talking about how important her father was or something she'd done.

"How you holding up?" Meredith asked, pressing out her lip in a pout. "You look miserable."

Nate nodded and shoved his hands into the pockets of his dress pants, the sport coat loose at his shoulders.

"I'm going to slip out of here in a minute," he said. Before he threw up all over Corrina's pâté and crab puffs. Just his luck this was a dry affair.

"Where you going to go?" Ren asked.

He didn't have a car yet. And a taxi back to Arlington was as insane as him calling Corrina's driver. Something he'd never do.

And there she appeared on the little winding staircase that led up to the second floor of the suite, her thin legs fluid as she pranced down the stairs in her cotton candy pink Versace. She pressed a hand against her bobbed hair, a few strands woefully out of place, that ever-present grin on her face as she sashayed down. Looking like a pathetic imitation of Daisy Buchanan. She lacked both poise and grace.

Tall and preppy, his eyebrows too bushy, Bradley chased after her in a black suit. Armani, from the look of it. His shirt tails were untucked, his jacket askew, a sloppy smile on his long face. Nate's face burned. He was almost certain they'd had sex upstairs.

"Anywhere but here," said Nate, feeling nauseated as he turned away from the stairs.

"Nate, my wuv!" Corrina called, clattering across the floor toward him in her size five stiletto heels.

He cringed, his body lurching away from the touch of her hands against his arms, her arms sliding across his chest. He smelled the gardenia sweet of her cologne tinged with...he recoiled. With men's aftershave lotion. Something he never wore.

"I've looked everywhere for you," she said as he untangled her octopus grip on him.

"Been right here the whole time," he snapped.

"Why's my Nate so cross?" she asked, pouting a moment then smiling, her sugary pink lip gloss thick.

He always got cross when his fiancé left parties to bang another guy then flaunt the aftershave in his face.

"That's a new perfume, isn't it?" Nate said, a faint smile on his face.

Planted only for Ren and Meredith's benefit. "What is it? Chanel and Axe? Red and Drakkar?"

Ren bit back a snort, Meredith covering her mouth as Corrina's cheeks reddened.

"No, silly, it's Obsession—what I always wear."

"His and hers?" Nate asked and Ren walked away, his shoulders shuddering as he fought down a laugh.

Corrina just smiled, reaching her hand toward Nate's face, but he stiffened, pulling away. She stared at him a moment, looking confused by his actions.

"What's the matter, wuv?"

"Nothing," he said then glanced at his watch. "I'm taking off now. Got a client dinner in less than an hour."

It was a lie, but he'd keep telling it if it got him out of here.

"Will I see you tomorrow?" She grinned at him, tilting back and forth like a child. "Will I see you on Saturday?"

He cringed at the realization. On Saturday, he'd be married. The thought made him shake all over.

"I'll be here," he said as she leaned toward him.

"Kissies," she said to him, puckering up.

Kissing the same lips that Bradley had probably just slobbered on made him queasy. He leaned over and kissed her on top of the head and turned away toward the door.

"Nate," she called, "that wasn't a kiss."

He kept walking, feeling like he'd suffocate, and hurried out the door. Once he was on the street, he tugged the knot loose on his tie and dropped down on the stone fence outside, staring out at the traffic.

"His and hers?" Ren snickered behind him.

Nate let out a chuckle and glanced up at Ren who was standing beside him. His best friend was still laughing.

"I nearly busted my gut when you said that to her. Is she really that dense? Or does she think you are?"

"Wasn't I?" Nate said, rolling his eyes. "She's probably been banging that guy the entire year we've dated."

Ren squeezed his shoulder. "Nate, man—I'm telling you, it's not too late to escape. You've still got tomorrow to catch a flight out of here."

"My Dad would hunt me down."

Ren plopped down on the stone fence beside him. "Let him. What can he do? Fire you?"

*No, just you, Ren*, he wanted to say. *And Kadence.* He couldn't take that risk.

Meredith pulled around to the curb in Ren's Land Rover. Ren tugged on Nate's sleeve.

"C'mon, the getaway car's here," he said.

Nate rose from the fence and climbed into the Land Rover and Meredith took off.

"Where to, boys?"

"The office," said Nate, slumping against the backseat.

"You're not going to work tonight, are you?" Ren asked, a sour expression on his face.

Nate pinched the bridge of his nose, a headache beginning between his eyes.

"No, I just want to pick up a few things. So, I'll have something to do on my honeymoon."

Meredith and Ren laughed, but he saw Meredith wince in the rearview mirror and cast a sad look at Ren. Ren just shook his head and stared out the window, his elbow resting against the glass.

In fifteen minutes, Meredith pulled into one of the reserved parking spaces in front of Logan Financial and shut off the motor. Nate hopped out, Ren behind him. He fished out his keyring, the keys to his SUV still bobbling beside his house key, almost like it was still parked in the garage somewhere. He unlocked the glass doors and the three of them walked in, heading for the elevator.

His office was on the tenth floor. He stepped out of the elevator and across to the glass doors bearing the red Logan Financial logo: a lightship. He unlocked the doors and stepped into the entryway with its rich cherry wood and round reception desk. The air smelled sweet and familiar with citrus as he moved down the hall to his office. Meredith sat down at the reception desk and bumped over a pile of orange, While You Were Out messages onto the floor.

"Oh, Ren—help please!" she called.

Nate rounded the hall and pushed open the door to his office. The red voice mail light on his phone pulsed steadily, even despite the greeting that said he'd be out of the office until January third.

He hit the speaker phone button and pressed the voice mail playback, entering his code.

"You have twelve messages. Press seven to play the first message."

He tapped the seven and someone from his insurance company had left a message about his totaled SUV (and the subsequent raising of his insurance rates). He deleted the message.

The next four were client messages, telling him they'd contact Ren. The next three were caterers, tuxedo fitting, and the jeweler about the wedding bands. He found the two ring boxes with diamond studded platinum wedding bands in the locked drawer of his desk as the message indicated. Disgusted, he shoved them in his coat pocket, not wanting that gaudy thing around his finger.

The next one was Bill Simon and he smiled.

"Nate, this here's Bill Simon. From N'Orleans. Listen, I just wanted to say thank you for all you done for Sarah and me. Thanks to you, she had a lovely service and there's a nice bench where I can sit and talk to her every day. God bless you, son."

He'd wanted to do so much more than that.

The next message was a hang-up. But the next one was from the young couple he'd given money to get back on their feet.

"Nate, dis here's Andy, from St. Bernard's Parish. Remember, you helped my Terri and me. We wanted to say thanks for all you did. We got us a nice apartment here in Baton Rouge and the money you give us got da baby's room all nice again. Thank you."

He leaned against the desk, remembering that day as a mixture of pain and suffering. The memory of Bill Simon sitting with his dead wife would always stay with him and it would humble him.

The next message was another hang-up. But he jolted when Elsie's voice echoed from the speaker.

"Nate, it's Elsie. It's powerful lonely without you 'round here. Me and dem cats miss you lots. And so does Kadence."

His chest burned in a raw ache and he sat down heavily in his desk chair.

"I wanted to see how you was doin' and if'n you married that girl yet. Honey, marriage ain't no good if there's no love there. I hope you don't go makin' that mistake when I know your heart's still here in Hackberry. Here's our phone number if'n you're a mind to call. Three three seven, four nine one, five five five five. Bye, honey!"

He saved Elsie's message.

The phone rang and he snapped his hand to the talk button, the phone still on speaker.

"Nate." It was a statement, not a question. And he was gloating. Nate glared at the phone.

"Dad."

"I thought you'd be in the office today as I directed."

"Any other directives to hand me? Dad."

"Nate, I know you're angry at me right now, but down the road, you'll thank me. Trust me. This is a powerful alliance. With Judge Coleridge's backing, you could run for president."

Nate exhaled sharply. "I already told you, Dad, that's your dream, not mine."

"Nonsense! Once you get a taste of politics, it'll be in your blood."

*Not in this lifetime,* Nate thought with a scowl.

"Look, Dad…I don't think I can go through with this."

"Now you listen to me, young man. You *will* go through with this. You'll show up at that wedding on Saturday and you *will* marry Corrina Coleridge. If you don't, so help me God, Ren will be in the employment line for McDonalds first thing Monday morning. And then I go after your little professor. Understand me, son?"

Nate snapped up from his chair, knocking it over. His pathetic show of rebellion would accomplish nothing. He had no choice but to obey. And his dad knew it.

"See you on Saturday, son."

The dial tone blared back at him as he slammed his fist against the speakerphone button.

That's when he heard his office door creak open. He looked up and there stood Ren, a look of horror on his face. Nate cringed, turning away. He couldn't face Ren now. He hadn't wanted him to know any of that.

"My God, Nate," he said, at last finding his voice. "You were going to marry that bitch to save my lousy-ass job?"

He nodded, feeling like an idiot. Ren slid his arm around Nate's shoulders and pulled him into a hug.

"Don't you sweat it, buddy. I'm not letting you throw away your life like this."

Nate stepped away from him, turning to face his best friend. "Even if he hadn't threatened your job, he's threatened to ruin Kadence, too. And I can't let that happen." He sighed. "I love her and you too much to let that happen."

"Well, you're off the hook in my case, Nate, because I quit. I'm drawing up the papers tonight and FedExing them to your old man."

"Ren, no!" Nate shouted. "It won't change anything.

Meredith hugged the door frame, her eyes glassy with tears, a handful of phone messages in her hands.

"Oh, Nate—we'd never forgive ourselves if you were forced to marry Corrina to save a stupid job."

He laughed. "Come to think of it, guess I'm out of a job, too if I don't marry her." He shook his head. "But if I don't go through with this, he'll ruin Kadence."

Meredith rushed over and hugged him. "I wish there was something I could do."

He held her tightly. "Be there at the airport when our flight to Bali leaves. If I run fast enough, we can be away from the curb before Corrina notices I'm gone."

Ren laughed, but Nate saw the pain in his eyes.

"Come on," said Ren, motioning them toward the door. "Let's get out of here."

Nate walked out behind Ren. Either way, he would never set foot in Logan Financial again. Ren was resigning, so he was out of here, too. He grabbed his notebook computer and charger off the desk. His mother's picture was still on the desk, so he swept up the frame and shuffled out beside Meredith, headed for the elevator.

# TWENTY-SIX

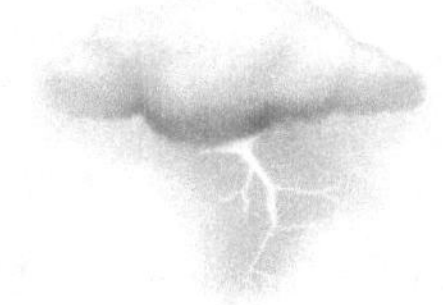

Kadence slumped on the couch beside Elsie, watching some talk show and missing Hackberry. Missing that old house. Missing Nate. It had been a month since he'd slipped away unseen in Marty's Grand Prix for Baton Rouge. She'd left a dozen messages at his office, but he'd not returned one of her calls. She and her big mouth had ruined her last hope with him.

At least tomorrow was Friday. Made it to one more weekend.

Jim sat in a brown recliner, a Pepsi in his hand, pretending to watch the television, but his worried gaze kept flicking from the talk show to Kadence. He'd been here a lot lately, trying to get her out of the house, out doing things, but she'd resisted all his attempts except visiting her ruined property. She knew he was concerned about her and was trying to be a supportive friend, but Jim couldn't fix all her losses.

The phone rang and she jumped up from the old beige couch and shuffled into the Harvest Gold kitchen. A green phone was mounted on the wall, the room smelling warm with fresh brewing coffee as she picked it up.

"Hello?"

"Kadence?"

Kadence frowned. The voice almost familiar, but she couldn't place it.

"Yes? Who's this?"

"This is Meredith Hudson. Remember, one of Nate's friends?"

Her heart leaped, the grin spilling across her face. "Meredith, hi! Of course, I remember you. How are you? How's Nate?"

Meredith chuckled. "I'm fine. But Nate's not so fine, I'm afraid. That's why I'm calling."

Her stomach fell. "Oh, God—is he sick? Did he have an accident?"

"No, no, physically he's fine. But he's about to make the most terrible mistake of his life."

A cold wind brushed across her heart. The wedding. It had to be this weekend.

"The wedding?" she said, trying hard not to let her voice crack.

"Saturday afternoon at the Four Seasons Hotel in D.C."

She couldn't say anything, the awful image burning into her head of Corrina Coleridge and her over-processed blond hair and condescending attitude.

"See, Kadence, I found all your phone messages for Nate at his office, but he never got them."

"No?" She wanted to cry out with relief. He hadn't rejected her. He hadn't gotten her messages.

"And even worse," Meredith continued. "Nate's trying to be everyone's protector."

"What do you mean protector?" Kadence asked, squinting.

"Nate's father plans to fire Ren if Nate doesn't marry Corrina on Saturday."

She gasped. "What?" Nate was being forced to marry that woman?

"That's not the worst part," said Meredith.

"What's worse than that?" she demanded.

"Nate's Dad also said he'd ruin you at the college if Nate broke off the engagement."

Kadence sank down in a gold vinyl dining chair, feeling sick. "Oh, my God…he was trying to protect me?" Her eyes welled with tears. She'd been so awful to him.

"You know Nate."

She did. She remembered him throwing himself into flood waters to save her. And he was doing it again. But this time, she wouldn't be there to grab his wrists and pull him out of the storm surge.

She grinned. But she could be by tomorrow night.

"Meredith, can you do me a huge favor?"

"Anything," said Meredith.

"Pick me up at Dulles tomorrow night."

"I've already booked you a flight, Kadence. You just get to Baton Rouge and I'll see you at Dulles."

Kadence wiped back tears. "I don't know how to thank you."

"Just stop him from marrying that evil woman. That's all I ask. She's been cheating on him, Kadence, and practically flaunting it in his face. He's miserable. You've got to save him."

She would. After all, it was her turn.

"Thanks, Meredith," she said and hung up the phone.

"Elsie, Jim, I've got to go out of town," she called from the kitchen as she grabbed a Pepsi and hurried out of the kitchen.

Grinning, Elsie clapped her hands together. "You goin' to Arlington?"

Kadence grinned. "I've got to go stop a wedding."

"'Bout time somebody come to that conclusion," she said. "Take a nice dress now. That's a fancy hotel."

"Kay? Are you crazy?"

Jim was on his feet, moving toward her as she rushed past. He took hold of her shoulders, turning her around.

"I'm going, Jim," she said in a firm voice. He'd better not even think of trying to talk her out of this.

"But he lied to you," said Jim, shaking his head.

She nodded. "He did it to protect me, Jim. His father promised to ruin me, get my fired unless Nate went through with the wedding."

Jim sighed and brushed the wisps of red hair out of her eyes. "What if you're wrong?"

"What if I'm not?" she said in a hushed voice. "I love him, Jim."

At last, a smile curved across his tanned face. "He was protectin' you, huh?"

"Kinda like you," she said, poking him. "You know he's a good man, Jim. He didn't mean to hurt me. You didn't know this, but the night Rita made landfall, I fell into the flood waters."

"What?" Jim winced, squeezing his eyes closed, his Adam's apple bobbing.

"Nate jumped into the current and saved me. I was trapped under debris, but he pulled me out. He nearly drowned twice, but fought his way back to the surface and I got him back onto the landing. If he didn't love me…"

Jim sighed. He bowed his head, nodding as he stared at his feet. Finally, he lifted his head to look her in the eye. He looked sad. "Looks like we misjudged Nate."

"Terribly," she replied, feeling the guilt burn her stomach.

He smiled and patted her on the sleeve. "Guess you'd better get to packin'. Got a weddin' to stop."

Grinning, she rushed into the tiny bedroom and shoved open the closet door.

"Tell him I'm sorry for schoolin' him, too," Jim called to her.

"I'll apologize for everything, don't you worry, Jim," she called as she thumbed through her clothes, smelling the lavender sachet that she'd hung in the closet. To remind her of home.

She'd take a nice dress. Something nice and sexy and slinky that would pop Nate's eyes out of his head and turn Corrina green with envy. It was so impolite to look hotter than the bride. She couldn't wait.

# TWENTY-SEVEN

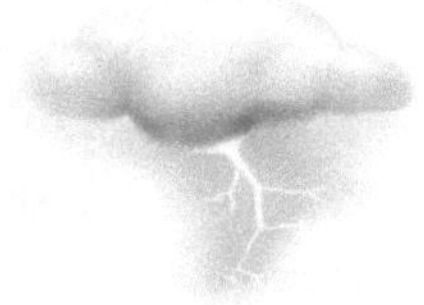

Nate stood at the end of the long, rose-laden aisle, Ren his best man, his Dad a groomsman and waited for his life to end.

A white lattice pergola stretched the length of the long banquet room, the minister standing at the far end, Nate and his groomsmen to the minister's right. Corrina's bridesmaids, dressed in pale pink, strapless gowns hugged massive bouquets of pink roses against their chests as they eagerly awaited the bride.

Any moment, Corrina would appear on that white carpet in her Vera Wang dress and flowing lace train, led by the Honorable Judge Coleridge.

Guests packed into the room, fidgeting in the white folding chairs on either side of the vine-draped pergola, rose petals and glitter spread across the white carpet. Dad's political cronies watched the spectacle on one side, Corrina's friends and family (including the ubiquitous douchebag, Bradley Wilcox) on the other. Why did he feel so outnumbered?

A four-piece quartet lamented *Wind Beneath My Wings* from somewhere behind the bridesmaids, the air sweet with roses. It was the only pleasant thing in the room, Nate thought, scowling.

Ren leaned forward as Nate tugged at the grey ascot choking him.

He wished it would do the job right and cut off all his air so he wouldn't have to go through with this sham.

"You okay?" Ren asked.

"No," he snapped, glaring at his best friend. "Do I look okay?"

"Just checking to make sure you weren't trying to strangle yourself."

"Can't get it tight enough," he said and stopped pulling on the ascot. He leaned back toward Ren. "Promise me when the time comes, you'll smother me on the way to the limousine."

Ren snickered, patting him on the shoulder. "If given the choice, I'm going to smother her," Ren whispered, pointing toward Corrina who stood at the edge of the pergola.

"All rise," said the minister, motioning the packed roomful of guests to their feet.

Nate stiffened, his hands going cold, the shakes beginning. His stomach roiled as he gritted his teeth, watching Corrina prance down the aisle on her father's arm. The long lacy train of her gown rustling above *Hear Comes the Bride*.

He couldn't go through with this. He couldn't!

He cast a panicked look at Ren, who laid a sympathetic hand on his shoulder and shook his head.

And suddenly, Corrina was beside him, bouncing as the Judge, a tall, stern-looking man with thinning white hair, raised her veil and kissed her on the cheek. Then he turned her toward Nate who froze. The Judge cast a look of triumph at Nate's father, shorter with thick salt and pepper hair, who stood behind Ren.

"Take her hand, son," said the Judge to Nate.

Nate swallowed hard and took hold of her hand, turning her toward the minister. Where his life started flashing before his eyes.

Stepping off the plane in Lake Charles. Rusty red hair and freckles, pert little nose, large brown eyes. And that wonderful bright smile that had made him feel immediately welcome. Kadence Harlowe.

"Marriage is a sacred vow, not to be entered into lightly," said the minister, holding out his arms as he addressed the room.

"Or stupidly," Ren whispered in his ear.

Those cutoff shorts and long, long legs, rushing into flood waters beside her, those hip-waders so sexy on those slim hips. He smiled. Sam Adams and kisses by firelight. The feel of her hands against his bare chest.

"Do you Corrina, take Nate to be your lawfully wedded husband, to have and to hold…"

The soft feel of her body pressed against his, the porch swing creaking in the sultry night air, smell of lavender and sandalwood in that rusty red hair tangling around his face as he leaned down to kiss her neck.

"I will," said Corrina.

"And do you Nate, take Corrina as your lawfully wedded wife, to have and to hold…"

Brush of warm wind against creamy white skin and green string bikini, sting of saltwater in his eyes as she sank into his arms in the warm surf. The brush of her lips against his, warm and inviting. His breath caught. The comfort of her hand against his burning forehead, the fever stirring up pain and accidents.

"Nate?" the minister whispered.

His gaze flicked to the minister.

"Do you?" he asked.

"I uh…" Nate stared at Corrina's vacant eyes looking past him, seeing only the illusion of flowers and party dresses and rose petals, and her on center stage—all of which would disappear by Monday. What was left? A wrought alliance between two politicians and a woman who saw him as just another Gucci purse.

"Nate," his Dad snapped in a harsh whisper. "Answer the man."

Nate let out the faintest hint of a sigh. A sigh of defeat. "I uh—will."

Corrina gave him that condescending little smile of hers. *There, that didn't hurt so much, did it? Step into my web, Nate my wuv. You won't mind Bradley joining us in Papua, will you?*

"The rings, please," as the minister, a fortyish, round faced man with wire-rimmed glasses and a too-pleasant smile.

Ren handed off the two rings and with shaking fingers, Nate slid the gaudy platinum band onto Corrina's finger. She took his hand and slid the band onto his finger as he fought down the urge to flinch.

This would seal the deal. He couldn't go back from here.

The minister cast a look around the room. "Is there anyone who can show just cause why these two people should not be bound in the sanctity of marriage?"

Nate cast a desperate look at Ren, but Ren shook his head, looking defeated.

"How about breach of contract?" a voice shouted from the back of the room.

Nate turned around as murmurs rose, Corrina's face turning red with fury.

Kadence stood at the back of the room, a silky mint green dress hugging every amazing curve, a slit letting those long legs peak out as she stepped down the carpet of glitter and rose petals toward him.

He couldn't hold back his grin as he stepped back from Corrina, walking down the carpet toward her.

"What do you mean, breach of contract?" he asked, still smiling.

"Yes, young lady," the minister replied, looking less than pleased with this interruption. "Explain yourself."

She stared at Nate a moment then focused on the minister. "I bought this man off the internet."

Whispers and conversation buzzed through the room.

"Rent an executive for a term of thirty days," Kadence continued. "Signed a contract and everything. For charity. But see, Mr. Logan here walked out with two days left." She crossed her arms.

Judge Coleridge stormed down the aisle toward Kadence, but she didn't give an inch of ground.

"Young lady, whatever this nonsense is, it can be settled later. You're ruining a wedding."

Kadence shook her head. "No, I demand this situation be resolved right now. See, there's a little more to the contract than those two days."

Nate took hold of her hands and Corrina shrieked.

"There is?" he asked, still grinning at her. "Like what?"

"Like an option on the next thirty years. With the possibility of purchase." She grinned at him.

"What's the interest rate?" he asked, leaning toward her.

"Through the roof. At least a hundred percent."

"Then I'll take it," he said and kissed her as hard as he could.

Corrina screamed in rage and rushed down the aisle toward Nate.

"You pig! You horrible pig!" She swung her fist out toward Nate's head, but he blocked her punch with his palm. "I hate you!" she shrieked.

Kadence handed Nate a piece of paper and he glanced at it, nearly gagging. An image of Corrina on the floor with Bradley in all their glory. In full, graphic color. Behind Kadence, Meredith walked up the aisle, prancing, a stack of papers in her hands.

"I'm the pig?" Nate snapped, thrusting the paper into Corrina's face.

Her face flushed bright red, her mouth bobbing like a fish. The Judge turned purple, livid at the compromised image of his daughter.

"Now, we can settle this peacefully," said Nate, turning to the Judge, "or we can settle this badly." He pointed to the huge stack of papers in Meredith's hands.

"What are you suggesting?" the Judge sputtered, glaring at Nate.

"I'm going to walk out now," said Nate to the Judge, "but I can walk out quietly or not so quietly when we scatter these pictures through the room like confetti. Your choice."

The Judge glared at his sobbing daughter for several long moments. Finally, he pointed at the door. "Just go and take those horrid things with you." He slid his arm around Corrina's waist as she threw herself into her father's arms.

Meredith leaned toward the Judge. "Buy her a new Prada purse and she'll be fine." She motioned at Ren who ran down the aisle.

Nate popped the ring off his left hand and plopped it into the Judge's hand. He turned to Kadence and slid his arm around her waist, picking her up in his arms and carrying her out of the room. She threw her arms around his neck, kissing him again as Meredith led them out the back to the waiting Land Rover.

"This is cool," Ren said, climbing into the passenger side. "We're fugitives."

Meredith climbed in and started the Land Rover as Nate lifted Kadence into the backseat.

"How'd you get here?" he asked, wrapping his arms around her, holding her against his chest, never wanting to let go of her.

She kissed him again. "Meredith told me how your Dad threatened Ren…and me if you didn't marry Corrina. I had to stop you."

"Why?" he asked, grinning at her.

"Because I love you, Nate," she said in a quiet voice. "But I was afraid you didn't love me."

"I couldn't love you more," he said, cradling her against him. "I didn't want my dad to cause you harm. He's more than capable of it."

"So, what happens now?" Ren asked. "Now that we're both out of jobs."

Nate thought a moment, but he already knew his answer. "I want to rebuild that house, Kadence."

She held onto him, her arms around his neck as she pulled his face closer to hers. "So do I. More than ever now. But why do you want to rebuild it, Nate?"

He laid his hand against her face, against that wavy rust-red hair. "Because that's where you saved me, Kadence. Back there in Hackberry. I didn't know how lost I was until you found me."

She brushed her lips against his, kissing so gently it stung his eyes.

"I know where you can get a good deal on a slightly used executive," he said with a wink.

"I'll take him. By the way, Jim says he's sorry for schooling you."

Nate winced, remembering Jim kicking his butt in the backyard for not telling Kadence he was engaged.

"It's okay. Guess I had some of that coming." He studied her loving brown eyes. "I should have told you and avoided this whole mess. We'll settle it over a beer some night, okay."

She nodded, smiling.

"I want to open a restaurant," said Meredith, glancing at Ren, taking hold of his hand as she drove.

"Really?" said Ren, nodding. "You and me in the restaurant business…I love the idea," he said as Meredith's eyes lit with excitement. "Where? In D.C.—or Arlington?"

"Lake Charles," she said and glanced back at Kadence. "Think anybody could show us around?"

"I'll get my rented executive on the job," said Kadence.

Nate pressed his lips to hers in a quick kiss, holding her tight. She leaned into him, nuzzling her face against his neck and he smelled her calming lavender scent. He couldn't wait to get back to his life. And the rest of his thirty days. With an option on the next thirty years. How could he pass that up?

**The End of LANDFALL**

*If you enjoyed this book, check out Lisa's Contemporary Celestial Romantasy series:*

**THE CINDERELLA HOUR: Book One, A Game of Lost Souls**

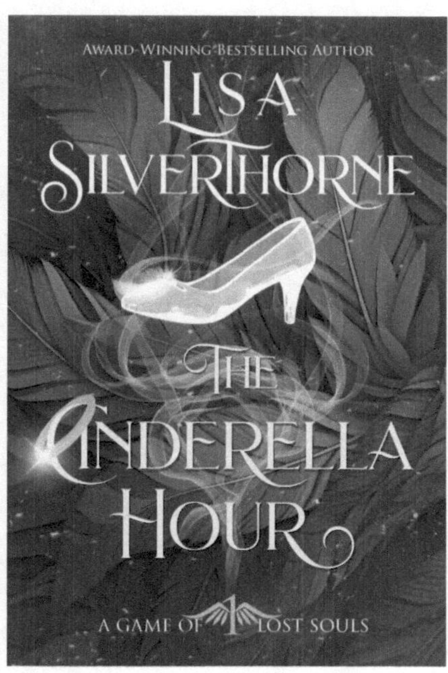

**Novels by Lisa Silverthorne**

***A Game of Lost Souls* series:**
*Contemporary Romantasy*
THE CINDERELLA HOUR
THE PRINCE CHARMING HOUR
THE EVER AFTER HOUR
THE FALLEN HEARTS SEASON
THE RISING SPIRITS SEASON
THE ETERNAL SOULS SEASON
THE ROYAL WEDDING HOUR
THE HEAVENLY HONEYMOON HOUR
THE DIVINE NEWLYWEDS SHOW
THE CELESTIAL COUPLES SHOW
THE ENOCHIAN APOCALYPSE SHOW
THE ANGELIC ANNIVERSARY SHOW
THE PERDITION PICTURE SHOW
**Complete Series!**


***Curse and Crown* series:**
*Epic Romantasy*
THORN & BLADE
STORM & STEEL
FLAME & DAGGER (2026)


***The Spiral* series:**
*Dark Contemporary Fantasy*
BETWEEN
REPRISE
AVENGE

*The Resurrectionist Papers*
*Paranormal Romystery*
GRAVE RECKONING


***Standalones:***
ISABEL'S TEARS
LANDFALL
PACIFIC BLUE TATTOO


**Short Story Collections**
THE SOUND OF ANGELS
THE MAGIC OF ORDINARY THINGS
TIMELESS
WINTER'S EMBRACE

---

**Science Fiction Writing as L.S. Silverthorne**

*Experiencing True Purple series:*
RECOMBINANT, Book 1
HELIX, Book 2
SPLICE, Book 3

*Standalones:*
REDISCOVERY

# ABOUT THE AUTHOR

LISA SILVERTHORNE, an award-winning author, has published over 30 novels and 150 short stories and novelettes in many genres. She is the author of *A Game of Lost Souls*, *Experiencing True Purple*, *The Spiral*, *The Resurrectionist Papers*, and *Curse and Crown*.

Before you go, you are invited to please leave a **review of this book**!

Reviews are a wonderful way to help an author and share your thoughts with other readers, so **please post yours,** in as many places as possible!

 ***ONLINE STORE!***
*For Ebook Bundles, book swag, and beautiful*
***Special Edition*** *hardcovers (coming soon), visit:* **LisaSilverthorne-Books.com**